Benjamin G. Lovejoy

Francis Bacon - (Lord Verulam)

A Critical Review of His Life and Character -With Selections From His Writings

Benjamin G. Lovejoy

Francis Bacon - (Lord Verulam)
A Critical Review of His Life and Character -With Selections From His Writings

ISBN/EAN: 9783337053895

Printed in Europe, USA, Canada, Australia, Japan

Cover: Foto ©Raphael Reischuk / pixelio.de

More available books at **www.hansebooks.com**

FRANCIS BACON

(LORD VERULAM)

A CRITICAL REVIEW

OF

HIS LIFE AND CHARACTER

WITH

SELECTIONS FROM HIS WRITINGS

BY

B. G. LOVEJOY, LL. B.

" The brightest, wisest, meanest of mankind."—POPE

LONDON

T. FISHER UNWIN

26 PATERNOSTER SQUARE

1888

DEDICATION.

————

PREFACE.

Three of the most interesting, and, in some respects, most influential writers of earlier English prose, were Johnson, Addison and Bacon. The last is having his revival in America through his Essays, which are being adopted as a text-book in English literature in many of our Colleges and High Schools.

A comparatively recent life of Bacon attracted the writer's attention in one of these nurseries of American citizenship, and he was impressed with the hero-worship prominent in every paragraph, — how admiration of the philosopher's intellect made the biographer blind to the man's frailty, how every comment seemed to be a compromise with, or apology for, just such individual and official corruption as is now awakening the American mind to a just appreciation of public and private honesty and integrity.

Impressed with the idea that there is room for a sketch of this great type of official bribe-takers, the writer has exhibited this extraordinary man climbing to the Wool-sack and descending to the prison-cell, through the channels of unsatisfied ambition and greed for wealth, while giving to the world principles of philosophy and morality which conferred immortality alike upon his fame and his infamy.

In this estimate of Bacon's character, his actions are tested by his own rules of right, and his conduct is subjected to the touchstone of his own code of morality.

The selections contained in this volume are intended to illustrate the truth of his sentiments and the beauty of their expression.

B. G. L.

WASHINGTON, June 1, 1883.

CONTENTS.

PART I.

FROM THE BIRTH OF BACON TO THE DEATH OF ELIZABETH.

The tribute paid to Bacon by succeeding ages; his life as instructive as his pen; object of this sketch to outline him in his two rôles of place-hunter and truth-seeker; contemporary history essential to acquaintance with the individual; his political, religious and intellectual surroundings glanced at; Queen Elizabeth, her embarrassments and policy; the literature of the period; Bacon's mother one of the "learned ladies;" Bacon's father; Bacon born January 22d, A. D. 1560; his precocity; early education; enters the University of Cambridge, aged thirteen; university education unprogressive; Bacon's opinion of the teachers and methods at the universities; contrast between home surroundings and college life; in his sixteenth year accompanies Sir Amias Paulet, English ambassador, to Paris; possible bad influence of Elizabethan diplomacy on his youthful nature; his residence abroad and its results; summoned home by the sudden death of his father; confronted by poverty; seeks office, and failing, enters upon the study of the law; state of religious feeling; Bacon seeks a short path to the bar; how he regarded the profession of the law; Burghley's rebuke; full admission to the bar, A. D. 1586; sits in the parliament, 1586; is a speaker in debate on execution of sentence against Queen of Scots; Martin Marprelate, Bacon enters the controversial contest; his pen employed by the Queen; rewarded for his services by gift of a place in reversion; intimacy with Earl of Essex; new parliament, February 19, 1592; Bacon as a reformer, and speech on law reform; his "patriotic" but unfortunate speech against granting three subsidies to the Queen;

Elizabeth's anger at his course; what inspired this speech; the "three-pound men"—"*Dulcis tractus pari jugo;*" he contemplates retirement, but is restrained by Essex; he is financially embarrassed; his contradictory impulses; he fastens his eye on the Attorney-Generalship; writes to Burghley's sons, Sir Thomas and Sir Robert Cecil; letter to the Queen, disavowing the pressing of his suit on the Queen; Essex supports him, but is confronted by Bacon's anti-subsidy speech; Sir Edward Coke is made Attorney-General, notwithstanding the "uttermost credit, friendship and authority" of Essex; Bacon turns to the Solicitor-Generalship, and is supported by Essex; he tells Essex to disparage competitors for the position; the Queen sends him on a mission; he borrows from Anthony Bacon to pay his travelling expenses; is taken ill; returns, taking "A. M." on the way, from Cambridge; Essex acquaints Elizabeth with Bacon's threat of retirement if he does not receive promotion; the Queen's anger; Bacon's interview with Sir Robert Cecil; they part "in kindness, *secundum exterius;*" Essex presses Bacon's suit in vain; Fleming made Solicitor-General, A. D. 1596; Bacon's dejection and retirement to the villa of Essex; the Earl's sympathy; gives Bacon an estate worth £1,800; publication of essays, "Colors of Good and Evil," "*Meditationes Sacræ;*" Essex's successful expedition against the Spaniards and Cadiz; Bacon's letter of advice to the young Earl; its moral tone, or, rather, immoral tone; Queen's opinion of his legal ability: "excellent gift of speech, but in law she rather thought he could show to the uttermost than that he was deep;" vindicates his legal ability by writing his "Maxims" and "Use of the Common Law;" proposes to relieve financial embarrassments by marriage of convenience; Lady Hatton—her character; letter to Essex, asking his backing; good advice to the Earl; Coke runs off with Lady Hatton; seven matrimonial objections to Coke; Lady Hatton's married life; parliament of 1597; Bacon an active member; votes for large subsidies; Essex's return from unsuccessful naval adventure; Raleigh second in command; his success; Essex's injustice; Queen displeased; Essex sulks, is forgiven and restored to favor; is adviser to the Queen during Cecil's absence; Bacon's letter to Essex touching Irish affairs; Bacon arrested for debt; spunging-house; presents the Queen with an embroidered petticoat; coolness between Essex and

PART II.

FROM THE ACCESSION OF JAMES TO THE PUBLICATION OF NOVUM ORGANUM, OCT. 12, 1620.

Elizabeth on the succession; correspondence of Anthony Bacon, Essex, Cecil and others with the Court of Scotland; Bacon trades on the capital of his dead brother and his dead patron; James continues regular appointees of the Crown in office, which leaves Bacon out; Southampton visited in the Tower; Bacon writes to him, "I may safely be now that which I was truly

PART III.

FROM THE PUBLICATION OF THE NOVUM ORGANUM, OCT. 12, 1620, TO BACON'S DEATH, APRIL 9, 1626.

Bacon celebrates his sixtieth birthday, as Lord Verulam and Lord Chancellor; Ben Jonson's ode; the Elector Palatine par-liament; monopolies, grievances; Mompesson, Mitchell, "Over-reach" and "Greedy;" Edward Villiers diplomatized; Bacon

ESSAYS.

EXTRACTS.

FRANCIS BACON.

HIS LIFE AND CHARACTER.

PART I.

FROM BIRTH OF BACON TO DEATH OF QUEEN ELIZABETH.

Nearly three hundred years ago, Francis Bacon died, and was buried in the country church of St. Michael's.

The solemn sentence — "Dust to dust, ashes to ashes," has long since been fulfilled, and all that was mortal of a great philosopher has become as earthy as the remains of the pauper whom the same inevitable event consigned to the potter's field.

The memory of a bad man is sometimes preserved for a time to point a moral; that of a philanthropist lives in his monuments to the brotherhood of humanity; the memories of kings and conquerors flit like troubled ghosts through the pages of history; but it is only the name of the thinker of great thoughts, the writer of profound and beautiful truths, the pioneer of principles reaching in their beneficent benevolence to remote generations, that foreign nations and after ages cherish with intellectual veneration.

This is the tribute paid to Francis Bacon.

His essays are recognized as a source of the soundest principles of social and moral philosophy; his Advancement of Learning as a most able and eloquent defense of the utility of knowledge ; his *Novum Organum* as the missionary of philosophical inquiry among English-speaking people ; his Church Controversies and other religious tracts as abounding in golden maxims of Christian conservatism ; his Orders in Chancery as the basis of equity practice in English jurisprudence ; * his legal tracts and speeches as giving an impulse to the study of law as a science, and as suggesting many wise reforms in legislation ; his political tracts and speeches as inculcating principles of wise government ; his thoughts on education as anticipating some of the successful experiments of later times ; and his Apothegms as a clever jest-book.

To read his works and not know the author is treading but an arc of the circle. His life teaches as profound lessons as his pen. And when the frailty and folly of the man are contrasted with the morality and wisdom of the writer, a most curious exhibition of inconsistency is presented to the student of human nature.

The object of this sketch is to outline him in his two rôles of Truth-seeker and Place-hunter, in his courage and cowardice, strength and weakness, glory and shame. To form a fair estimate of any historical character, it is necessary to consider the times in which he lived; to know something of those who guided his infancy, influenced his youth, surrounded his manhood, and with whose destinies his own fate was interwoven. For, although we come into this world alone, and go out of it alone, none of us live in it alone. Our lives are mingled together as warp and woof ; in every stage

---

* Campbell's " Lives of the Lord Chancellors," vol. ii., p. 434; Basil Montagu's " Bacon's Works," vol. xvi., p. 242.

of existence we are involuntarily influencing others, and unconsciously being influenced by others.

A storm of political and religious agitation preceded the birth of Bacon, and its clouds, though broken, were not scattered until the last of the Stuarts made the final and fruitless attempt to solve with arms the problem which the Tudors had devised.

After Henry the Eighth had dragged the Pope from the spiritual throne of England, and created a very good new church, which he supplied with a very indifferent head, he was occupied in efforts to completely disestablish one hierarchy and firmly establish another, to silence one class of consciences by tests that were martyrdom, and reconcile another with bribes that were bishoprics. His death handed over country and church to a boy-successor, who soon followed his father to that bourn where all kings go crownless. But not until he had out-Henried Henry in his new departure, and, under the protectorship of Somerset and Warwick, substituted sectarian fanaticism for his father's State-craft, and "reformed" his people almost into rebels and revolutionists.

Queen Mary signalized her succession to the throne by undoing all that her brother had done, and as vigorously and more viciously attempting to force upon the body of the people one faith, one baptism, one sacrament. But she was fortunately summoned to join her father and brother before she had accomplished her mission, and at the very stage when she had prepared England to receive Elizabeth as the heir to Henry the Eighth's throne and Henry the Eighth's policy.

The new church received new life under a ruler who, to the courage of a Boadicea, added the cunning of a

Machiavelli. Unlike her brother and sister, she was conservative; and her task was not only to soothe, or sacrifice, as a last alternative, the Catholics,— it was to cool the ardor of reformers, and to deal with troublesome spirits, who, while supporting secession from the Church of Rome, refused adhesion to that of England.

With unparalleled skill she nationalized every warring sect; so that they who, under Edward and Mary, were ready to burn each other at the stake, stood shoulder to shoulder upon the decks of Drake's fleet, or the plain of Tilbury, to defend Elizabeth and England from foreign foes. The danger past, they renewed their bickerings, and she resumed her rôle of moderator.

Throughout her reign she was confronted by fears of Spanish invasions, papal plots, Irish rebellions, church controversies. And the task of her life was to evoke inward patriotism, command outward conformity, and to establish England upon a foundation which nothing could have sapped but the folly of her successor. In this object she was seconded by councillors whom the times begot for the times. These she used and abused. For she possessed, as Macaulay says of Louis XIV., the "two talents invaluable to a prince,— the talent of choosing her servants well, and the talent of appropriating to herself the chief part of the credit of their acts."

Of the literature which met the subject of this sketch upon the threshold of life, little now can be said than that it was very meagre. The spirit of the age favored the pen dedicated to theological controversy. Although the Queen might reward a Spenserian sonnet, her chief adviser scorned the "old song," and begrudged the reward to the sweet singer. Although Elizabeth might indulge in a masque of Ben Jonson's, or command Burbage to produce before Her Majesty a play of Will Shakspeare, a philippic of Demosthenes, or the "Phæ-don" of Plato, was alone worthy of the scholarly con-sideration of the pupil of Roger Ascham, or a Latin argument in favor of her politico-spiritual supremacy, written by some courtly theologian, pliant relic of the last reign, whom Mary would have made a saint if his prudence had not postponed the canonization of stake and fagot.

Education was limited to the few, and that of the most cultured in degree. Greece and Rome reigned supreme; or if the ancients were neglected, not England but Italy, that "store-house of divine rites," as it was then called, supplied the place of Athenian orator and Latin poet.

The mass of English mothers were instructed in the practical duties of the household only.

The average husband found the average wife all that his fancy painted her, if she were

"Versed in the arts
Of pies, puddings and tarts."

When Sir Peter, in one of his delightful outbursts of bad temper, contrasts Lady Teazle's country existence with her town life, she replies :

"Yes, I recollect it very well. My daily occupations were to overlook the dairy, superintend the poultry, make abstracts from the family receipt book, and comb my Aunt Deborah's lap-dog. My evening's employments were to draw patterns for ruffles which I had no material to make up, play at Pope Joan with the curate, read a sermon to my Aunt Deborah, and perhaps be stuck up at an old spinet, to play my father to sleep, after a fox-chase."

Unintellectual as these occupations were, they were in advance of those of the average Elizabethan maid and mother.

But, among the exceptions was Lady Bacon, mother of Francis. She was a daughter of the learned tutor of Edward VI., Sir Anthony Cooke, of whom it was said, "Contemplation was his soul, privacy his life, and discourse his element; business was his purgatory, and publicity his torment." Which reveals a scholarly gentleman, revelling in retirement, reading, and such conversations as enlivened Cicero's retreat to his Tusculan villa.

Sir Anthony first gave his five daughters a good education, and then provided them with good husbands, thus performing the whole duty of man as a father. One daughter married William Cecil, who, as Lord Burghley, was Elizabeth's chief adviser through many years. Lady Anne married Sir Nicholas Bacon, who was the Queen's Lord Keeper.

Lady Bacon was one of the exceptionally learned women of the day. She was somewhat distinguished for her Italian and Latin translations, took a deep interest in theological discussions, was tinctured with Calvinism, and was both an imperious and an affectionate mother. Sir Nicholas comes to us through the channel of biography as a sound lawyer, tiresome orator, honest judge and faithful subject. Their second and favorite son was Francis Bacon, the subject of this sketch, who was born on the 22d day of January, A. D. 1561, at York House, his father's London residence. The great philosopher came into the world and went out of it as all mortals do,—his first cry a protest against living, his last moan a protest against dying. But to think of him as an ordinary child is difficult ; for, before reaching his teens, he indulged in investigations into the laws of sound and the mysteries of animal magnetism.* And when the Queen toyed with his curly locks and asked his age, he replied, with the easy sycophancy of a courtier, "Two years younger than your Majesty's most happy reign."

Brilliant minds are said to derive their gifts from the mother. What Lady Bacon may have contributed she cultivated. Her son's delicate constitution consigned him to her care and companionship. Aided by a private tutor, she superintended his education. His studies were probably confined to Greek, Latin, French and Italian literature. He and his contemporary, Shakspeare, were to furnish the two pillars upon which the literary fame of the Elizabethan period rests. The first twelve years of his life were spent thus at home ; but in an atmosphere of politics, in the company of distinguished men; and as persons of state discussed affairs of state, the precocious boy stood by, probably drinking in all that was said, nursing the seed of an ambition that was to color his after-life.

In his thirteenth year he entered Cambridge, where he remained about three years. The "New Learning"

---

* In the 10th century of the "Sylvia," he alludes to this, in connection with a juggler, whom he probably met in the servants' hall, practising on their credulity, who would tell them which of a pack of cards they thought. Bacon says he related the incident to "a man that was curious and vain enough in these things. This pretended learned told me it was a mistaking in me; for, said he, it was not the knowledge of the man's thought (for that is proper to God), but it was enforcing a thought upon him, and binding his imagination by stronger, that he could think no other card."

had, under Henry the Eighth, revolutionized the uni
versities; but subsequent religious, political and social
changes had checked progress, and stagnation was the
substitute for the enthusiasm of John Colet, Erasmus,
and his patron, Archbishop Warham.

A young mind of extraordinary originality and curi-
osity crossed the threshold of Trinity College, and was
required to don the intellectual straight-jacket of the
order which he joined. What they could teach he
mastered, but he despised their methods, and unjustly
identified their great master, Aristotle, with their
pedantic vanities and objectless labors. The impressions he then received he subsequently dwelt upon with
sharp criticism, referring to his masters and fellows
as —

" Men of sharp and strong wits, and abundance of leisure,
and small variety of reading, their wits being shut up in the
cells of a few authors, chiefly Aristotle, their dictator. And,
knowing little history, either of nature or time, did, out of
no great quantity of matter and infinite agitation of wit,
spin cobwebs of learning, admirable for the fineness of
thread and work, but of no substance or profit." *

Translation from his father's house, from conversation with a mother who employed her learning and gifts
in the sharp controversies, the living issues of the day,
exchanging the society of men dealing with the stern
realities, and working for the glorious possibilities, of
Elizabeth's reign, for the society of pedantic quibblers,
invited contrasts, awakened reflections, and, in the
end, inspired him to become the apostle of philosophic

* Contentious Learning,— Ad. of Learning.

and philanthropic truth. All of his biographers agree
that, as a boy at the university, Bacon contemplated
the revolution which he afterwards initiated.

In his sixteenth year he left Cambridge without
regret, and accompanied Sir Amias Paulet, the English
ambassador, to France. His father regarded the
opportunity as favorable for introducing his son into
the mysteries of diplomacy and state-craft. The Queen
lied at home, and her ministers lied abroad, for the good
of the country; so that the school was a good one for
the disciple in one sense, although probably a bad one
in another. It is likely that Bacon's moral nature
received an unfavorable bias from this early entrance
into diplomacy. He performed no service other than
bearing a dispatch to England, it is true; but it is
probable that his thirst for office was then awakened,
and his contemplation of the devious ways of the dip-
lomats familiarized him with the doctrine of any means
to attain an end.

His stay in the country of Montaigne doubtless suggested his "Essays." His treatises on the state of
Europe, and on cipher-writing, were subsequent fruits
of his pen. His elegant and charming manners, and
brilliant conversation, may be credited, in part, to his
residence among a people whose national mission seems
to be that of polishing the universe.

After an absence of about two years, he was recalled
by the sudden death of Sir Nicholas, and returned to a
fatherless home and friendless court.

Lawyer-like, the Lord Keeper was more prompt in
drafting other people's wills than his own, so he died
intestate. The estate he had intended to purchase for
Francis was never bought; and the father, who had

provided for the sons by his first marriage, and even for Bacon's own brother, neglected to secure anything to his favorite child, and left him to confront comparative poverty on the threshold of manhood.

Possessing rare gifts, which had received flattering recognition and encouragement, reared in ease, and assured of competency, Bacon had, previous to his father's death, never seriously contemplated other than scholarly and philosophical pursuits, and political employment, as the road to honors and fame, rather than livelihood. But now, in his own words, he was constrained to "think how to live, instead of living only to think." And his first move seems to have been an application, through his uncle, the Lord Treasurer, to the Queen for preferment at court. An answer appears to have been given which encouraged hope for awhile; but whether his confidence in his uncle's sincerity wavered, or he thought voluntary application to the study of the legal profession would evidence his alacrity and ability for self-denying industry, and favorably impress both Queen and minister, does not appear. However, he became a student at Gray's Inn, Basil Montague and Lord Campbell say, reluctantly; but Mr. Spedding tells us that "his intention was to study the common law as his profession." In a letter to Lord Burghley, from Gray's Inn, September 16th, 1580, Bacon renewed his appeal to his uncle:

"My letter hath no further errand but to commend unto your lordship the remembrance of my suit, which then I moved unto you; whereof it also pleased your lordship to give me a good hearing, so far forth as to promise to tender it unto Her Majesty, and withal to add, in the behalf of it, that which I may better deliver by letter than by speech, which is, that although it must be confessed that the request is rare and unaccustomed, yet if it be observed how few there be which fall in with the study of the common laws, either being well left or friended, or at their own free election, or forsaking likely success in other studies of more delight, and no less preferment, or setting hand thereunto early, without waste of years: upon such survey made, it may be my case may not seem ordinary, no more my suit, and so more beseeming unto it."

Whether he meant to express to his uncle his distaste for the profession of the law, or to exhibit himself boldly entering upon its study to prepare himself for employment in the Queen's service, is, as far as light can be obtained from his letter, left to conjecture ; but his subsequent career seems to afford conclusive proof that he had neither an ambition nor the fitness to become a common-law practioner.

This early correspondence, urging the Lord Treasurer to use his influence with the Queen, and urging Lady Burghley to use her influence with the Lord Treasurer, in his behalf, exhibits him, for the first time, in the rôle of a place-hunter. It also indicates, by its unsuccessful issue, the reluctance on the part of his powerful relative to afford him any assistance in the direction of preferment under the crown.

Although Bacon had fixed his eye on a place at court, his disappointment did not prevent him from bending to the oar of uncongenial labor. When we reflect on his vast attainments, we must credit him with diligence in every undertaking. Close application to year-book, report, and the few text-books then extant, relieved by occasional excursion into the pleasant fields of philosophy, occupied the period embraced between

the years 1580 and 1584, when he took his seat for
Melcombe in the House of Commons.   This parliament
is distinguished for the opposition which the Lower
House displayed to the Queen on the question of
church government.   The Act of Uniformity and plots
against the Queen's life made all its members Protestants ; the intense anti-protestantism of the continent
made a majority of its members sympathizers with the
Non-conformists.

"Puritanism," says the historian Green, "was becoming
the creed of every earnest Protestant throughout the realm;
and the demand for a further advance towards the Calvin-
istic system, and a more open breach with Catholicism
which was embodied in the suppression of the 'superstitious usages,' became stronger than ever.   But Elizabeth
was firm, as of old, to make no advance.   Greatly as the
Protestants had grown, she knew they were still a minority
in the realm.   If the hotter Catholics were fast decreasing,
they remained a large and important body.   But the mass
of the nation was neither Catholic nor Protestant.   It had
lost its faith in the Papacy.   It was slowly drifting to a new
faith in the Bible.   But it still clung obstinately to the past;
it still recoiled from violent change ; its temper was religious
rather than theological, and it shrank from the fanaticism of
Geneva as it shrank from the fanaticism of Rome.   It was
a proof of Elizabeth's genius, that, alone, among her councillors, she understood this drift of opinion, and withstood
measures which would have startled the mass of Englishmen
into a new resistance."

Through the Ecclesiastical Commission and Whit-
gift she repressed Puritanism.   She scotched the snake,
but did not kill it.   She postponed English reformation
to a time when its success would assure the preserva-

tion, not the destruction, of English liberties. But, in the meanwhile, those church controversies which were to enlist Bacon's pen grew warmer.

Bacon had served a part of his apprenticeship at the bar, and in this period mastered whatever difficulties confronted the ordinary student, and which may have required of such continuous application through the five preparatory years which were the prerequisite to the admission to practice. But that his heart was not in his profession is evident from the somewhat desperate tone of his letter to Walsingham, whom he puts in remembrance of the suit for court service which he had previously pressed on Burghley's notice.

"The very stay," he says, "doth in this respect concern me, because I am thereby hindered to take a course of practice, which, by the leave of God, if Her Majesty like not of my suit, I must and will follow. Not," he disingenuously adds, "for my necessity of estate, but for my credit's sake, which, I know, by living out of action will mar."

Disingenuously, because his father's failure to make provision for him made a profession or office absolutely necessary. For, in his own language, he had to think how to live instead of living only to think.

When Mrs. Shandy could not go up to London, she declined the services of Dr. Slop. Whereupon the autobiographer exclaims, "Now, this I like. When you cannot get the thing you want, never be satisfied with the next best thing to it." This Shandean theory had no place in the Baconian philosophy, for when the would-be courtier was disappointed in one direction, with characteristic facility he turned his face in another. His suit, whatever it was, failed. Now he applied to be admitted to active practice by a short cut, which would lop off two of his five years' probation.

Professional men are generally conceited respecting the exacting claims, as well as ennobling characteristics of their callings. Blackstone dabbled in verse until he took up "Coke on Littleton," when he wrote a farewell to his muse, lest she should charm him from his more serious studies. Fearne, the celebrated author of "Contingent Remainders," delighted in philosophy, and wrote his "Anti-Tooke" in reply to the "Diversions of Purley;" but destroyed every vestige of his pleasant pursuit when he took up "Special Pleading."

Bacon differed from this class in regarding his profession but as a branch of that universal knowledge within the reach of a comprehensive and diligent mind. His position is evidenced by his passing from the law's dry details to philosophy, and by his writing, as a law-student, his "Masculine Birth of Time," the foreshadowing of his "Novum Organum."

The long apprenticeship which bench and bar then required grew irksome to him. Had not his wonderful mind mastered all that book and instructor could teach? Why should he not enjoy some of the fruits of being a Lord Keeper's son, a Lord Treasurer's nephew? It was natural enough for him to apply to his uncle to facilitate his entrance upon active professional life. And he did apply,—heedless of Lord Burghley's indisposition to help him. Instead of encouragement and aid, he received a lecture for his arrogancy, to which he replied with that humility which never takes offense, because it is always fearful of offending.

The probability is that Burghley dreaded to bring

his nephew in contact with his son, Robert Cecil; the contrast would have been apparent and damaging. Hence, repression came to Bacon from a quarter where advancement might have been confidently expected.

But, notwithstanding Burghley's rebuke, his desire was finally gratified; and, sometime in the year 1586, he became a full-fledged lawyer.

But of his professional career, for awhile, if he had one, nothing is known, and the history of his legislative career is almost as vague. He sat in the parliament which succeeded the trial of Mary, Queen of Scots; he spoke on "The Great Cause," and joined in the unanimous vote for plucking the thorn from the side of Elizabeth; he was one of a committee of conference to offer the Queen a benevolence in the place of an additional subsidy; and in the discussion of this subject became, probably, impregnated with certain patriotic notions against increasing taxation beyond the limits of time-honored precedents.

He was prominent in the next parliament, which granted a double subsidy, with a precautionary clause that it should not be considered as establishing a precedent.

About this time, the unquenchable energy of Puritanism burst forth and expressed its opinions in a flood of secretly-printed pamphlets. The first champion was one Penry, a Welchman, who, under the *nom de plume* of Martin Marprelate, provoked the Bishop of Winchester to religious controversy. Penry subsequently enjoyed the distinction of being hanged, which was a reflection upon the bishop's controversial powers. Bacon seems to have been of the opinion that the controversy needed volunteer pens, for he now wrote his admirable paper entitled "An Advertisement touching the Controversies of the Church of England," which was, years after, revived to allay the radicalism as well of the Long Parliament as of the Restoration.

The ability displayed in this pamphlet led to the employment of his pen in the preparation of a paper to impress on the continental mind that, although English sectaries were apparently on the eve of cutting one another's throats, they would forego this luxury and coalesce, rather than the throne should be endangered by domestic dissension becoming an ally to foreign invasion.

This service may have propitiated his uncle; for, a few years afterwards, Bacon received the reversion of a place worth sixteen hundred pounds a year; but he was kept out of its enjoyment by an incumbent who lived and enjoyed the office during twenty years succeeding.

From a letter to the Earl of Leicester, written in 1588, in which Bacon asks for something, it appears that the acquaintance with the Earl of Essex had been initiated, which was to ripen into a disinterested friendship on the Earl's part.

Bacon's brother, Anthony, had resided abroad for many years, where he had employed his time and talents in the rôle of an amateur diplomat,— just as George Selwyn was an amateur headsman. In 1592 Anthony returned to England, and he locked hands with Francis, and Francis' young friend, the Earl of Essex. The information which Anthony had supplied to his uncle Burghley was now given to Essex, who was aspiring to rivalry with the Lord Treasurer for influence over the Queen.

A profitless reversion, and an appointment as
Counsel Extraordinary to the Queen, the reward of
which was one of Elizabeth's faded smiles, were all
that Bacon had received in the line of preferment at
court. When he entered on his thirty-second year he
again addressed himself to his uncle, whom he calls
"the Atlas of this Commonwealth, the honor of my
house, and the second founder of my poor estate."
After referring to the meanness of his estate, he tells
Burghley that if he will not "carry him on," he will
sell what he has, and "become some sorry book-
maker."

Neither flattery nor threat seems to have moved the
Lord Treasurer. Bacon returned to Gray's Inn, and
employed his pen in his "Observations on a Libel,"
and his "Discourse in Praise of his Sovereign." The
only fruits either bore were rhetorical, unless the
refusal of recognition on the part of his uncle resulted
in knitting him closer to Essex, which is more than
probable; since, many years after, upon sending Buckingham the patent creating him a viscount, he wrote:
"In the time of the Cecils, the father and the son, able
men, were by design and of purpose suppressed."

It is a popular belief that queens who love their
people must have a special single object for their
superfluous affection. Some love their husbands, some
love their lovers, others love their lap-dogs. Elizabeth
had neither husband nor lap-dog; but the Queen's
lover was as essential to her court as the king's jester
to that of her father. Nor was she fastidious respecting the status of her favorite as another woman's
husband. She apparently applied the principle of
eminent domain to the marital relation, and regarded

every wife as the mere sub-tenant of a husband's affection.

Robert Devereaux, Earl of Essex, was now the Queen's favorite. He was handsome, brave, impulsive and headstrong; generous to his friends and followers, jealous of, and unjust to, his rivals. His relations with the Queen were a compound of comedy and tragedy.

Now fondling an old woman's bony hand, next rebelling against an old woman's bad temper; while she, on her part, to-day admitted him to the familiarity of a lover, and to-morrow required the obedience of a subject and obsequiousness of a courtier. Sometimes she granted his most extravagant demands; at others refused his most reasonable requests.

His ambition was insatiate. The Queen had conferred military honors and offices upon him which were envied by veteran soldiers; and now, at the age of twenty-three, he entered the lists against Burghley for civil employment, influence and power.

It was at this period of the Earl's career that the friendship between him and Bacon reached its height. About the same time, the intrigues of Spain with Scotland inspired the summoning of a parliament; which was informed by the Lord Keeper, the Queen being present, that supplies were wanted to confront the threatening dangers; that there was no need of new laws, the superfluity of old ones requiring abridgment.

The admirers of Bacon point, with pardonable pride, to the fact that he seized the opportunity for a speech on law reform, in respect to which he was far in advance of his contemporaries.

He was a law-maker as well as lawyer, and suggested

improvements which tardy legislation has, within comparatively recent times, adopted.

His second speech in this parliament had a serious
influence upon his after-life. The demand of the
Queen was, after an altercation between the two houses,
responded to by a motion for the grant of an unprecedented supply, collectable in a brief period.

Bacon, in a moment of impulsive patriotism, or,
willing to resent the neglect he had suffered at the
hands of the government, spoke against the motion,
and said, "It is impossible; the poor men's rent is
such as they are not able to yield it, and the general
commonalty is not able to pay so much upon the
present. The gentlemen must sell their plate, and the
farmers their brass pots ere this will be paid."

Such language was strange to the time and the place.
It was paralleled by Colepepper, speaking of monop-
olists, in the Long Parliament, when he said, "They
sup in our cup; they dip in our dish; they sit by our
fire; we find them in the dye-fat, the wash-bowls, and
the powdering-tub." Hence, it must have electrified
Bacon's contemporaries, stricken Burghley dumb, and
loosened the Queen's tongue, and made her profanely
voluble.

She conveyed her displeasure to the nephew through
his too-willing uncle; and Bacon replied, in a letter to
Burghley, in which he claims the inspiration of the best
motives for his speech, and begs him to continue him
in his good opinion, "to perform the part of an honest
friend towards your poor servant and ally, in drawing
Her Majesty to accept of the sincerity and simplicity
of my heart, and to bear with the rest, and restore me
to Her Majesty's favor."

If it be just to test a man's sincerity by contrasting his conduct in after-life, and under similar circumstances, with a position formerly assumed, Bacon's sympathy for the poor would appear to have been assumed, and his respect for precedents affected. In the parliament of 1601, when the largest grant ever received by the Queen was voted, Bacon opposed a proposition to exempt the poor tax-payer,— "the three-pound men," and said "it was *dulcis tractus pari jugo*, and therefore the poor, as well as the rich, not to be exempted." In other words, he answered his own early arguments, and voted against his own early principles.

After having been rendered unhappy by the Queen's anger, and consequent exile from her presence, it seems that he contemplated some change in his life, which, however, was not carried into execution, because of the disapproval of Essex, to whom Bacon yielded, "because it is the best wisdom in any man, in his own matters, to rest in the wisdom of a friend; but, also, because my affection to your Lordship hath made mine own contentment inseparable from your satisfaction."

In the meantime, Bacon was embarrassed by a limited income and unlimited debts.

"If a young man has parts and poverty he can get along at the bar," says an old English judge. Bacon was provided with these prerequisites, but had no success in his profession commensurate with his abilities. He was a little Cosmos of contradictions. His heart was enslaved by philosophy, yet the tool of an office-seeking ambition. He sighed for a contemplative life, while aspiring to a prominent place among his busiest contemporaries.

Amid contradictory desires and embarrassing surroundings, instead of centering his hopes and endeavors
in a single direction, he was subservient to every breeze
which seemed to blow from a favorable quarter. In
1593 a vacancy was about to occur in the office of
Attorney-General; and Bacon, an almost briefless barrister, at the age of thirty-three, fixed his eye upon the
place. Essex probably encouraged him with assurances
more sanguine than certain.

The candidate's experience discouraged him from
addressing Burghley directly, so he sought to propitiate
the Lord Treasurer's sons,—Sir Thomas and Sir
Robert Cecil. His letter to his cousin Robert, whom
he calls "your honor," is in an humble strain, and is
replied to in a frank, friendly form, as insincere as
Bacon's.

Essex, with characteristic generosity, became his
warmest advocate with the Queen. Bacon wrote Elizabeth a letter of a manly tone, which contained an
assurance that if his friends pressed his suit his spirit
was not with them,—an assurance irreconcilable with
the facts, incompatible with the truth.

Nothing but the friendly enthusiasm of Essex could
have excused his application to an unforgiving woman
with an unforgetting faculty, for a favor such as he now
asked. And, as might have been expected, she confronted his friend with the speech against granting the
Queen what she most needed in a perilous situation.

Sir Edward Coke, Bacon's life-long rival, was made
Attorney-General, in spite of the "uttermost credit,
friendship and authority" which Essex, as favorite and
a Privy-Councillor, pledged in Bacon's behalf.

A fresh scent was taken up as soon as the old was

dropped, by Bacon pursuing the Solicitor-Generalship.

He received the same hearty support from Essex,
and more encouragement from other influential men
who had access to the Queen. In a letter, thanking
Essex, he repeats his threat of retirement to private
life, and devotion to studies and contemplation; but,
with this inviting and, to Bacon, appropriate career
before him, he descends to the ignoble suggestions of
a place-hunter. "The objection to my competitors
your Lordship knoweth partly. I pray, spare them not,
not over the Queen, but to the great ones, to show
your confidence, and work their distaste."

The Queen postponed the selection of a Solicitor-
General, but became reconciled sufficiently to employ
Bacon as Counsel-Extraordinary, sending him on a
journey at his own cost, which compelled him to call
his brother Anthony's better credit in play, to borrow
the wherewithal to meet his travelling expenses.

He was halted by sudden illness. From his sick-
room he wrote to the Queen: "Most gracious and
admirable Sovereign, as I do acknowledge a providence
of God towards me that findeth it expedient for me
tolerare jugum in juventate mea, so this present arrest of
me by *His Divine Majesty*, from *your Majesty's* service,
is not the least affliction I have proved," etc., bringing
the two sovereignties in a juxtaposition, as he repeatedly
did afterwards in royal correspondence, in a manner
shocking to all sense of propriety.

Without fulfilling his mission, he returned to London,
having, on the way, received the degree of Master of
Arts from Cambridge. He closed the year in writing
the part of a discourse touching the safety of the Queen

against conspiracies, in the examination into a plot for the murder of Elizabeth; and in the preparation and conduct of elaborate holiday festivities at Gray's Inn.

Essex, being of the opinion that the Queen really set a high price on Bacon's services, acquainted her with his threat of retirement should he fail in procuring the long-sought preferment. This, it seems, produced a summons of Bacon to court. He did not see the Queen, but had an interview with his cousin, Sir Robert Cecil, who entertained him with a report of Elizabeth's anger that he should have presumed to hasten her decision. "Then Her Majesty sweareth that if I continue in this manner she will seek all England for a solicitor rather than take me; that she never dealt so with any as with me; she hath pulled me over the bar (note the words, for they cannot be her own). We (*i. e.* Bacon and his cousin) parted in kindness *secundum exterius.*" Thus he writes to his brother, Anthony, and we infer that he suspected his cousin of secret enmity; and, instead of then replying to what Sir Robert said, he craved the privilege of putting his answer in writing, which he did in a letter to his cousin, disclaiming his purpose of travelling to have been a "present motion," or that he authorized Essex to make known his resolve, and referred to the latter for substantiation of this statement.

The favorite pressed his friend's suit urgently and eloquently, but in vain; for, on November 5th, 1596, Sergeant Fleming became Solicitor-General.

Disappointed and dejected, Bacon sought retirement and consolation. The villa of Essex afforded him an asylum, and philosophy gave him comfort.

The warm-hearted Earl shared his chagrin and

soothed his sorrow by giving him an estate worth £1,800. This, Bacon coquetted about accepting, but accepted.

The embittered spirits of the two friends yielded to the influences of time, and Essex, with the aid of Bacon, celebrated the Queen's birthday, after the former had allayed her suspicious mind respecting his patronage of a book on the forbidden question of the succession.

The publication, about this time, of Bacon's first edition of his Essays, ten in number, the "Colors of Good and Evil," and the "*Meditationes Sacræ*" proclaimed to the world that the place-hunter was not only a place-hunter; and their reception must have more than consoled and comforted the author.

His friend Essex, in 1596, returned from the successful expedition against Cadiz, which might have conferred additional lustre on English arms if the Earl's advice had been followed, and Spain's Indian fleet engaged. As it was, Essex was met by rumors of charges against him, at court, by rivals jealous of his success and the fame it procured him; which was increased when it was discovered that Spain's Indian fleet placidly sailed into the Tagus, when it might have been intercepted, if the advice of Essex had prevailed.

A thorough appreciation of the Earl's impulsive nature, of his frank and unguarded conduct, of the jealousy which too great popularity with the people might excite in the Queen's breast, inspired Bacon to now write his friend a long letter of advice, which has more the tone of a Machiavelli than a moralist.

After asking the Earl "to consider, first, whether I have not reason to think that your fortune comprehendeth mine," he urges him to "win the Queen;" then, picturing what an unfavorable turn to his relations with Elizabeth might be brought about by his enemies using and abusing his popularity, his military renown, his very nearness to the Queen, he proceeds to advise how he may render the Queen unsusceptible to such influences, commending, in brief, a course of deceit. He says : —

"Next, whereas I have noted you to fly and avoid (in some respect justly) the resemblance or imitation of my Lord of Leicester and my Lord Chancellor Hatton; yet I am persuaded (howsoever I wish your Lordship as distant as you are from them in points of favor, integrity, magnanimity, and merit,) that it will do you much good between the Queen and you, to allege them (as oft as you find occasion) for authors and patterns. For I do not know a readier mean to make Her Majesty think you are in your right way."

Next, he criticises his method of flattering the Queen, and commends a better course : —

"Fourthly," he says, "your Lordship should never be without some particulars afoot, which you should seem to pursue with earnestness and affection, and then let them fail, upon taking knowledge of Her Majesty's opposition and dislike. . . . A less weighty sort of particulars may be the pretense of some journeys, which, at Her Majesty's request, your Lordship mought relinquish; as if you would pretend a journey to see your living and estate towards Wales, or the like; for, as for great foreign journeys of employment and service, it standeth not with your gravity to play or stratagem with them."

The teacher was a thoughtful, contemplative, delib

erate man, a professed moralist and philosopher; the
scholar was some years his junior, impressible, with a
native-born disposition towards courageous frankness,
and towards the taking of straight paths to a wished-
for goal.

A few years later, Bacon protested "that he had
spent more time in vain in studying how to make the
Earl a good servant to the Queen and State than he
had done in anything else."

An appeal from Bacon to Bacon never fails to
condemn the courtier out of the mouth of the
philosopher.

Twenty years later he addressed a letter of advice to
the favorite of another sovereign :—

"You are now the king's favorite, so voted and so
esteemed by all. . . . You are as a continual sentinel,
always to stand upon your watch, to give him true intelligence. If you flatter him, you betray him. If you conceal
the truth of those things from him which concern his justice
or his honor, although not the safety of his person, you are
as dangerous a traitor to his state as he that riseth in arms
against him. A false friend is more dangerous than an open
enemy. . . . . Let him (the king) take on him this
resolution, as King *David* did. '*There shall no deceitful
person dwell in my house.*' . . . . But neither in jest
nor earnest must there be countenance or ear given to flatterers or sycophants, the bane of all courts." *

The two letters differ in tone, because Bacon knew
that Elizabeth would not see one, and that James I.
would see the other.

Before dismissing the consideration of this remark-

* Advice to Villiers.

able letter to Essex, a further quotation will throw more light upon the almost inconceivable inconsistency between Bacon in politics and Bacon in the closet : —

"Lastly, to be plain with your Lordship (for the gentlemen are such as I am beholden to), nothing can make the Queen or the world think so much that you are come to a provident care of your estate, as the altering of some of your officers, who, though they be as true to you as one hand to the other, yet *opinio veritate major.*"

My singular good Lord! some of your officers have placed me under obligations to their kindness; they are as true as steel to you, but their dismissal from your service would be favorably commented on by the gossips, whose opinion is greater than truth; therefore I advise you to reward their consideration for me and faithfulness to you by turning them out into the cold.

During the chase for the place of Solicitor-General, the enemies of Bacon under-estimated his legal lore and ability to the Queen, so that she told Essex, that, while she acknowledged his friend's "excellent gift of speech, that in law she rather thought he could show to the uttermost than that he was deep."

Bacon now vindicated himself from this charge by writing his "Maxims" and "Use of the Common Law," — very valuable expositions of law as a science, as far as they went, and far more philosophical in treatment than contemporary works on the same subject.

His fortune did not keep pace with the fame which attended his writings; his practice, never lucrative, must have suffered from neglect incident to pursuit of office; and, failing to obtain relief by preferment, he concluded to try the last resort of a respectable beggary,— marriage for money.

The object of his speculative design was Lady Hatton, a lively young widow, sandwiched between a great fortune and a bad temper. He enlisted Essex in this enterprise : —

"My suit to your Lordship," he writes, "is for your several letters to be left with me, dormant, to the gentle-woman, and either of her parents; wherein I do not doubt but as the beams of your favor have often dissolved the coldness of my fortune, so, in this argument, your Lordship will do the like with your pen."

With commendatory forethought, in order to provide for more than a single path to support, he adds : —

"My desire is, also, that your Lordship would vouchsafe unto me a general letter to My Lord Keeper, for his Lord-ship's holding me from you recommended,— both in the course of my practice and in the course of my employment in Her Majesty's service."

The letter closes with some wise and friendly hints to the Earl, who was about setting out in charge of an expedition against the Spanish treasure-fleet. Bacon's timid and prudent nature regarded the eminence of his friend as a dangerous height, from which he might, at any time, have a fatal fall; and, therefore, did not approve, in his heart, of his undertaking. Essex, in the midst of his busy preparations, wrote a warm, earnest and eloquent endorsement of the suitor, who must have been a cold lover, for nothing came of his marital candidacy. The lady shortly afterwards ran off with Sir Edward Coke, to whom she was married. Thus was another victory secured for the lawyer over the philosopher.

The ways of widows are inscrutable. Bacon was younger than Coke, was handsome, amiable and agreeable; Sir Edward was an ill-tempered, overbearing widower. There were, it was said, seven comprehensive and conclusive marital objections against Coke,—his six children and himself.

The loss of this lady was Bacon's first stroke of good fortune. Her disagreeable qualities amounted to disagreeable abilities. She led her husband such a life, that, had he been a more sensitive man, he must have sought relief in death or Doctor's Commons.

Bacon was a disappointed suitor, not a dejected lover. It is doubtful whether the author of the essay on "Marriage and Single Life" ever felt the tender passion, or confessed to the soft impeachment. Apropos to the runaway match of the great English lawyer, the following anecdote is recorded in Mr. F. F. Heard's "Oddities of the Law."

"In the year 1598, Sir Edward Coke, then Attorney-General, married the Lady Hatton, according to the Book of Common Prayer, but without banns or license, and in a private house. Several great men were there present, as Lord Burleigh, Lord Chancellor Egerton, etc. They all, by their proctor, submitted to the censure of the archbishop, who granted them an absolution from the excommunication which they had incurred. The act of absolution set forth that it was granted by reason of penitence, *and the act seeming to have been done through ignorance of the law.*"

In the parliament of 1597, to which Bacon was now
returned, he became one of the most active and prominent members. He voted for a subsidy equal to the
one he had opposed in his unfortunate speech; and his
whole career indicated that he possessed the confidence
and respect of the House, while it must have propitiated the Queen, and subdued her lively recollection
of his early opposition to large grants and quick
payments.

Essex, in the meanwhile, returned from his naval
expedition, which was unsuccessful, as he failed to
intercept the Spanish fleet. Sir Walter Raleigh, second
in command, however, was fortunate enough to meet
with three stragglers; he improved the opportunity for
bravery and enterprise, as was his custom, and compelled them to strike their colors. He received, for
his reward, the jealous enmity of the impulsive Essex,
who was irritated by his own failure.

The Queen was not pleased with the result, nor
with the management of Essex; for his fleet strag-
gled home, and found the south coast alarmed by
fears of dangers, from the channel being left entirely
unprotected.

Essex retreated to his favorite asylum,—the sulks,
from which he was lured by the Queen's partiality, who
restored him fully to her good graces, honored him
with promotions, and employed him to perform the
offices of Secretary, in the absence of Sir Robert Cecil,
who had been sent on a special mission to France. In
his new capacity, Essex was called on to deal with
affairs in Ireland which were of a serious nature.
Bacon volunteered his advice, which was of a cautious
character. The closing paragraph of the letter indi-

cates a desire, on Bacon's part, for his friend to improve the opportunity, and a belief in his fitness to deal with the subject-matter : —

"If your Lordship," he writes, "doubt to put your sickle in another's harvest; first, time brings it to you in Mr. Secretary's absence; next, being mixed with matter of war, it is fittest for you; and, lastly, I know your Lordship will carry it with that modesty and respect towards aged dignity, and that good correspondence towards my dear kinsman and your good friend now abroad, as no inconvenience may grow that way. Thus have I played the ignorant statesman, which I do to nobody but your Lordship; except the Queen, sometimes, when she trains me on. But your Lordship will accept my duty and good meaning, and secure me touching the privateness of that I write."

Essex was pleased with Bacon's friendly interest and the sound advice; and, in reply, acquainted him with the situation, so that he might no longer play the "ignorant statesman," but advise from a more intelligent standpoint. Bacon replies; and, after saying, "I will shoot my fool's bolt, since you will have it so," proceeds to submit suggestions well worth the consideration of all concerned in the important issue. One paragraph of his letter is quoted, because it may throw some light on the question of what was Bacon's exact relation to Essex in this affair.

"And, but that your Lordship is too easy to pass, in such cases, from dissimulation to verity, I think if your Lordship lent your reputation in this case,— that is, to pretend that if peace go not on, and the Queen mean not to make a defensive war, as in times past, but a full re-conquest of those parts of the country, you would escape the charge,— I think it would heip co settle Tyrone in his seeking accord, and win you a great deal of honor *gratis*."

The remainder of this letter abounds in wise counsel for establishing peace and prosperity in the rebellious isle.

Sir Robert Cecil having returned from France, the subject was further discussed, especially in respect to the selection of an officer 'for Ireland.

On this question, Essex quarrelled with the Queen, who boxed his ears. Then, of course, came the customary retirement from court, sulks, and reconciliation, which inspired a letter of congratulation from Bacon, in which, for the first time, he congratulated Essex as second to another in his consideration : "And, therefore, bearing unto your Lordship, *after Her Majesty*, of all public persons, the second duty, I could not but signify unto you my gratulation."

While Bacon was shooting his "fool's bolt," and playing "the ignorant statesman," his obligations were maturing. Extravagance, improvidence, attention to everything but nursing his paying practice (for he got nothing for his services to the Queen), laid him at the mercy of a money-lender, who consigned him to a sponging-house, for the non-payment of a debt of £300. He was released through the interposition of friends, but probably entered into liberty as a candidate for the debtor's gaol.

Cruel, indeed, would have fortune been to Bacon, if, in the midst of financial embarrassments and his lack of briefs, she had not cheered him with a single smile. The fact is that he was consoled by the consideration which he received at the Queen's hands. It put no

money in his purse; it brought no lucrative preferment. She accepted his services, which were valuable
and untiring; she fed his hopes, and he was happy.
Elizabeth was appeased by a consistent course of subserviency; she admitted him into her presence, and
graciously accepted his gifts, one of which was a
"pettycoat of white sattin, embroidered all over like
feathers and billets, with three broad borders, fair
embroidered with snakes and fruitage, emblems of
wisdom and bounty."

About the year 1598, the intimacy between Bacon
and Essex seems to have cooled; for, although there
was considerable controversy and excitement at court
over the selection of a commander of the forces to be
sent against the Irish rebel Tyrone,— a controversy in
which Essex displayed more than ordinary wrong-head-
edness,—we have no information of Bacon taking any
hand in the affair, or interposing, to check or direct his
hasty and high-tempered friend. It is true that, in the
paragraph from Bacon's letter heretofore quoted, which
was written under different circumstances and before
the expedition was determined on, he advised him to
lend his reputation in the crisis, as calculated to fright-
en Tyrone to terms, provided the Earl would not pass
from dissimulation to verity. This letter, and this
paragraph specially, are quoted in connection with
Bacon's apology; by some, to prove that Bacon
urgently opposed Essex taking command of this expedition. But the letter of March, 1598, indicates that
Bacon thought that, by letting Tyrone know of warlike
preparations, which, however, should be confined to
England, while a peaceful policy should be pursued,
the object desired might be secured. What he may

B

have meant, and probably did mean, by fearing his Lordship might pass from dissimulation to verity, was not to warn or advise the Earl against taking the command of such an expedition, but against espousing the expedition as necessary. For, when Essex was occupying Cecil's relationship to the Queen, during the Secretary's absence, Bacon advised him to "put his sickle into another's harvest," because of its "being mixed with matter of war, it is fittest for you." Taking this in connection with Bacon's opinion that the name of Essex would be a terror to Tyrone, it is, to some minds, hardly reconcilable with the proposition that Bacon earnestly advised Essex not to take the command. If matters of war were fittest for him in council, they were fittest in the field; if, in addition, his mere name, or "reputation," would be a terror to the rebels, what man so suitable to take the command, from Bacon's standpoint? Yet, if Bacon had been consulted, not when the question of how to deal with Tyrone, whether by force or with persuasion, was debated, but when the expedition was determined on, he would have probably advised the Earl not to accept the command, if he could bring himself to directly oppose such a man's desire, which is doubtful. He was, however, apparently not consulted, and did not proffer his opinion or advice. This seems evident from his letter, supposed to have been written in March, 1599,—the month in which the Earl set out. It seems to have been drawn from him because of his reticence : —

"MY SINGULAR GOOD LORD : — Your late note of my silence in your occasions hath made me set down these few wandering lines, as one that would say somewhat and can say nothing touching your Lordship's intended charge for Ireland."

Then follow reflections on "the great merit and peril of the service: a presage of success; divination of good from inwardly knowing his Lordship; his fitness proved by the choice of Her Majesty, known to be one of the most judicious princes in discerning of spirits that ever governed." Next he descants upon the character of the country and the enemy; then adds some excellent hints as to prudent carriage, and closes with wishes for the Earl's success.

In his apology, Bacon says: "Touching his going into Ireland, it pleased him expressly and in set manner to desire mine opinion and counsel. At which time I did not only dissuade, but protest against his going." Then he recites the arguments he used, "with much vehemency and asseveration." These arguments, recited in the apology, are almost identical with a portion of the contents of the letter last referred to, but, in the letter, disconnected with any protest against Essex proceeding with the expedition.

This much space is given to this matter because the lives of Bacon and Essex were so interwoven, that the biography of one involves that of the other. And no element of their history has provoked more discussion than the conduct of Bacon towards his friend, from the time Essex took command of this expedition to the tragic hour when the young Earl faced death so heroically upon the block.

Reference was made to happy relations between the Queen and Bacon; "but," says a clever writer, "prosperity never points its sunshine in our faces, without adversity, as our shadows, ever being at our heels."

Essex, having obtained the leadership of the Irish expedition, demanded and received those extraordinary powers which increase the responsibility of a commander, add nothing to the glory of success, and intensify the disgrace of failure.

His campaign was disastrous. Time, troops and money were wasted, instructions were not strictly adhered to, an interview with the rebel chieftain in the middle of a stream, out of ear-shot, supplied his enemies with a text for suspicion and misrepresentation; and, altogether, the enterprise ended most unfortunately for the young Earl. Contrary to orders, yet confident of sympathy and forgiveness, Essex conceived and executed the sudden plan of hastening to England and throwing himself at the feet of Elizabeth.

"Without stopping to change his dress, travel-stained as he was, he sought the Queen in her chamber, and found her newly-risen, with her hair about her face. He kneeled to her, and kissed her hands. Elizabeth, taken by surprise, gave way to her old partiality for him, and the pleasure she always had in his company. He left her presence much pleased with her reception, and thanked God, though he had suffered much trouble and storm abroad, that he had found a sweet calm at home."

The voice of one of his enemies enlisted her ear, even, probably, while the tones of her favorite's still lingered in her boudoir. The Queen was jealous of her own affections, and self-suspicious of forgiving favorites too easily; so, the next day, Essex was ordered into the custody of the Lord Keeper.

In order to justify, or rather excuse, the conduct of Bacon at the subsequent trial of Essex for treason, it is necessary to demonstrate that the Earl fell from the grace of loyalty while in Ireland, and that this vile beginning concluded in his tragic end.

Of the indictment now brought against the Earl, that he contemplated treason when the Queen most trusted him, of the charges which are now said to have been laid before the Queen, and which excited her suspicion and procured his qualified imprisonment, Bacon had no information. He was not in attendance upon the court at Nonsuch, and was informed, the day after the Earl's arrival, that he had returned. He wrote him a welcoming letter: "I have committed," he says, "to this poor paper the humble salutations of *him that is more yours than any man's; more yours than any man.*"

The most that Bacon knew was that Essex had not been successful, and that the Queen was disappointed and his rivals were rejoicing. So he hopes "it is a little cloud that will quickly pass away," and that his "Lordship's wisdom and obsequious circumspection and patience will turn all to the best."

He went to Nonsuch and had an interview with Essex. What occurred at this quarter of an hour's talk we know nothing save what is gathered from Bacon's "Apology," written after the Earl was in his grave. He says he told him it was "a little cloud which would soon pass away,—but a mist," and added to this consultation advice which Essex did not follow. The quasi-disgrace of Essex occasioned murmurs among the people whose idol he seems to have been; and as he was neither released nor brought to trial, the populace were informed, by the declaration of the principal counsellors in the Star Chamber, "what the Earl had been sent out to do, what means they had provided, and what he had done."

As he was not prosecuted, the people busied themselves about the problem of why the proceedings stopped where they did; why, if punishment was not meted out, pardon was not granted. Popular indignation, hungering and thirsting for some one to blame, is not very eclectic. Bacon fell under their suspicion because, say his defenders, it was given out that the council favored Essex; the masses could not suspect the Queen of voluntary injustice or unkindness to her favorite; but as Bacon now enjoyed frequent access to the Queen's presence, being employed in law and revenue matters, the people made him their victim, and held him responsible for arresting the Queen's full forgiveness of, and entire reconciliation with, Essex.

The opportunity for innocence to vindicate itself by an explanation was a fine one, but Bacon did not seize on it; he wrote but one public "Apology," in which he defined his relations as the link between Essex and the Queen, and that was done when the two were dead.

He wrote, it is true, letters to Sir Robert Cecil and to Lord Henry Howard, the latter the friend of Essex, who retired from court when Essex was forbidden its precincts. Both letters indignantly spurned the "tale shaped in London's forge," charging that Bacon represented to the Queen that Essex's offense "was first *premunire*, and now, last, that it was high treason." Adding: —

"For, my Lord Essex, I am not servile to him, having regard to my superior's duty. I have been much bound unto him; and, the other side, I have spent more time and more thoughts about his well-doing than ever I did about mine own. I pray God, you his friends amongst you, be in the right. For my part, I have deserved better than to have my name objected to envy, or my life to a ruffian's violence; but I have the privy coat of a good conscience. I am sure these curses and bruits hurt my Lord more than all."

On the 5th of June, 1600, Essex was formally brought before a special commission, formally tried, lightly prosecuted and lightly sentenced. He was suspended from the execution of his offices, and imprisoned in his own house during the Queen's pleasure. Bacon performed the part assigned him, as Queen's Councillor, along with Coke, in as humane a manner as the Queen designed it should be done. But we cannot forget that he stood among the prosecutors of Essex. The romantic friendship was near its end. The prisoner was not in the situation to be a patron. The client who, in the last of November, 1599, wrote, "I am more yours than any man's; more yours than any man," in the last of July, 1600, writes: "I love few persons *better* than yourself."

This letter and the reply present the strong contrast between the two characters of the men, when the wheel of fortune had reversed their lots. Essex is now a petitioner. He wants strong, disinterested friendship, an advocate with the Queen, who is surrounded by his secret enemies; he must depend on the unselfish devotion of a person of influence, who, in the language of Bacon, will "opportune and importune;" who, to remove a stain from the Earl's character, a suspicion of his sincerity, a doubt of his loyalty, a coldness from the heart of his Queen and mistress, will spend "all his power, might, authority and amity," as Essex did to obtain a paltry place for Bacon, so antagonizing the Queen in his zeal for his friend that he wrote to Bacon: "The Queen was not passionate against you until she found I was passionate for you."

But the Earl had no such friend at court, although Bacon was daily there. And Bacon, to disabuse a sanguine mind of too great expectations, wrote his former patron and friend the following letter, after allowing nearly two months to elapse since his trial and sentence, the worst feature of which was exile from the presence of Elizabeth:—

"MY LORD,— No man can better expound my doings than your Lordship, which maketh me to need say the less. Only I humbly pray you to believe that I aspire to the conscience and commendation, first, of *bonus civis*, which, with us, is a good and true servant to the Queen; and next, of *bonus vir*, that is, an honest man. I desire your Lordship, also, to think, that though I confess I love some things much better than I love your Lordship,— as the Queen's service, her quiet and contentment, her honor, her favor, the good of my country, and the like, yet I love few persons better than yourself, both for gratitude's sake and for your own virtues, which cannot hurt but by accident or abuse. Of which my good affection I was ever, and am ready to yield testimony by any good offices, but with such reservations as yourself cannot but allow; for as I was ever sorry that your Lordship should fly with waxen wings, doubting Icarus' fortune; so, for the growing up of your own feathers, specially ostrich's, or any other, save of a bird of prey, no man shall be more glad. And this is the axletree whereupon I have turned and shall turn; which, to signify to you, though I think you are yourself persuaded as much, in the cause of writing; and so I commend your Lordship to God's goodness. From Gray's Inn, this 20th day of July, 1600.
"Your Lordship's most humbly,   FR. BACON."

"My singular good Lord" no longer heads Bacon's letter; no unqualified pledge of friendship is tendered; no more comprehending of fortunes is recognized; no first love is declared; but the old friendship is subordinated now to Queen's service, quiet and contentment, to country's and an unenumerated "the like." A "few persons" have taken precedence of Essex; "good offices" are tendered with "a reservation;" and the fallen friend compared to the classic fool who flew with waxen wings. Bacon, in his "Apology," calls the Earl's reply "a courteous and loving acceptation of my good will and endeavors."

It is the answer of a generous and magnanimous mind. And yet, there are parts which seem to be inspired by prudent reflection upon the change in their relations to the Queen, upon the power possessed by Bacon to hurt or help, while here and there is a delicate touch of irony:—

"MR. BACON,— I can neither expound nor censure your late actions, being ignorant of all of them save one; and having directed my sight inward only, to examine myself. You do pray me to believe that you only aspire to the conscience and commendation of *bonus civis* and *bonus vir;* and I do faithfully assure you, that while that is your ambition (though your course be active and mind contemplative), yet we shall both *convenire in eodem tertio;* and *convenire inter nosipsos.* Your profession of affection and offer of good offices are welcome to me. For answer to them I will say but this: that you have believed I have been kind to you; and you may believe that I cannot be other, either upon humor or my own election. I am a stranger to all poetical conceits, or else should say something of your poetical example. But this I must say, that I never flew with other wings than desire to merit, and confidence in, my sovereign's favor; and, when one of these wings failed me, I would light no where but at my sovereign's feet though she suffered me to be bruised with the fall. And till Her Majesty that knows that I was never bird of prey, finds it to agree with her will and her service that my wings shall be *imped again, I have committed myself to the mire. No power but my God's and my sovereign's can alter this resolution of   Your retired friend,   ESSEX.'

Bacon claims, in his "Apology," that he used the frequent opportunities which he enjoyed of access to the Queen's presence to bring about reconciliation, and that he conceived and executed the following scheme: He wrote a diplomatic letter to Essex, which Anthony Bacon fathered and forwarded, and a diplomatic answer, which Essex signed and sent. There is ground in this correspondence to infer that the honest spirit of it was inspired by Anthony Bacon.

This correspondence is very curious, and some extracts may both entertain and enlighten the reader, if it be borne in mind that Bacon is the writer. He makes his brother Anthony say: —

"But to be plain with your Lordship, my fear rather is because I hear how some of your good and wise friends, not unpractised in the court, and supposing them not to be unseen in the deep and unscrutable centre of the court, which is Her Majesty's mind, do not only toll the bell, but even ring out peals, as if your fortune were dead and buried, and as if there were no possibility of recovering Her Majesty's favor; and as if the best of your condition were to live a private and retired life, out of want, out of peril and out of manifest disgrace."

* A term in hawking.

He then advises Essex against despair, praises the kind and faithful nature of the Queen: —

"Her Majesty, in her royal intention, never purposed to call your doings into public question, but only to have used a cloud without a shower, and censuring them by some restraint of liberty, and debarring from her presence. For both, the handling the cause in the Star-chamber was enforced by the violence of libelling and rumors, wherein the Queen thought to have satisfied the world, and yet spared your appearance. And then, after, when that means which was intended for the quenching of malicious bruits, turned to kindle them, because it was said your Lordship was condemned unheard, and your Lordship's sister wrote that private letter, then Her Majesty saw plainly that these winds of rumors could not be commanded down without a handling of the cause, by making you party and admitting your defense. And to this purpose, I do assure your lordship, *that my brother, Francis Bacon, who is too wise to be abused*, though he both reserved in all particulars more than is needful, yet, in generality, he hath ever constantly, and with asseveration, affirmed to me that both those days, — that at the Star-chamber and that at the Lord Keeper's, — were, of the Queen, wholly upon necessity and point of honor, against her inclination."

In the next paragraph personal to Bacon in this letter which he dictated, Anthony says: "And were it not that I desire and hope to see my brother established by Her Majesty's favor, as I think him well worthy for which he hath done and suffered, it were time," etc.

We have, in this letter, Bacon asserting that the Earl's enemies at court were rejoicing over his banishment from the Queen's presence, Bacon asserting that he himself is "too wise to be abused;" and that, when he says that the Queen consented to any proceedings against Essex because she was "won to it, against her inclination," he tells the truth of his own knowledge.

The answer of the Earl, which also was dictated by Bacon, says :—

"I believe most steadfastly Her Majesty never intended to bring my cause to a public censure; and I believe as verily, that, since the sentence, she meant to restore me to tend upon her person; but those which could use occasions (which it was not in me to let), and amplify and practice occasions to represent to Her Majesty a necessity to bring me to the one, can and will do the like to stop me from the other. You say, my errors were my prejudice, and therefore I can mend myself. It is true; but they that know that I can mend myself, and that if I ever recover the Queen that I will never lose her again, will never suffer me to obtain interest in her favor . . . Sure I am the false glass of others' informations, must alter her when I want access to plead mine own cause. . . . . Thanks be to God that they which can make Her Majesty believe I counterfeit with her, cannot make God believe that I counterfeit with him. . . . . . *For your brother, I hold him an honest gentleman, and wish him all good, much rather for your sake.* Yourself, I know, hath suffered more for me, and with me, than any friend that I have."

It will be seen that Bacon puts in the Earl's mouth the assertion that enemies at court prevent him from gaining access to the Queen, which, if accomplished, would restore him to favor that would never be lost; and in a counterfeit letter makes the Earl protest to God he does not counterfeit with the Queen. And as the correspondence was cunningly devised for the Queen's eyes, it introduces a saving clause to remove any impression on her mind that Bacon was the Earl's closest friend, who had suffered more than any other for his sake, since Elizabeth suspected, or pretended to suspect, at that time, every friend of the Earl to be an enemy of the Queen.

Yet for this correspondence Bacon takes great credit unto himself in his "Apology." There is no evidence, except in this "Apology," that Bacon employed himself in the interest of the Earl any further. Essex enjoyed liberty and everything else save employment at court and access to the Queen's presence. The impatient disposition of a young and impulsive nature fretted itself, and vibrated between prayers and curses. He made the renewal of a valuable patent the final test of the Queen's disposition towards him. She refused the late favorite's petition with the ungracious reply: "No; an unruly beast must be stinted of his provender." While the price of her favor seems to have been submission, the reward of submission appears to have been insult. If history furnishes a parallel to Elizabeth for badness and quickness of temper, strength and obstinacy of will, the annals of America supply it. Andrew Jackson in petticoats was Elizabeth. Elizabeth in trousers was Andrew Jackson.

Essex, thus exiled from court by the Queen's pride and his own sulkiness, excited the sympathy of a little coterie of disinterested friends, who clung to him in adversity as well as prosperity. About this nucleus gathered discontented and dangerous men. They fed the Earl's anger, and indulged in magnifying the acts and antagonism of his enemies at court, who, as Bacon's letters show, were really the barrier between him and restoration to favor and employment.

The conclusion reached at the Earl's Twickenham

villa was that pleasant relationship between him and
the Queen could be restored if he would obtain an
audience by force, and make love or peace at leisure.
This seems to be the substance of the most foolish plan
ever conceived or ever attempted to be executed by
men of brains and bravery.

One fine Sunday morning the Earl advanced through
the city, followed by two or three hundred adherents.
He and they endeavored to raise the populace with
drawn sword, and the cry that the life of Essex was in
danger. Everything in London wore a peaceful aspect
save this cavalcade, and no one apparently knew the
object of the strange procession save those engaged
in it.

Not a citizen joined the mob of gentlemen. The
Queen's forces met them, drove them back, followed
them to Twickenham, surrounded the villa of the misguided young man, planted cannon upon a neighboring
church tower, and demanded an unconditional surrender. The Lord Keeper and three other lords, who
had been sent to investigate this assembling of discontented spirits, were released from the imprisonment to
which they had been subjected, and in a few hours the
favorite was in the Tower of London. His imprisonment was shared by the Earl of Southampton, dear to
every English and American heart as the patron of
Shakspeare.

Elizabeth's heart was hurt and temper aroused by
the appearance of her young favorite in the rôle of
conspirator, and she became suspicious of every courtier who had ever been on friendly terms with Essex.
On February the 8th, 1601, the Earl was taken and
imprisoned. On the 11th of the same month, Bacon,

along with the other Learned Counsel, entered upon the investigation of the conspiracy. On the 18th some of the followers of Essex confessed. On the 19th the Earl and Southampton were arraigned on the charge of treason. Coke and Bacon appeared as prosecutors.

Coke opened in his characteristic and vigorous style, swelling with rhetorical violence, charging the Earl with the worst species of treason. Essex was permitted to interrupt him with protests of innocence, asseverating that the only object he had in view was security against his enemies and access to the Queen's presence. The Earl's interjections and interruptions prevented all regularity of proceedings. Coke wandered from the gist of the case, to the great advantage of the accused, when Bacon interposed and said:—

"In speaking of this late and horrible rebellion which hath been in the eyes and ears of all men, I shall save myself much labor in opening and enforcing the points thereof, insomuch that I speak not before a country jury of ignorant men, but before a most honorable assembly of the greatest Peers of the land, whose wisdom conceives far more than my tongue can utter; yet with your gracious and honorable favors I will presume, if not for information of your honors, yet for the discharge of my duty, to say thus much.

No man can be ignorant that knows matters of former ages, and all history makes it plain, that there was never any traitor heard of that durst directly attempt the seat of his liege prince, but he always colored his practices with some plausible pretense. For God hath imprinted such a majesty in the face of a prince, that no private man dare approach the person of his sovereign with a traitorous intent. And, therefore, they run another side course, *oblique et a latere;* some to reform corruptions of state and religion;

some to reduce the ancient liberties and customs pretended to be lost and worn out; some to remove those persons that, being in high places, make themselves subject to envy; but all of them aim at the overthrow of the state and destruction of the present rulers. And this, likewise, is the use of those that work mischief of another quality: as Cain, that first murderer, took up an excuse for his fact, shaming to outface it with impudency. Thus the Earl made his color the severing some great men and councillors from Her Majesty's favor, and the fear he stood of his pretended enemies lest they should murder him in his house. Therefore he saith he was compelled to fly into the City for succor and assistance; not much unlike Pisistratus, of whom it was so anciently written how he gashed and wounded himself, and in that sort ran crying into Athens that his life was sought and like to have been taken away; thinking to have moved the people to have pitied him, and taken his part, by such counterfeited harm and danger. Whereas, his aim and drift was to take the government of the City into his hands and alter the form thereof. With like pretenses of danger and assaults, the Earl of Essex entered the City of London and passed through the bowels thereof, blanching rumors that he should have been murdered and that the state was sold; whereas, he had no such enemies, no such dangers; persuading themselves that if they could prevail, all would have done well. But now *magna scelera terminantur in hæresia;* for you, my Lord, should know that though princes give their subjects cause of discontent, though they take away the honors they have heaped upon them, though they bring them to a lower estate than they raised them from, yet ought they not to be so forgetful of their allegiance that they should enter into any undutiful act, much less upon rebellion, as you, my Lord, have done. All whatsoever you have, and can say in answer hereof, are but shadows. And, therefore, methinks it were best for you to confess, not to justify."

This was certainly an ingenious speech. The skillful flattery of the introduction must have propitiated the triers. The example of Pisistratus was a powerful picture, but not a parallel. And as far as the remarks go, they were calculated to interfere with the favorable impressions which the excuses and explanations of Essex may have made upon his judges. The Earl appreciated this, and immediately endeavored to qualify their effect by saying:—

"To answer Mr. Bacon's speech at once, I say thus much; and call forth Mr. Bacon against Mr. Bacon. You are then to know that Mr. Francis Bacon hath written two letters, the one of which hath been artificially framed in my name, after he had framed the other in Mr. Anthony Bacon's name to provoke me. In the latter of these two *he lays down the grounds of my discontentment*, and the reasons I pretend against my enemies, pleading as orderly for me as I could do myself. . . . . If those reasons were then just and true, not counterfeit, how can it be that now my pretenses are false and injurious? For then Mr. Bacon joined with me in mine opinion, and pointed out those to be mine enemies, and to hold me in disgrace with Her Majesty, whom he seems now to clear of such mind towards me; and, therefore, I leave the truth of what I say, and he opposeth, unto your Lordships' indifferent considerations."

Bacon, in his letter to the Earl, when acting during Cecil's absence in France, and in the two letters above referred to, not only acknowledged that the Earl had dangerous enemies at court, but aggravated the Earl's fears and suspicion of them. He must have recognized the inconsistency, and for want of a better explanation he replied:—

"Those letters, if they were there, would not blush to be seen for anything contained in them; and that he had spent more time in vain in studying how to make the Earl a good servant to the Queen and state, than he had done in anything else."

The letters, however, were not produced or offered to be produced, although they were in Bacon's possession. The evidence was proceeded with, but the zealous Coke got into another controversy with the accused on matters foreign to the issue, the tendency of which was beneficial to the Earl. Bacon, seeing this, interrupted his senior and leader to say : —

" I have never yet seen in any case *such favor shown to any prisoner;* so many digressions, such delivering of evidence by fractions, and *so silly a defense of such great and notorious treasons.* May it please your Grace, you have seen how weakly he hath shadowed his purpose and how slenderly he hath answered the objections against him. But, my Lord, I doubt the variety of matters and the many digressions may minister occasion of forgetfulness, and may have swerved the judgments of the Lords. . . . . . Now, put the case that the Earl of Essex's intents were, as he would have it believed, to go only as a suppliant to Her Majesty. Shall their petitions be presented by armed petitioners? This must needs bring loss of liberty to the Prince. *Neither is it any point of law, as my Lord Southampton would have it believed, that condemns them of treason.* To take secret counsel, to execute it, to run together in numbers armed with weapons, what can be the excuse? Warned by the Lord Keeper, by a herald, and yet persist! Will any simple man take this to be less than treason ? "

The Earl answered by referring to the smallness of his following as inconsistent with the probability of a treasonable intent. Bacon replied : —

"It is not the company you carried with you, but the assistance you hoped for in the City which you trusted unto. The Duke of Guise thrust himself into the streets of Paris on the day of the Barricados in his doublet and hose, attended only with eight gentlemen, and found that help in the City which (thanks be to God!) you failed of here. And what followed? The King was forced to put himself into a pilgrim's weeds, and in that disguise to steal away to escape their fury. Even such was my Lord's confidence, too, and his pretense the same, and all-hail and a kiss to the City. But the end was treason, as hath been sufficiently proved. But when he had once delivered and engaged himself so far into that which the shallowness of his conceit could not accomplish as he expected, the Queen for her defense taking arms against him, he was glad to yield himself; and thinking to color his practices, turned his pretexts, and alleged the occasion thereof to proceed from a private quarrel."

Both Essex and Southampton were convicted and sentenced, but the former went to the block alone.

In discussing the conduct of Bacon at the trial of Essex, a defense of the Earl is not necessary to the condemnation of Bacon. Let the Earl's guilt be admitted; yet if there is anything in the tie of friendship or the obligation of gratitude, the post of prosecutor was the one which Bacon, of all men, should not have occupied. He was not of the *sworn* Learned Counsel, therefore came as a volunteer, not under the sacred obligation of an official oath.

From the moment Essex took the friendless place-hunter under his protection we have seen how disinterested were the Earl's actions, speeches and letters, how warm the protestations, pledges and acknowledgments of Bacon. But what a contrast is here offered between the Earl risking his favor with the Queen in

order to get Bacon a pitiful place, and Bacon, prosecuting his patron to the death, lest the Queen should
suspect him of a merciful sentiment for a misguided,
ill-advised, impulsive young man!

How false is the unreserved confession, "I am
more yours than any man's, more yours than any man,"
when compared with the sneers, the attacks, the disingenuous allusions, the cold and heartless efforts to
draw the vindictive Coke into the path that led to
conviction, to smother the sparks of mercy which the
youth and earnest eloquence of Essex kindled in the
breasts of his judges!

Who, unless blinded by the brilliant intellectual
qualities of the man, can excuse or justify Bacon for
thus confronting him who had labored in his interests,
sympathized with his disappointments, soothed his
sorrows, relieved his necessities, nursed his hopes?
And having so confronted him, he prosecuted his
young patron with a sworn prosecutor's vigor, a courtier's ardor, a barrister's coolness, and with the bitterness of an ingrate conscious of returning evil for
good.

History, it is true, does not abound in exhibitions of
disinterested friendship at courts and in palaces; but
to the credit of the human race there can generally be
found a set-off to treachery as base as Bacon's; and
the reign of the Queen's father exhibits a refreshing
contrast when it pictures Thomas Cromwell, a black-
smith's son, a soldier of fortune, sharing the Cardinal's
banishment, influencing the imperious Henry to spare
his patron's life, and resisting and defeating the bill in
Parliament for disqualifying Wolsey from all employment under the crown:

"For his honest behavior in his master's cause he was esteemed the most faithfullest servant, and was of all men greatly commended."

The execution of Essex occasioned murmurings among the people. These expressions of discontent must have been directed against the principal actors at the trial, and against the government. Bacon must have had his share of unpopularity. The Queen deemed it advisable to allay public discontent by publishing a "Declaration of the Practices and Treasons Attempted and Committed by Robert, late Earl of Essex, and his Complices." Bacon was selected to draft this paper, and accepted the office of pursuing his patron in the grave, of demonstrating to the English people, if possible, the inexcusable, unpardonable guilt of his late friend, the Earl, and the justification of his new friend, the Queen.

Yet, in his "Apology" to the English people, when Elizabeth was gone, and the name of Essex again heard in connection with words of praise, of sorrow, of anger, Bacon says:—

"For the time which passed, I mean between the arraignment and my Lord's suffering, I was but once with the Queen, at what time, though, I durst not deal directly for my Lord as things then stood; yet generally I did commend Her Majesty's mercy, terming it to her as an excellent balm that did continually distil from her excellent hands, and made an excellent odor in the senses of the people."

If Bacon thought that Essex's conduct was worthy of mercy at the Queen's hands, between the prison and the block, how much worthier was it of mercy at a friend's, between the charge and the sentence!

Let us endeavor to analyze his conduct in the light of his characteristics, and of his career from his early entrance into the arena.

The weakness of Bacon's nature, as a man in the battle of life, was want of self-reliance, a constant dependence upon and looking towards others, a willingness to become the instrument of smaller men, whose abilities were more practical or whose lots were more fortunate. He was constantly looking about him for some one to tie to, as a patron, and his letters convey pledges, which, if made to be kept, would destroy individuality of opinion and action. After seeking the patronage of the Cecils, and failing, he turned to Essex and succeeded. With gratitude for past and hope of future favors, he tells the Earl, "I am more yours than any man's," etc. When in pursuit of the Solicitor-Generalship, and asking the aid of Lord Keeper Puckering, he says:—

"My affection inclineth me to be much (your) Lordship's, and my course and way, in all reason and policy for myself, leadeth me to the same dependence; hereunto if there shall be joined your Lordship's obligation in dealing strongly for me as you have begun, *no man can be more yours.* . . . . *I hope you will think I am no unlikely piece of wood to shape you a true servant of.*"

And after a quarrel with Coke, to whom he addressed a letter of expostulation, we find him hinting how much he might have been that man's, his life-long enemy's, who bullied him and thwarted him at every step, whenever an occasion offered. "If you had not been shortsighted in your own fortune (as I think), you might have had more use of me."

This quarrel between Bacon and Coke occurred in the Exchequer, and the latter was, as usual, the assailant, and his language and conduct were as coarse as customary. He sneered at Bacon for being an *unsworn* Counsel of the Queen, and alluded to the affair of the spunging-house. Bacon set down all that either of them said. And now that Essex was gone, having apparently turned to Secretary Cecil as the most available patron, he furnished Sir Robert with a transcript, in order to anticipate at headquarters the report of his enemy or of the court gossips. The letter to his cousin, written from Gray's Inn, April 29th, 1601, contains a statement of their relations, strikingly at variance with the truth:—

"I am bold now to possess your Honor, as one that ever I found careful of my advancement, and yet more jealous of my wrongs."

Seven years had elapsed since Anthony Bacon transmitted to Lady Bacon this picture of Sir Robert's care and jealousy for Francis:—

"'If your Lordship had spoken of the Solicitorship,' said Sir Robert to the Earl of Essex, 'that might be of easier digestion to the Queen.' 'Digest me no digesting,' said the Earl; 'for the Attorneyship is that I must have for Francis Bacon; and in that I will spend my uttermost credit, friendship and authority. . . . And for your own part, Sir Robert, I do think much and strange both of my Lord, your father, and you, that can have the mind to seek the preferment of a stranger before so near a kinsman; namely, considering if you weigh in a balance his parts and sufficiency in any respect with those of his competitor, excepting only four poor years of admittance, which Francis Bacon hath more than recompensed with the priority of his reaaing, in all other respects you shall find no comparison between them.'"

With this certain knowledge of his cousin's antagonism from the lips of Essex, with the equally certain knowledge derived from a long and fruitless chase after-preferment which the Cecils could have secured for him, with his own conclusion, expressed afterwards to Villiers, heretofore quoted, complaining of the Cecils, father and son, for repressing men of merit, this paragraph becomes one of the many witnesses furnished by Bacon that testify to his disingenuousness and to his sacrifices of personal honor and resentment upon the shrine of official patronage.

This year, 1601, must have been a troubled one. His peace of mind was further clouded by the death of Anthony Bacon, who seems to have been an exceptionally devoted brother. He died, as Francis lived, in debt; and it is probable that the latter received comparatively little from the estate, after the demands of creditors had been satisfied, and the bills of doctors and undertaker paid.

But his services against Essex were not altogether unremunerated. Heavy fines had been imposed on many of the Earl's co-conspirators, and of this money, £1,200 were assigned to Bacon by the Queen's order.

Elizabeth now met, for the last time, her people in parliament. A fresh invasion of her realm, the landing of a Spanish army in Ireland, occasioned the demand of money, and inspired a patriotic response.

Bacon appeared in the House of Commons in the graceful rôle of a law-reformer, and presented a bill for the regulation of weights and measures, — a wise and

beneficent proposition, which met with no encouragement, and was postponed for a future generation of
legislators to enact as a blessing to their country; for
it did not receive the attention it deserved until William
IV. was on the throne.

A most generous supply was granted the Queen,
greater than was ever before proposed. A motion was
made to exempt the poorer classes, "the three-pound
men;" but Bacon opposed any exemption. He had
grown wiser, or less sympathetic, than when he antagonized a smaller imposition: because of its "impos-
sibility, the poor men's rent is such as they are not able
to yield it." Now, this was his language: "It was
dulcis tractus pari jugo, and therefore the poor as well
as the rich not to be exempted."

The Queen could not find fault with this speech, as
she did with the former, and although it subjected
Bacon to the sarcasms of Sir Walter Raleigh, who
revived and quoted his early speech about the tax-
payer selling his "pots" and "pans," it insured him
against the frowns of Elizabeth.

The question of monopolies, or grants by the Queen
of exclusive rights to certain individuals or companies,
to deal in certain commodities, was raised in this parliament, and threatened to bring the Commons and
Crown in collision. That this royal custom of parcel-
ing out the privileges of supplying the necessities of
whole peoples, at prices which unrivaled patentees and
grantees chose to demand, was not only a wrong, but a
much-abused wrong, every member of both Houses
knew; and when a bill was proposed to stamp it, both
as opposed to law and as a cruel grievance, Bacon stood
up as the Queen's advocate, defended the custom as a

part of her prerogative, and maintained that if her grantees and patentees abused her favors, she should be appealed to by the House, in the form of a petition:—

"The use hath been ever by petition," he said, "to humble ourselves to Her Majesty, and by petition to desire to have our grievances redressed; especially when the remedy toucheth her so nigh in point of prerogative. . . . . I say, and I say again, that we ought not to deal, or judge, or meddle with Her Majesty's prerogative."

The prerogative which Bacon defended was born of the times when English liberty lay smothered in the ashes of the War of the Roses.

"With the closing years of his [Edward IV.] reign," says a recent popular and philosophical writer, "the monarchy took a new color. The introduction of an elaborate spy system, the use of the rack and the practice of interference with the purity of justice, gave the first signs of an arbitrary rule which the Tudors were to develop. It was on his creation of a new financial system that the King laid the foundation of a despotic rule. . . . . Sums were extorted from the clergy; *monopolies were sold.*" *

It will be seen, not only from this instance, but from others which will appear as the scroll of Bacon's life is unrolled, that as a law-reformer he did not deal with the great questions which involved collision between crown and people, out of which sprang some new principle of freedom, or which emitted sparks that kindled after-glows upon the altar of constitutional

* Green's Hist. Eng. Peop., Vol. II., p. 51.

liberty. Unlike the martyr upon this shrine in the reign of Henry VIII., Sir Thomas More,

> "He ne'er with patriot fires had warmed his youth,
> Or staked existence on a single truth."

And if the reader finds his moral instincts blunted for the instant by the brilliancy of Bacon's intellect, he can take no surer guide to lead him back to paths of courageous honesty than the man whose life, as well as pen, set example for future ages:—

> "There will never be wanting some pretense for deciding in the King's favor," wrote More, "as, that equity is on his side, or the strict letter of the law, or some forced interpretation of it; or, if none of these, that the royal prerogative ought, with conscientious judges, to outweigh all other considerations."

The committees who were to give, in some form, an expression to the grievance of the people, delayed reporting to the Commons, and the Queen, anticipating their action and wish, announced that she had given orders to have some of the abuses reformed, others were to be revoked, and all were to be suspended for examination and report.

An enthusiastic, grateful and loyal Commons then greeted their great Queen for the last time.

Bacon's services in this parliament, upon the heel of his services at the trial of Essex, supplementing, also, the devotion of his pen to the Queen, deserved some special recognition for their earnestness alone, even if they had not been valuable, which, however, they must have been. Yet he continued on his unrewarded course, volunteering elaborately-written advice to his

cousin, Sir Robert Cecil, now chief adviser of the
Queen and anxious candidate for the same place under
him who was to be her successor.

Elizabeth was old, and her strength began to yield
to time and the anxieties which were incident to a reign
unparalleled in so many respects. It only needed some
acute illness to irritate her bad temper and excite her
stubborn will. She had survived the great men who
surrounded her throne at her accession. When Burghley yielded to age and disease, she lost the service of
one of the wisest and most conservative statesmen that
had ever stood by a monarch's side. His son was his
successor, but could not be his substitute. He was
impregnated by education with his father's ideas and
policy, and endeavored to walk in the same path; but,
in the forcible words of Bacon, "As, in Egypt, the seven
good years sustained the seven bad, so governments,
for a time well grounded, do bear out errors following." * The policy of Burghley ran through the entire
reign of Elizabeth, and overlapping into the early part
of that of James, sustained for a time the station of
England among her contemporaries.

Elizabeth, declining all medical aid, grew worse day
by day, and yielding to a settled melancholy, faded
rapidly away. In three weeks from her attack she
reached the border, and on the 24th day of March,
1603, crossed over to join the spirits of her beautiful
young rival and handsome young favorite, whose death-
warrant she had signed.

At the time of the Queen's death Bacon was fifty-
three years of age. As he stood by her bier he must

---

* Advancement of Learning. Vol. II., 257.

have reflected how long and anxiously he had sought her favor and smile, what sacrifices he had made in vain, what slight recognitions she had given of his ability and ardor! And yet her death came when he was highest in her good graces; a little time might have crowned his long waiting. Now that she was gone, and he was brought face to face with the waste of precious moments, the opportunity was offered for retirement from a stage which held out no encouragements to the society of that divine philosophy which never ceased to be his first love, although he had so often turned his back upon her and closed his ears to her voice. But the breath was hardly out of the body of Bacon's "most gracious mistress" before he sent a skirmish line of propitiatory letters to meet his most gracious master, who, with a Scotch mob at his heels, was heading for the throne of England

PART II.

Elizabeth, throughout her reign, would never permit the question of succession to be mentioned or discussed. A dying nod in the direction of Scotland was her only confirmation of the divine right of James.

> "A mouse that trusts to one poor hole
> Can never be a mouse of any soul."

So thought the statesmen and courtiers, great and little, who advised, obeyed and flattered the great Queen and vain woman.

Sir Robert Cecil, the Earl of Northumberland, and others, had, for years previous to the Queen's death, been in secret correspondence with James.

Anthony Bacon, who, as an amateur, was dabbling in all politics, had, in connection with the Earl of Essex, also established a correspondence with certain persons around King James. Francis Bacon, who was cognizant of this, now proposed to utilize whatever capital his brother had accumulated under Essex. On this capital of his dead brother and dead patron he now traded. To one of his brother's correspondents he inclosed a letter to the King himself, in which he pays this tribute to the memory of Elizabeth: "A princess happy in many things, but most happy in her successor." Yet he must have known James to have been a pedant, a coward and a trifler; a man whose defects and deficiencies were aggravated by contrast with the woman who had preceded him. Bacon next proceeds to invite the King's kindly glances to himself:—

"And yet further and more nearly, I was not a little encouraged, not only upon a supposal that unto Your Majesty's sacred ears (open to the air of all virtues), there might perhaps have come some small breath of the good memory of my father, so long a principal counsellor in this your kingdom; but also by the particular knowledge of the infinite devotion and incessant endeavors (beyond the strength of his body and the nature of the times) which appeared in my good brother towards Your Majesty's service; and were, on Your Majesty's part, through your singular benignity, by many most gracious and lively significations and favors, accepted and acknowledged, beyond the merit of anything he could effect. *All which endeavors and duties were for the most part common to myself with him, though by design (as between brethren) dissembled.*

"And therefore, most high and mighty King, my most dear and dread sovereign Lord, since now the corner-stone is laid of the mightiest monarchy in Europe, and that God above, who is noted to have a mighty hand in bridling floods and fluctuations of the seas and of people's hearts, hath by the miraculous and universal consent (the more strange because it proceedeth from such diversity of causes), in your coming in, given a sign and token what he intendeth in the continuance. I think there is no subject of Your Majesty's who loveth this island and is not hollow and unworthy, whose heart is not set on fire, not only to bring you peace-offerings to make you propitious, but to sacrifice himself a burnt-offering to Your Majesty's service; amongst which number no man's fire shall be more pure and fervent than mine. *But how far forth it shall blaze out, that resteth in Your Majesty's employment.*"

Bacon's next step was to address the Earl of Northumberland, who was thought to stand highest with the King, a letter inclosing the draft of a proclamation to be issued by the King, upon his entrance. It is an able state paper because of its fitness for the times and probable acceptability to the people of England, to whom the praise of Elizabeth which it contained would have been especially grateful. Whether Bacon really expected that the King, surrounded by old and new friends greedy for favor, recognition and employment, would accept the advice and service of a private man in so important a matter, is unknown; but the offer would evidence his zeal, and the writing evidence his capacity.

King James, before his arrival at London, and his coronation, directed that all persons in office when the Queen died should continue until he should determine otherwise. Bacon, by this order, was deprived of the shadow which he had accepted in lieu of the substance, for he never was, in law, the Queen's counsel, never having been sworn or received his warrant as such. But he was not idle in preparing himself as a candidate for royal favor. The Queen's death was the signal for the revival of the hopes and prospects of the friends of the Earl of Essex. The release of the Earl of Southampton was a foregone conclusion; and he wrote to this nobleman, who had identified himself with Essex, been tried and condemned with Essex, whom Bacon had prosecuted together with Essex.

C

"Neither is it any point of law," said Bacon, at the trial, "as my Lord of Southampton would have it believed, that condemns them of treason. To take secret counsel, to execute it, to run together in numbers armed with weapons,—what can be the excuse? Warned by the Lord Keeper, by a herald, and yet persist! Will any simple man take this to be less than treason?"

The friends of Southampton were visiting him in the Tower, and conveying their hearty congratulations upon the freedom which he was soon to enjoy. Bacon substituted a letter for a call, in which he said:—

"I would have been very glad to have presented my humble service to your Lordship by my attendance if I could have foreseen that it should not have been unpleasing to you. And therefore, because I would commit no error, I chose to write, assuring your Lordship (how credible soever it may seem to you at first, yet it is as true as a thing that God knoweth), that this great change hath wrought in me no other change towards your Lordship than this, that I may safely be now that which I was truly before."

The extract above given from Bacon's speech against Southampton is an answer to this letter; and unless we judge him by an entirely different standard than we do other men, we cannot escape the conviction of insincerity, either at the trial or in this letter. Southampton was as guilty at one time as at another.

"And so, craving no other pardon," concludes Bacon's letter, "than for troubling you with this letter, I do not now begin, but continue, to be your Lordship's humble and much devoted."

Always your servant, although once your merciless prosecutor!

Bacon's pen was busy during these excited times. Having been admitted to the King's presence, he gave an immediate account of it to Northumberland. He had "no private conference to any purpose. No more hath almost any other English." But he describes him after a courtier's fashion.

Bacon, on the King's arrival, was continued an unsworn counsellor, which meant little or nothing. This must have been a disappointment to him who had volunteered to write royal proclamations. That he was again in that depressed state which always inspired him to persuade himself, or try to convince others, that he had given over the pursuit of political place and honors, is evident from a letter to Sir Robert Cecil, dated July 3d, 1603.

One of the earliest acts of sovereignty on the part of King James was the confirming of knighthood upon a troop of three hundred gentlemen, who were marched up like a drove of cattle to be branded, and were assessed so many pounds for the honor conferred upon them.

When there was anything to get, Bacon was on hand to ask. Besides, his activity as Queen's counsel had involved the neglect of his practice, and periodical embarrassment was again disturbing him. A second courtship proclaimed the narrowed condition of his finances, all of which appears from the letter to his cousin, Sir Robert, above referred to: —

"For my purpose and course," he writes, "I desire to meddle as little as I can in the King's causes, His Majesty now abounding in counsel, and to follow my private thrift and practice, and to marry with some convenient advancement. For, as for my ambition, I do assure your honor, mine is quenched. In the Queen's, my excellent mistress's, time, the *quorum* was small; her service was a kind of freehold, and it was a more solemn time. All these points agreed with my nature and judgment. My ambition now I shall only put upon my pen, whereby I shall be able to maintain memory and merit of the times succeeding. Lastly, for this divulged and almost prostituted title of knighthood, I could, without charge, by your Honor's mean, be content to have it, both because of this late disgrace " [something he had suffered, it is presumed, at the hands of a creditor], "and because I have three new knights in my mess in Gray's Inn's commons; and because I have found out an alderman's daughter, an handsome maiden to my liking."

Another letter to Sir Robert Cecil, touching money matters, closes his correspondence of this period as far as we are informed. In public affairs immediately succeeding the accession of James, he took no part, although his pen contributed a valuable paper to the religious controversies which were revived with renewed ardor by the accident of a new reign and a new sovereign. "Certain Considerations Touching the Better Pacification and Edification of the Church of England" should be catalogued with his "Church Controversies," as a philosophical contribution to a discussion which commenced with Cain and Abel in the Garden of Eden, and which will continue until theology yields to Christianity, or an infallible church absorbs all races under its government, or every individual rejects all intermediaries between himself and a personal God.

Charles I., writing to Wentworth, then in Ireland, concludes his letter by saying, "I will end with a rule that may serve for a statesman, a courtier or a lover: Never make a defense or apology before you be accused." This rule of action is one which most thoughtful men observe, one which all innocent men instinctively obey. But as Bacon, about this time, wrote his famous "Apology in Certain Imputations Concerning the late Earl of Essex," the inference is that he had been accused of conduct inconsistent with the commonly-accepted notions of right. The title of the "Apology," and the introductory paragraph, prove that the tongues which the death of Elizabeth had loosened revived the tales which had been more quietly circulated to Bacon's detriment. Instead of suffering an old story to be buried beneath the accumulation of new events, he wrote, published and circulated this history of his con-nection with the prosecution of his friend and bene-factor. It was addressed to the public through the Earl of Devonshire. Two editions were printed and distributed by Bacon, one in the year 1604, the other in the year following. Yet Bacon proclaims his inde-pendence of popular censure, and that his desire to stand well with a few persons is what alone inspired his "Apology."

"It may please your good Lordship," he says, "I cannot be ignorant, and ought to be sensible of the wrong which I sustain in common speech, as if I had been false or un-thankful to that noble but unfortunate Earl, the Earl of Essex. And for satisfying the vulgar sort, I do not so much regard it; though I love a good name, but yet, as an hand-maid and attendant of honesty and virtue. . . . But, on the other side, there is no worldly thing that concerneth my-self which I hold more dear than the good opinion of certain persons, among which there is none I would more willingly give satisfaction unto than to your Lordship. First, because you loved the Lord of Essex, and therefore will not be par-tial towards me, which is part of that I desire; next, because it has ever pleased you to show yourself to me an honorable friend."

Then follows statement of fact and argument. Like most personal explanations to the public, it is probable that this one was not altogether satisfactory. Yet little or nothing is known of its effect, and the opinions of writers differ in respect to it, as they differ in respect to the original transaction which inspired it.

The most interesting incident of the beginning of the new sovereign's reign was the trial of Sir Walter Raleigh for participation in the Arabella Stuart fiasco, whom the reader will recall as the most unfortunate victim of the conspiracy to dethrone James and enthrone one to whom the Tower of London became both a prison and an insane asylum.

Sir Edward Coke and Bacon were the prosecutors of this great Englishman, and fortunately for the unfavored King's counsel, he was not called on or permitted to take an active part in the disgraceful scene. But the Attorney-General surpassed himself in zeal and brutality. He assailed one of the brightest ornaments of the age with the vile vocabulary of a Scroggs or Jeffries, and rendered himself immortally infamous by a coarseness and cruelty unparalleled and never imitated.

Bacon's next appearance in public was as a member of the House of Commons in James' first parliament, which convened March 19th, 1604. The King's address commended the consideration of the subject nearest to his heart, — the union of the two kingdoms; also the settlement of religious controversies, and the amendment of the laws.

Bacon divided his attention between the King's pet project and the popular cry for reform of laws, whose improvement would insure redress of grievances. With extraordinary industry, characteristic ability and great tact, he labored to accomplish objects nearest to the hearts of sovereign and people, and the close of the session found him in the enjoyment of a prominence and popularity which he had hitherto never reached. Unbegged recognition of his worth and services, though meagre in its quantity and quality, for the first time cheered his hopes. He received from the King a warrant as one of the Learned Counsel, with a small salary, and was thus fortified against the sneers with which Coke welcomed the "unsworn" servant of the crown. To this was added a pension of £60, which did little to relieve the embarrassed lawyer, but did much to encourage the persistent place-hunter. Yet here the new departure for a time was checked, and in such a way, in all probability, as to dampen the hopeful impression made on Bacon's mind.

The object of the writer has been to sketch truthfully the public career of Bacon, and to comment on the *morale* of the individual as it is exhibited in the light of his relations to others, his writings, sayings, correspondence, personal and political. These present the picture of a timid, time-serving, unsuccessful place-hunter, whose repeated failures took something each time from the dignity of his character. But the most extraordinary chapter of his life, and one which lifts the office-seeker from the slough in which he seems to have passed his whole existence, is that which presents him to us in enforced retirement from public affairs, meditating, between disappointments at court, in the closet of the philosopher, and now, as the result, dazzling the intellectual world with his "Advancement of Learning."

The fame which he acquired through his parliamentary career, and by his last, and as yet greatest, contribution to philosophy, must have won over the "handsome maiden, to my liking," whom three years before he had designed "to marry for convenient advancement." For now, on the 10th of May, 1606, he became the husband of the beautiful and wealthy Alice Barnham, daughter of a London alderman. A contemporaneous letter-writer gives an account of the wedding:—

"Sir Francis Bacon was married yesterday to his young wench, in Maribone Chapel. He was clad from top to toe in purple, and hath made himself and his wife such store of fine raiments of cloth of silver and gold that it draws deep into her portion."

Sir Robert Cecil was now Prime Minister and the Earl of Salisbury. Bacon had, as we have seen, made warm protestations of confidence in his cousin's goodwill, and even indulged in expressions of a gratitude which seems to have responded to Walpole's definition, "a place-expectant's lively sense of future favors," for he had received no promotion of any real dignity at the hands of his cousin, whose kindness appears to have been limited to procuring him knighthood, not as he wanted it, but in the crowd of three hundred, who had to pay for what had, under the Tudors, been conferred as an honorable distinction. His warrant as Learned Counsel, and the small annuity, were trifles in view of his services. A loan of money, or the offer of a loan, was about the only independent personal favor which Bacon had ever received at his cousin's hands; and although of late he had been more profuse than ever in encouraging expressions, when the time arrived to give substantial proof of his sincerity, Salisbury suffered his cousin to have the door shut again in his face when he stood on the threshold of the coveted Solicitor-Generalship. On the 29th of June, 1606, Coke was made Chief Justice of the Court of Common Pleas. The custom under Queen Elizabeth was to promote the Solicitor-General to the office of Attorney-General; and this had been done on three occasions. But as this order of succession was not a rule, and the matter depended on the King's pleasure, the indifference or treachery of Salisbury, supplemented, probably, by the ill-will of Coke, resulted in the selection of Sir Henry Hobart for the Attorney-Generalship, and the retention of the Solicitor-General in his place. But as Bacon made every exertion for the position, believing that a vacancy was inevitable, addressing petitioning letters to the King, Lord Chancellor and Salisbury, he is again presented in the familiar rôle of a disappointed yet persistent place-hunter. The king and those around him probably realized, after their adverse action, that they were guilty of impolitic and unjust conduct towards Bacon; and when the Chief Justice of the Court of King's Bench, in an accommodating spirit, died and opened a path to the long-sought place, promotions made way for Bacon, and on the 25th of June, 1607, he obtained the place upon which he had fixed his eye in the year 1593, and upon which he had kept it fastened ever since.

His exertions in the House of Commons on the heel of this appointment, in favor of the union of the two kingdoms, in behalf of which he had already labored as one of the commission to digest a scheme for that purpose; his efforts to persuade parliament to take the first step by the passage of an act of naturalization;

and, on failing to accomplish this, his device to con-
summate the King's wish by the decision of the courts;
his brilliant argument before the judges in what is
known as the case of the *Post-nati;* and his untiring
zeal and superior ability in advancing the King's wishes,
all gave assurance to James that he had not made a
mistake in the choice of this servant, whatever doubts
he may have had of others whom he had hastened to
recognize and promote.

These years of political and professional activity in
the life of this extraordinary man were also years of
profound philosophical thought, and enthusiastic philosophical labor.

The hours stolen from sleep, the breathing spaces
between sessions of parliament, the holidays, few in
number, of his busy career, were dedicated to the
development and elaboration of those theories and
methods which were afterwards to be known as
Baconian philosophy.

Here and there he would pause in his busy pursuit
of power, or its busy employment when obtained, to
devote his pen to historical, philosophical or legal subjects; and, as was said of Goldsmith, he touched nothing which he did not adorn.   His praise of Elizabeth's
name, and defense of her memory, a Latin treatise,
circulated in manuscript, his "*Cogita et Visa,*" and
"Wisdom of the Ancients," were written during the
early years of James' reign.   His mind, as a philosopher, dwelling all the time upon what he called his
"Great Instauration," under which title he compre-
hended whatever he should accomplish in revolutioniz-
ing English methods of scientific thought and investigation, in supplying proper classification of human

knowledge, and the dedication of all to the advancement of man's welfare.

The assembling of parliament in 1609 drew Bacon
into the whirlpool of political life; and until the dissolution, in 1611, his active loyalty was demonstrated in
every possible way. The crown and ·commons came
into collision respecting the prerogative, and when
Bacon failed to pour oil on the troubled waters, he stood
up for the King.

A negotiation between the King and the commons,
whereby he should surrender certain royal revenues and
feudal rights, and they should secure him a compen-
satory supply of money, failed; and in this parliament
Bacon fought stoutly for the King's right to "set
impositions upon merchandises without the assent of
parliament."

Now that his arena of political activity was closed
by the dissolution of the parliament, he resumed his
pen, and the result was a new edition of his "Essays,"
enlarged and revised, which was published in 1612.

The same pen that re-cast the "Essays," about the
same time addressed a letter to the King asking for
another office, to wit, the Attorney-Generalship, when
it should become vacant. After referring to how "pre-
ferments of the law fly about mine ears, to some above
me and some below me," and assigning this neglect to
the account of his modesty in asking, he repeats, in
this request, the almost inseparable threat of retirement
contingent on failure :—

"I may be in danger to be neglected and forgotten. And
if that should be, then were it much better for me, now while
I stand in Your Majesty's good opinion (though unworthily),
and have some little reputation with the world, to give over

the course I am in, and to make proof to do you some honor by my pen."

A promise of the succession detained him as a philosopher-in-waiting. This effect of his appeal to the King indicates his growth in influence; but the scheme which he soon accomplished presents him as something of a power behind the throne.

Coke, when he left the bar for the bench, left also his bad manners behind him. He was a bullying Attorney-General; but his conduct as Chief Justice of the Court of Common Pleas not only endeared him to the practitioners, it contributed to the estimation in which he was held as a learned lawyer. He had become wedded to his court. Bacon contrived to have him transferred to the Court of King's Bench, to have Attorney-General Hobart succeed Coke, and himself succeed Hobart. Coke is said to have wept — tears of rage, probably — at thus being kicked up-stairs, and it must have added no little to the antagonism he had always exhibited toward Bacon.

In haste to follow Bacon in his rapid ascent, reference to events previous to his last promotion was omitted. The chief of these were his efforts to divest the charity of one Thomas Sutton, whose fortune was devised in a channel which has since fed the charter-house. He came forward as a volunteer, advising the King to make a better will for the testator, and argued the cause instituted by a pretended heir to break the will. For this he has been much censured by his critics, and excused by his apologists.

But there is a position taken, in his letter of advice to the King, which exhibits that inconsistency so often met with in his career.

In his "Advancement of Learning" he submits this answer to the objections of politicians:—

"It is without all controversy that learning doth make the minds of men gentle, generous, maniable and pliant to government, whereas ignorance doth make them churlish, thwarting and mutinous."

Yet one argument he used with James, to encourage the monarch to an illegal interference with the testator's disposition of his own in his own way, is thus expressed:—

"For grammar schools there are already too many, and therefore no providence to add where there is excess. For the great number of schools which are in Your Highness' realm doth cause a want, and doth cause likewise an overflow, both of them inconvenient, and one of them dangerous. For by means of them they find want in the country and towns, both of servants for husbandry and apprentices for trade; and on the other hand, there being more scholars bred than the State can prefer and employ, and the active part of that life not bearing a proportion to the preparative, it must needs fall out that many persons will be bred unfit for other vocations, and unprofitable for that in which they are brought up, which fills the realm full of indigent, idle and wanton people. Therefore, in this point, I wish Mr. Sutton's intention more exalted a degree, that that which he meant for teachers of children, Your Majesty should make for teachers of men."

Bacon had undertaken to establish the foundation of a new organ in philosophical investigation, a new system of study, and he wanted money and men to assist in the accomplishment of this enterprise; and to reach his end, he did not hesitate to use any means. This is the natural inference, or the alternative conclusion is, that a politician, philosopher, and historian, wise in most matters above his fellows, could stultify himself. It was the mass of the people who, when ignorant, were "churlish, thwarting and mutinous," and when elevated, "maniable and pliant to government." The value of the citizen to the State he knew depended on his intelligence. "Now, the empire of man consists in knowledge; for his power is what he knows," he says, in his "Interpretation of Nature." *

Under the reign of Henry VIII., Colet, in 1510, founded the first grammar school, near St. Paul's. We are told that the image of the child Jesus was over the master's chair, and beneath that image the words "Hear ye Him;" and that the Dean thus wrote to the little souls whom he desired so to disenthrall and free from the ignorance which defiles and degrades: "Lift up your little white hands for me, for me which prayeth for you to God." And Bacon knew, when he stood between the fountain of free knowledge and the thirsting channels which waited to be filled, that, in the language of a later historian, "the grammar schools of Edward the Sixth and Elizabeth, in a word, the system of middle-class education, which, by the close of the century had changed the face of England, were the outcome of Colet's foundation of St. Paul's." †

Another questionable course on the part of Bacon was that which he took to recommend himself to James' favor, to a promotion above the flight of ordinary ambition.

His cousin, the Earl of Salisbury and Lord Treasurer, died May 24th, 1612. On the first of the year,

---

* Montagu's Edition. Vol. XV. p. 35.
† Green's History of English People. Vol. II. p. 86.

in making acknowledgment of Salisbury's assurance of aid in obtaining the Attorney-Generalship if Hobart died, as he was expected to do, but did not, Bacon indulges in this enthusiastic outburst:—

"And I do protest before God, without compliments or any light vein of mind, that if I knew in what course of life to do you best service, I would take it and make my thoughts, which now fly to many pieces, be reduced to that centre."

A few days after the death of one who inspired such protestations, he wrote to the King in the following strain about him:—

"Your Majesty hath lost a great subject and a great servant. But if I should praise him in propriety, I should say he was a fit man to keep things from growing worse, but no fit man to reduce things to be much better. For he loved to have the eyes of all Israel a little too much about himself, and to have all business still under the hammer and like clay in the hands of the potter, to mould it as he thought good; so that he was more *in operatione* than *in opere*. And though he had fine passages of action, yet the real conclusion came slowly on."

Is this not faint praise from a source so grateful three months previous? Not an expression of commendation without a detrimental qualification. On the heel of this ubiquitous obituary notice of his dead cousin, he calls attention to his own fitness for the King's service. After suggesting the propriety of leaving, for the time, the two vacancies—that of Lord Treasurer and Secretary—unfilled until the King had considered how and when to summon parliament for the increase of James' purse and popularities, he says:—

"Now, because I take myself to have a little skill in that region, as one that ever affected that Your Majesty mought, in all your causes, not only prevail, but prevail with the satisfaction of the inner man; and though no man can say but that I was a perfect and peremptory royalist, yet every man makes me believe that I was never one hour out of credit with the lower house. My desire is to know whether Your Majesty will give me leave to meditate and propound unto you some preparative remembrances touching the future parliament.

"Your Majesty may truly perceive, that though I cannot challenge to myself either invention or judgment, or elocution or method, or any of those powers, yet my offering is care and observance. And as my good old mistress was wont to call me her watch-candle, because it pleased her to say I did continually burn (and yet she suffered me to waste almost to nothing), so I must much more owe the like duty to Your Majesty, by whom my fortunes have been settled and raised. And so, craving pardon, I rest

"Your Majesty's most humble servant devote,

"F. B."

This letter was followed by another, in which he offered himself for the position of Secretary. In this he gives more importance to his diplomatic education, or experience, in France, than it has received at the hands of his biographers :—

"I was three of my young years bred with an ambassador in France, and since I have been an old truant in the school-house of your council-chamber; though on the second form, yet longer than any that now setteth hath been on the head form."

His offer to be promoted was not accepted ; but his services in various ways were, especially in the consideration of ways and means to relieve His Majesty from monetary embarrassments.

His criticism of his dead cousin has already been referred to. In a letter to the King, on the subject of his estate, the following censure of Salisbury's course in the matter of negotiating between James and his parliament for money supply in exchange for the surrender of feudal rights which had grown into grievances:—

"My next prayer," writes Bacon, "is that Your Majesty, in respect of the hasty freeing of your State, would not descend to any means, or degree of means, which carrieth not a symmetry with Your Majesty's greatness. He (Salisbury) is gone from whom those courses did wholly flow. To have your wants and necessities in particular as it were hanged up in two tablets before the eyes of your lords and commons, to be talked of for four months together; to have all your courses to help yourself in revenue or profit put into printed books, which were wont to be held *arcana imperii;* to have such worms of aldermen" [very disrespectful to his father-in-law,] "to lend for ten in the hundred upon good assurance, and with such entreaty as if it would save the bark of your fortune; to contract still where mought be had the readiest payment, and not the best bargain; to stir a number of projects for your profit, and then to blast them and leave Your Majesty nothing but the scandal of them; to pretend even carriage between Your Majesty's rights and the ease of the people, and satisfy neither; these courses and others, the like I hope are gone with the deviser of them, which have turned Your Majesty to inestimable prejudice."

What a picture of such a minister as Salisbury is this to hold up before such a King as James! But that Bacon should volunteer this terrible philippic against the dead whom he had praised and thanked, and protested to "before God!" Such tergiversations from dependence, humility and gratitude when a man is alive, to license, bravery and abuse when he is dead, are what almost excuse Pope's extravagant declaration that he was "the meanest of mankind."

The wise councillors whom James inherited from Elizabeth were now either dead or past the age of active usefulness. The King's conceit made him, for a time, his own minister. The Scotch favorite, Carr, the Earl of Somerset, had no capacity; so that circumstances were favorable for Bacon's obtaining, if not place and power, at least a hearing in the affairs of State.

James was very much embarrassed financially, and the summoning of parliament seemed inevitable; but it meant scrutiny into the King's expenditures, complaints on their part, concessions on his, and after these, a subsidy, which would have to be purchased by a slice of the prerogative. Bacon came forward at this juncture, and in a long and elaborate paper tendered his advice. Pending the consideration of this subject, he became Attorney-General, and a contemporary letter-writer—Chamberlain—thus comments on his appointment: "There is a strong apprehension that little good is to be expected by this change, and that Bacon may prove a dangerous instrument." This inference was probably drawn from the ultra-royalty of his later years, in and out of parliament, his unreserved protestations of devotion to the King and his prerogative, coupled with his now universally recognized ability and pliability. The opinion of this writer receives additional weight from the fact that, in the parliament which was now—1614—summoned, opposition was made to Bacon taking his seat, on the ground that he was Attorney-General, and as such, though it was not openly said, too much the King's own. The motion did not, however, prevail. The King confronted the House of Commons with the urgency of his necessities, and the House confronted him with the people's grievances. The sound of monopoly and imposition drowned the voice of supply, and the King lost his temper and sent the representatives back to their constituents.

And to these constituents the King decided to appeal for that relief which the commons hesitated about granting on demand. In other words, he proceeded to replenish his exhausted exchequer by means of "Benevolences," or loans from the citizens requested through sheriffs and other officers. The scheme started with a free offering from the bishops, which was supplemented by contributions from some of the lay-lords. Even the parsimonious and money-loving Coke gave £200; but the twenty-pound tender of other judges was rejected. It is difficult to reconcile these offerings, coming on the heel of a parliament dissolved by the King in anger, with the crudest notions of constitutionality. The parliament had been called to supply the King with means to carry on the government; and the constitutional provision for such a supply was parliamentary taxation. Parliament had not refused to make the necessary grant; it had only postponed it in order to consider other subjects of the first importance, in its opinion; and while acting within constitutional limits, the King lost his temper, and an abrupt dissolution followed. Under these circumstances, any contribution on the part of an individual was calculated to release the King from all dependence on parliament, for the money power of the House of Commons was then developing into the great bulwark of English liberty; its judicious exercise was to purchase that liberty, and was to protect it.

These voluntary contributions did little toward satisfying the necessities of James, so it was decided to send letters throughout England asking relief for the royal beggar. These letters would have gone forth under the Great Seal if Coke had not declared such a course to be illegal. Bacon objected to the proposition as impolitic. His idea was that they should not have any official character, lest they might subject the King to misconstruction. But they went forth from the council addressed to sheriffs, justices of the peace and mayors.

The relief dictated by Mr. Richard Turpin, on Hounslow Heath, was hardly less voluntary, hardly less of a benevolence, than the aid thus demanded by the King.

Edward the Fourth is credited with the usurpation of contracting loans without the assent of parliament, with being the author of "benevolences." Although reluctantly submitted to under him, to his successor a protest was made against them, as "extortions and new impositions against the laws of God and man, and the liberty and laws of this realm," and the parliament of Richard the Third declared them to be illegal. Henry the Seventh returned to benevolences as one of the instruments which might serve to make him independent of the parliament. It was in this spirit that they originated; it was because of this tendency they were declared illegal. Henry the Eighth, through Wolsey, improved upon the plans of his predecessors, and reduced the raising of benevolences to a system, and extended the arm of confiscation deeper into the coffers of the citizens. He was finally met by a general and powerful resistance: "The political instinct of the nation discerned, as of old, that in the question of self-taxation was involved that of the very existence of freedom." Elizabeth, although frequently involved in financial difficulties which endangered her crown, always a poor queen without ever being an extravagant woman, never once descended to this measure, the last resort of a royal beggar or a royal usurper. Even when a parsimonious parliament voted a subsidy inadequate to the demands of the occasion, and supplemented their too cautious economy as a legislative body with a suggestion that it would rejoice the hearts of wealthy individuals to supply the lack with loans, the offer was rejected.

When these letters were issued by the Council of King James, addressed to the King's servants in the various shires, it would be absurd to regard them in the light of requests which might be refused without incurring the displeasure of royalty, if more serious penalties would not follow a rejection.

When a second circular, inspired by the want of enthusiasm on the part of the involuntary creditors of the King, reached the town of Marlborough, in Wiltshire, the mayor asked advice of an impulsive English squire named Oliver St. John. This gentleman replied by letter for the enlightenment of the justices, and gave it as his opinion that the whole affair was a breach of *Magna Charta*, that James was guilty of a breach of his oath, and that every lender would render himself liable to excommunication as an accessory to a foresworn King. He stated the law and the facts in too plain

English, and was summoned to the Star Chamber, where Attorney-General Bacon prosecuted him successfully. A heavy sentence followed, the spirit of independence was bowed, St. John acknowledged his offense, submitted to the King's mercy, and was pardoned.

That there were no limits to Bacon's official zeal, that he was therefore likely to "become a dangerous instrument," was further illustrated by his conduct in the Peacham prosecution. In the study of this aged divine and staunch puritan a sermon was found which contained reflections upon the King and government,— the froth of a religious enthusiast; but it had never been preached or published. The writer was hurried to the Tower. Evidence independent of this manuscript was wanting. The rack was called in to supply the deficiency. Bacon went, with seven others, and they interrogated the venerable and feeble prisoner "before torture, during torture, between torture, and after torture." His aged limbs were crucified, but his stubborn spirit would not yield, and an unsatisfactory report had to be made to "His most Christian Majesty."

The too partial biographers of Bacon do not dwell upon this incident in his career, and pass lightly over his presence at this scene, credit him with one-eighth of the responsibility, and surmise that if he had had the sole management he would not have pursued this course. His own pen not only justified the torture of this weak old man, but commended its application as a sovereign remedy for loosening the tongue of another who declined to furnish evidence that was wanted to secure his conviction and punishment. In a letter to the King, touching a case and prisoner under examination, he says:—

"But I make no judgment yet, but will go on with all diligence; and, if it may not be done otherwise, it is fit Peacock be put to the torture. He deserveth it as well as Peacham did. I beseech Your Majesty not to think I am more bitter because my name is in it; for, besides that I always make my particular a cypher when there is a question of Your Majesty's honor and service, I think myself honored by being brought into so good company. And as, without flattery, I think Your Majesty the best of Kings, and my noble Lord of Buckingham the best of persons favored, so I hope, without presumption, for my honest and true intentions to State and justice, and my love to my master, I am not the worst of chancellors.

"God preserve Your Majesty.

"Your Majesty's most obliged

"and most obedient servant,

"FR. VERULAM, Cauc.

"Feb. 10, 1619."

This was the opinion of Bacon six years later, as to the persuasive influence of torture, and its legality. It evidences, too, his willingness to promote its use, even in a case where, from his letter, it appears he had some personal animosity against, or at least had suffered some personal wrong at the hands of, this candidate for the rack.

Not being able to accumulate any evidence against Peacham other than that afforded by his unpreached sermon, it was resolved to consult the judges as to whether or not this amounted to treason,—whether the government could safely go to trial. Bacon undertook to deal with Coke: "Not being wholly without hope," he says, "that my Lord Coke himself, when I have, in some dark manner, put him in doubt that he shall be left alone, will not continue singular."

The other judges having been approached separately, yielded assent to the proposition. Coke at first hesitated about giving an answer, saying, "Such auricular taking of opinions was not according to the custom of the realm." And when he did reply, it was to the effect that "no words of scandal or defamation importing that the King was utterly unworthy to govern, were treason except they disabled his title."

Bacon, however, as Attorney-General, proceeded with the preparation of the case, and Peacham was sent down to Somersetshire, where he was tried, Sergeant Crew and Solicitor Yelverton prosecuting him. He was found guilty, yet was never executed, but died the following year in Taunton jail. It was the spirit of fear and not of mercy which saved him from the penalty of his alleged treason. The previous and subsequent history of the character of Peacham's offense is the guide which is safest to follow in passing judgment upon Bacon's conduct in bringing him to trial. With respect to precedents, there does not appear to have been any exactly in point. Blackstone refers to two persons executed in the reign of Edward IV.: —

" The one a citizen of London, who said he would make his son heir of the *Crown*, being the house in which he lived. The other a gentleman, whose favorite buck the King killed in hunting; whereupon he wished it, horns and all, in the King's belly. These were esteemed hard cases; and the Chief Justice Markham rather chose to leave his place than assent to the latter judgment. But now it seems clearly to be agreed, that by the Common Law and the statute of Edward III., words spoken amount to only a high misdemeanor, and no treason. . . . If the words be set down in writing, it argues more deliberate intention, and it has been held that writing is an overt act of treason; for *scribere est agere*. But even in this case, the bare words are not the treason, but the deliberate act of writing them. And such writing, though unpublished, has, in some arbitrary reigns, convicted its author of treason; particularly in the case of one Peacham, a clergyman, for treasonable passages in a sermon never preached; and of Algernon Sidney, for some papers found in his closet. . . . But being merely speculative, without any intention, so far as appeared, of making any public use of them, the convicting the authors of treason upon such an insufficient foundation, has been universally disapproved." *

Yet, notwithstanding these facts and legal conclusions, the indignant censure of Lord Campbell, in his "Life of Bacon," and of Macaulay, in his review of Montagu's life of him, a partial apologist has recently championed the subject of their condemnation in a consideration of their accounts and conclusions, and endeavored to excuse, if not justify, Bacon's course in this most disgraceful of his official acts.

The folly of "benevolences" in the England of James the First's time, was parallel with its illegality. The loans he obtained were exhausted in about a year, and so, probably, were his credit and the generosity of courtier and patience of people. The inevitable parliament had to be summoned; and little over a year after the dissolution of the last, the King was consulting his council about assembling the next. Bacon volunteered advice calculated to prevent the mistakes which marred the beginning of business in the late House of Commons, prolonged the exciting and boisterous session,

* Fourth Bl. Com. 80.

and brought it to an abrupt close. But the subject was postponed on account of the discovery that Sir Thomas Overberry, whom the favorite Somerset had imprisoned, had died in the Tower, of poison. The vulgar instruments of the horrid crime were tried, convicted and executed. The inspirers of it, the Earl and Countess of Somerset, were waiting trial. It only needed some such certainty to complete the downfall of James's first favorite. For a new sun was advancing to its meridian in the royal circle. Bacon's watchful eye was the first to catch its rays, as it rose above the horizon; and before other courtiers were aware of its presence, he had concentrated its warming and fructifying beams upon himself. It was thus that George Villiers, the King's cup-bearer, aged twenty-three, and Francis Bacon, the King's sense-bearer, aged fifty-four, became as substance and shadow. In less than a year after this young page's personal beauty and grace attracted the King's fancy, he received knighthood and a pension of £1,000 pounds; and added to this was the flattering attention of the middle-aged lawyer, statesman and philosopher. To this frivolous page the profound thinker and writer and wily politician attached himself as a follower, and to him, subsequently, addressed that famous letter, with its wealth of wisdom and morality, containing the best counsel that disinterested age could give inexperienced youth, basking in the sunshine of royal favoritism. This paper went further; it was a statesman's advice to a King whom he had not the moral courage to approach directly with counsel so opposite, in so many respects, to that King's habits of thought and action.

Having been drawn closer to the King by demonstrations of unquestioning obedience to every wish, by services which James valued in the degree that they degraded Bacon personally, and by the absence of able rivals, the Attorney-General began to renew his pursuit of place. The Lord Chancellor was old and feeble. An attack of extreme illness afforded Bacon an opening for presenting himself to the king. He first wrote:—

"My Lord Chancellor's sickness falleth out *duro tempore.* I have always known him a wise man, and of a just elevation for monarchy. But Your Majesty's service must not be mortal. And if you leese him, as Your Majesty hath now, of late, purchased many hearts by depressing the wicked, so God doth minister unto you a counterpart to do the like by raising the honest. God evermore preserve your Majesty.
"Your Majesty's most humble subject
"and devoted servant.
"Feb. 9, 1615."

But hearing that the King had written to the invalid, he re-wrote his own letter, substituting for the above paragraph, the following:—

"My Lord Chancellor's sickness falleth out *duro tempore.* I have ever known him a wise man, and of a just elevation for monarchy. I understand this afternoon, by Mr. Murray, that your M. hath written to him; and I can best witness how much that sovereign cordial wrought with him in his sickness this time twelvemonth, which sickness was not so much in his spirits as this is. I purpose to see my L. to-morrow, and then I will be bold to write to your M. what hope I have either of his continuance or of his return to business, that your M.'s service may be as little passive as can be by this accident. God have your M. in his precious custody.
"Your M.'s most humble subject
"and most bounden servant,
"1615.   FR. BACON."

He saw the Lord Chancellor, and read death and a
vacancy in his face; and this is the "hope of his continuance, or of his return to business," which was
promised the King.

"It may please your most excellent Majesty, your worthy
Chancellor, I fear, goes his last day. God hath hitherto
used to weed out such servants as grew not fit for Your
Majesty. But now he hath gathered to himself a true sage,
or *salvia*, out of your garden. But Your Majesty's service
must not be mortal.

"Upon this heavy accident, I pray Your Majesty, in all
humbleness and sincerity, to give me leave to use a few
words. I must never forget, when I moved Your Majesty
for the Attorney's place, it was your own sole act, more than
that Somerset, when he knew Your Majesty had resolved it,
thrust himself into the business for a fee; and therefore I
have no reason to pray to saints.

"I shall now again make oblation to Your Majesty, first of
my heart, then of my service, thirdly of my place of Attorney,
which I think is honestly worth £6,000 *per annum*, and
fourthly of my place of the Star Chamber, which is worth
£1,600 *per annum*, and with the favor and countenance of a
Chancellor much more."

Having laid at the King's feet himself and his be-
longings, he proceeds to assign reasons why James
should take him by the hand and lead him to the wool
sack :—

"I hope I may be acquitted of presumption if I think of
it, both because my father had the place, which is some civil
inducement to my desire (and I pray God may have twenty
no worse years in your greatness than Queen Elizabeth had
in her model, after my father's placing), and chiefly because
the Chancellor's place went to the law, it was ever conferred
upon some of the Learned Counsel, and never upon a judge.

For Audley was raised from King's Serjeant; my father from Attorney of the wards; Bromley from solicitor; Puckering from Queen's Serjeant; and Egerton from Master of the Rolls, having newly left the Attorney's place."

This list of precedents was designed to enforce a rule on the King's mind which would, if recognized, influence him to pass over all law officers until he reached that class at whose head stood the Attorney-General. His next step is to criticise each of his probable rivals in such a way as to excite the King's natural jealousy of his prerogative:—

"Now, I beseech Your Majesty, let me put you the present case truly. If you take my Lord Coke, this will follow: First, Your Majesty shall put an overruling nature in an overruling place, which may breed an extreme. Next, you shall blunt his industries in the matter of your finances, which seemeth to aim at another place. And, lastly, popular men are no sure mounters for Your Majesty's saddle. If you take my Lord Hubbard, you shall have a Judge at the upper end of your council board and another at the lower end, whereby Your Majesty will find your prerogative pent; for though there should be emulation between them, yet, as legists, they will agree in magnifying that wherein they are best. He is no statesman, but an economist, wholly for himself; so as Your Majesty, more than at outward form, will find little help in him for your business.

"If you take my Lord of Canterbury, I will say no more but the Chancellor's place requires a whole man; and to have both jurisdiction, spiritual and temporal, in that height, is fit but for a King."

He next offers himself, in contrast not only with these rivals, but with the then incumbent:—

"For myself, I can only present Your Majesty with *gloria in obsequio*. Yet I dare promise that if I sit in that place, your business shall not make such short terms upon you as it doth, but when a direction is once given it shall be pursued and performed, and Your Majesty shall only be troubled with the true care of a King, which is to think what you would have done in chief, and not how far the passages."

It will be recollected that in his letter of the 9th of February, and its substitute, he refers to the Lord Chancellor as a wise man, and one of a just elevation for monarchy; but now, in the belief that death's hand was upon Ellesmere, Bacon charges him with mismanagement of the King's business, and pledges that blind obedience to James which men feared would be his course when he was appointed Attorney-General, and when they expressed apprehension lest he should become a dangerous instrument.

Proceeding with his self-endorsement, he dwells on his parliamentary influence, and on the true rôle of a true servant of the King:—

"I do presume, also, in respect of my father's memory, and that I have been always gracious in the Lower House, I have some interest in the gentlemen of England, and shall be able to do some effect in rectifying that body of parliament men, which is *cardo rerum*. For let me tell Your Majesty that that part of the Chancellor's place which is to judge in equity between party and party, that same *regnum judiciale* (which, since my father's time, is but too much enlarged), concerneth Your Majesty least, more than the acquitting of your conscience for justice. But it is the other parts,—of a moderator amongst your council, of an overseer over your judges, of a planter of fit justices and governors in the country, that importeth your affairs and these times most.

"I will also add that I hope, by my care, the inventive part of your council will be strengthened, who now commonly do exercise rather their judgments than their inventions, and the inventors come from projectors and private men, which cannot be so well; in which kind my Lord of Salisbury had a good method, if his ends had been upright."

This final shot at his dead cousin closes this letter of abuse of others and praise of himself. The Lord Chancellor recuperated; but Bacon had not pleaded in vain. He received from Villiers a promise of succession, and expressed his gratitude to the favorite in even stronger language than he was wont to use to Essex :—

"I am yours," he writes; "surer to you than my own life. For, as they speak of the turquois stone in a ring, I will break into twenty pieces before you have the least fall. God keep you ever.

"Your truest servant,

"Fr. Bacon.

"Feb'y 15, 1615."

His postscript tells of a half-an-hour's visit to the Lord Chancellor: "We both wept, which I do not often." Servility parting with ambition's bauble—the Great Seal—wept! What was it that brought tears to Bacon's eyes? He had very recently contemplated Ellesmere's death with complacency. He had made him a curious call, and after diagnosis, had petitioned to succeed the presumably dying man, under whom the King's business made such short turns, etc.

At one of his levees, George II. noticed a stranger present, and asked Pulteney who he was. "That, sir," said the minister, "is Mr. Hely Hutchinson, Provost of Dublin, a man who, if Your Majesty should give him the United Kingdom, would ask you for the Isle of Man as potato-garden."

Of the same kidney was Bacon. Having thanked
Villiers on the 15th of February for the promise of the
Great Seal when death or resignation should retire
Ellesmere, on the 21st he asks Villiers to have him
made a Privy Councillor : —

"My Lord Chancellor," he adds, "told me yesterday, in
plain terms, that if the King would ask his opinion touching
the person he would commend to succeed him upon death or
disability, he would name me for the fittest man. You may
advise whether use may not be made of this offer.

"I sent, a pretty while since, a paper to Mr. John Murray,
which was indeed a little remembrance of some things past,
concerning my honest and faithful services to His Majesty;
not by way of boasting (from which I am far), but as tokens
of my studying his service uprightly and carefully. If you
be pleased to call for the paper, which is with Mr. John
Murray, and to find a fit time that His Majesty may cast an
eye upon it, I think it will do no hurt; and I have written
to Mr. Murray to deliver the paper if you call for it. God
keep you in all happiness.

"Your truest servant."

Trusting his cause to his autobiography and his friend,
he now was called upon to prosecute Somerset, the late
favorite, and his countess. Her guilt, as the instigator
of the poisoning of Overberry, admitted of no defense,
so she confessed, begged for mercy, and obtained it.
Somerset stood his trial, and was convicted. Bacon
prosecuted the feminine poisoner mildly, and afterwards
prepared the pardon which the King signed. The
merciful course of the King and his law servants towards the instigators of this vilest species of murder,
after, too, that their tools had been dealt with summarily; the hesitancy on the part of James to stand

aside and let the case take the ordinary course; the peculiar conduct of Somerset, which gave rise to a suspicion — whether well founded or not is hard to say — that he held some secret which intimidated the King, all involve the story in a cloud, so that no one of the participators is seen in a favorable light. Bacon's promise, "It shall be my care so to moderate the manner of charging him as it might make him not odious beyond the extent of mercy," takes the mind back to the time when it was his care so to aggravate the manner of charging Essex as it might make him odious beyond the extent of mercy.

The next correspondence supplying links in Bacon's career are two letters to Villiers, in the spring of 1616: the first urging the execution of the King's good intentions towards Bacon in respect to membership of the council; the second deciding to be sworn as Councillor, instead of accepting an assurance of succession to the chancellorship, which the tenacious Ellesmere still held. And so he became legally what he had so long a time been in fact, one of the King's advisers. In the dual capacity of Attorney-General and Councillor, his first service was to contribute to the degradation of his lifelong rival, Coke, who, with all his faults, was then regarded as the champion of an independent judiciary, and of the constitution against the encroachments of the executive, and for which his memory is now held sacred. In a case before Coke, the counsel denied that the King could make a certain grant. Bacon and the Lord Chancellor prepared a letter, which was sent under the Privy Seal, commanding the Chief Justice to suspend the hearing until James could be consulted. The ground assumed was that the King's prerogative

D

was involved in the question. Coke requested that like letters should be sent to the other judges, which was done. They all, after consultation, responded that the letters received required them to break their oaths, and that under the law the case must be heard. The King summoned them before him and scolded them for their disrespect. On their knees they apologized for the independent expressions they had used in giving their opinion, but did not retract. Coke offered no excuse, but a defense, saying, "The delay required was against law and their oaths."

Bacon, who, with the Lord Chancellor, was present, spoke up, antagonized Coke, and argued with the judges. Coke resented his interference, and these two exchanged hot words. The King and Lord Chancellor reinforced the Attorney-General. Then were the judges asked, if the King required them to stay a case pending, which involved his power or profit, until they could consult with him, would they do it. All save Coke said they would. His answer was: "When the case shall be, I will do that which shall be fit for a judge to do."

Mr. Hallam, in his "Constitutional History," gives a graphic sketch of this scene:—

"Having been induced, by a sense of duty, or through the ascendency Coke had acquired over them, to make a show of withstanding the Court, they behaved like cowardly rebels, who surrender at the first discharge of cannon, and prostituted their integrity and their fame through dread of losing their offices, or rather, perhaps, of incurring the un-merciful and ruinous penalties of the Star Chamber."

Coke was summoned before the Council, and made answer to a stale charge of some irregularity in money dealings, to the charge of disrespectful disregard of Bacon's argument in the King's presence, and his refusal to yield as the other judges had done. His defense was heard and reported to the King.

The prosecution did not stop here. The Lord Chancellor, Attorney-General Bacon, and Solicitor Yelverton, after overhauling Coke's "Reports," suggested to the King that his sacred prerogative had been assailed in those volumes. The result was that James, through his Council, directed the Lord Chief Justice to vacate for the present both his seat in the Council and on the Bench. He was ordered to employ his enforced holiday in overlooking his "Reports," for his "exorbitant and extravagant opinions set down and published for positive and good law." When Coke had finished this criticism of Coke, he was to "bring the same privately to himself (James) that he might consider thereof, as in his princely judgment should be found expedient."

James turned from disgracing Coke to honoring Villiers, whom he now, August 27, 1616, created a viscount. A favorite with James meant his familiar and inseparable companion, whom he fondled, kissed, and slobbered over in a disgusting way. In exchange for submission to these endearments the recipient enjoyed unbounded influence, personal and political, over the King. We have seen how long and persistent were the efforts of Bacon to obtain the least recognition of his great gifts and deserts at the hands of Elizabeth, and how she died without having advanced him many steps beyond the threshold of the door at which he stood knocking from youth to middle age. Upon James' accession he did not cease his efforts at preferment, and in this, as in the former reign, he placed his hopes and reliance on men younger than himself. Between his age and that of Essex there were but a few years, but he was nearly twice as old as Villiers, whom he now saw, in the short space of two years, advanced from the place of a page, the King's cup-bearer, to that of a peer of England. Villiers is described by his contemporaries as very handsome in form and feature, as personally brave, with a sort of chivalric frankness toward those against whom he used the influence he wielded. So well assured of the favor of James, he seems to have never feared the enmity of others; and when he struck, it was done after declaring his displeasure openly. He spent three years in France, and returned at the age of twenty-one a polished young courtier. Clarendon thus describes him : —

"In a few days after his first appearance in court he was made cup-bearer to the King; by this he was, of course, to be much in his presence, and so admitted to that conversation and discourse with which that prince always abounded at his meals. His inclinations to the new cup-bearer disposed him to administer frequent occasions of discoursing of the Court of France, and the transactions there, with which he had been so lately acquainted that he could pertinently enlarge upon that subject, to the King's great delight, and to the gaining of the esteem and value of all the standers-by to himself; which was a thing the King was well pleased with. He acted very few works upon this stage, when he mounted higher; and being knighted without any other qualifications, he was at the same time made Gentleman of the Bedchamber and Knight of the Order of the Garter; and in a short time (very short for such a prodigious ascent) he was made a baron, a viscount and earl, a marquis, and became Lord High Admiral of England, Lord Warden of the Cinque Ports, Master of the Horse, and entirely disposed of all the graces of the King, in conferring all the honors and all the offices of the three kingdoms, without a rival; in dispensing whereof in it as guided more by the rules of appetite than of judgment; and so exalted almost all of his numerous family and dependents, whose greatest merit was their alliance to him, which equally offended the nobility and the people of all conditions, who saw the flowers of their crown every day fading and withered, whilst the demesnes and revenue thereof were sacrificed to the enriching of a private family (how well soever originally extracted), scarce ever heard of before to the nation; and the expenses of the court so vast and unlimited that they had a sad prospect of that poverty and necessity which afterward befell the crown, almost to the ruin of it."

This was the man unto whom with a politician's prescience Bacon had attached himself. The attraction was mutual, and at first the young favorite looked up to the experienced lawyer and statesman for advice in a situation rendered somewhat trying by the suddenness of his rise. It was to furnish a lamp to his pathway that "A Letter of Advice, written by Sir Francis Bacon, to the Duke of Buckingham, when He became Favorite to King James" was composed. Bacon, it will be seen by the tone of his letter, recognizes the influence of the young favorite.

"Being overruled by your Lordship's command, first by word, and since by your letters, I have chosen rather to show my obedience than to dispute the danger of discovering my weakness in adventuring to give advice on a subject too high for me."

This, from one who had all his life been a volunteer of advice to secretaries of state and sovereigns, must be accepted as incense upon the altar of one who had already wielded, and was to wield, influence in the distribution of place and power.   He proceeds: —

"You are now the King's favorite, so voted and so esteemed by all.   You are as a continual sentinel, always to stand upon your watch, to give him true intelligence. If you flatter him, you betray him.   If you conceal the truth of those things from him which concerns his justice or his honor (although not the safety of his person), you are as dangerous a traitor to his state as he that resisteth in arms against him.   A false friend is more dangerous than an open enemy."

Proceeding with his subject, Bacon develops this letter into a series of golden rules, every one a light to the pathway of King as well as favorite.   It is a valuable essay upon the proper administration of public affairs, and serves to illustrate how the pen was to Bacon what the wonderful lamp was to Aladdin.   With that in his hand he seemed to live in another world, far from the one in which he played so often so ignoble a part.   It reads as a confession of what he would have done if the dream of his youth and manhood had been realized; like a promise of what he would do were they realized in the future.   When he laid aside his pen, he took up, by the King's command, the persecution, for it deserves no other name, of Chief Justice Coke, who appeared before the Lord Chancellor and Attorney-General to answer respecting the alleged errors in his "Reports."

Instead of humility and retraction, he told them in substance that he had found the legal treasures freer from errors than might have been expected.   After some further consideration and consultation, and when Coke had explained some misinterpreted expressions, the Chief Justice was removed from the Bench.

As a set-off to what modern lawyers agree in calling the disgraceful conduct of Bacon in the whole proceeding against the great judge, we have the wise and beneficent proposition of the first of England's reformers to recompile her laws; for as such reformer Bacon stands first. We have seen that his proposition to regulate weights and measures was renewed, and first enacted in the reign of William IV.; and in the parliament of 1614 he offered a bill for the reform of penal laws, which Sir Robert Peel read as a part of his argument in support of a similar measure, in 1826, saying :—

"The lapse of two hundred and fifty years has increased the necessity of the measure which Lord Bacon then proposed, but it has produced no argument in favor of the principle, no objection adverse to it which he did not anticipate "

The career of Bacon under Elizabeth was signalized by repeated disappointments. All that he attained to in office was the honor of Counsel Learned Extraordinary; that is a position which was without a commission or warrant, which subjected him to ill-natured remarks of Coke because he was an unsworn Counsellor, and therefore regarded from a professional standpoint as a sort of interloper, although he labored most diligently in the business of the Queen, whenever he was employed in her affairs. The only recognition he received by way of emolument was a reversion, whose enjoyment was postponed for the wearisome waiting term of twenty years.

But his rise under James illustrated the truth of the proverb that "nothing succeeds like success." The regular appointment of Learned Counsel was supplemented by a small annuity; then followed that of Judge of the Court of the Verge of the Palace, the Solicitor-Generalship, the Attorney-Generalship, the Chancellorship of the Duchy of Cornwall, thrown in as an incidental, the place of Privy Councillor, and at last, on the 7th of March, 1617, he became Lord Keeper of the Great Seal, one step removed from the goal of an English lawyer's ambition. To the young favorite he was indebted, and to him he poured out the flood of gratitude which swelled his bosom : —

"In this day's work," he writes to Buckingham, "you are the truest and perfectest mirror and example of firm and generous friendship that ever was in court. And I shall count every day lost wherein I shall not either study your well-doing in thought, or do your name honor in speech, or perform you service in deed.

"Good my Lord, account and accept me,
   "Your most bounden and devoted friend
        "and servant, of all men living,
              "Fr. Bacon, C. S."

His new position placed him at the helm of the ship of state, and the dream of his youth, the hope of his manhood was realized. If he had not been sandwiched between a conceited and cowardly king, and a willful, ignorant and selfish favorite; or if his devotion to place had been secondary to that courageous independence which must supplement wisdom in high places to make it available for the public good, the name of Bacon might have been associated with that of the greatest ministers of state. But his chief object was to please the King and oblige the favorite.

Yet, even when committing himself to these two ends, here and there is seen the spontaneous outcropping of his higher and better nature. An instance of this is furnished by his letter of advice to James, touching the contemplated marriage contract between Prince Charles and the Infanta of Spain. The King had entered into this negotiation of his own will and wisdom, and no one knew better than Bacon that such a marriage would be regarded by the mass of Englishmen as an insult to the memory of Elizabeth, with whom and for whom they and their fathers had fought Philip and the Pope, as a threat against Protestantism, as the death-blow to Puritanism, as endangering the liberties which Elizabeth had established and left for a birthright. Yet Bacon did not oppose the King's mad proposition. But he did urge James to broaden his negotiations with Spain. His first propositien was that the two sovereigns should unite for the extirpation of piracy, thus anticipating that international action which, centuries later, accomplished this great security to the commerce of the world.

His next proposition was the joint declaration of a holy war against the infidel Turk; not so profound and philanthropic a scheme, but a diplomatic effort to make oil and water mix, to overshadow the union of a Protestant prince to a Roman Catholic princess, by a union of a Protestant people and a Roman Catholic people against a common foe.

His third proposition was to establish an international tribunal for the settlement of mutual wrongs without going to war. It is true that he meant to narrow and confine the jurisdiction of this court to the two sovereigns, but it was the germ of that great victory over lingering barbarism which England and the United States, in the last half of the 19th century, have accomplished.*

His last proposition was aimed at crushing out the spirit of democracy by a union of monarchies against it: an idea acted upon, to some extent, indirectly at least, and which has served to deprive every European monarchy save England of the blessing of a free constitution.

On the 7th of May, 1617, Bacon was installed as Lord Keeper. The King, Buckingham and their retinue had recently left for a jaunt to Scotland; but the philosopher managed to arrange a showy procession and ceremony.

"Our Lord Keeper," says a contemporary letter-writer, "exceeds all his predecessors in the bravery and multitude of his servants. It amazes those that look on his beginnings, besides never so indulgent a master. On the first day of term he appeared in his greatest glory; for to the Hall, besides his own retinue, did accompany him all the Lords of his Majesty's Council and others, with all Knights and gentlemen that could get horses and foot-cloths."

The procession started from Gray's Inn, where, thirty-eight years before, Bacon had almost hopelessly entered upon the study of the law. After taking the oaths of office, he delivered an inaugural address, exhibiting his familiarity with and appreciation of the principles of law and equity; he indicated the course

* Referring national quarrels to an international tribunal instead of to the cannon, the *ultima ratio regum*.

which he would take, the improvements which he would initiate, and the rules he would prescribe for the facilitation of business and the administration of equity.

At the close of his speech he commenced business, and rather marred the effect of his eloquence by exhibiting an awkwardness in handling a motion made by a young lawyer. However, with a grateful and joyous heart he reported the day's doings to the favorite, and forwarded to the King a copy of his address.

After this he entered upon the practical duties of his office with great zest, and by great diligence disposed of many cases then pending and long delayed.

Upon Justice Hutton being called to the bench of the Court of Common Pleas, Bacon delivered an address which is unparalleled for its condensed characterization of all that goes to make up a good judge. His discriminating eye had detected, perhaps he had suffered from, the errors and faults most common to the judiciary, and he laid down eleven rules, which would to-day serve to elevate and purify the bench, if taken to heart. In fact, they are worthy of being engraved in golden letters upon imperishable tablets, and set up in every court-room as a constant admonition to the judicial mind.

In his subsequent address, upon the elevation of Sir John Denham to be a Baron of the Exchequer, he was not so happy, and declared himself in these unequivocal terms respecting the royal prerogative: —

"First, therefore, above all, you ought to maintain the King's prerogative, and to set down with yourself that the King's prerogative and law are not two things; but the King's prerogative is law, and the principal part of the law: the first-born, or *pars premia* of the law."

Everything that was done or said by Bacon was reported to the absentees, whose stay in Scotland was relieved of all anxiety by the diligence of so zealous a servant. But he whose ambition it is to please everybody must offend some. The Queen became dissatisfied with her Solicitor, Mr. Lowder, therefore Bacon sent him to the north, with a letter to Buckingham, in which he says: —

"Upon knowledge of her (the Queen's) pleasure he was willing to part with his place, upon hope not to be destituted, but to be preferred to one of the Baron's places in Ireland. I pray move the King for him, and let His Majesty know from me that I think (howsoever he pleased not here), he is fit to do His Majesty's service in that place ; he is grave and formal (which is somewhat there), and sufficient enough for that place.

"The Queen hath made Mr. Haskwell her solicitor, etc."

Later on it will be seen that Bacon's ready disposition to humor the Queen in this matter, furnished the King with his first ground of complaint and censure.

While Bacon was revelling in the rôle of Lord Keeper, the unfrocked Chief Justice was chafing in the retirement to which his rival had been so active in consigning him. Coke pretended to think little of Bacon's legal ability, had no sympathy with his philosophical predilections, was probably jealous of his fame as an author, despised his subserviency, and perhaps dreaded his pliability as instrumental for danger to England's liberties; for, with all his faults, the Chief Justice was a patriot.

Rage, jealousy and patriotism inspired him to look around for some escape from his inactive, powerless and distasteful retirement. Meditating over his own

wrongs and his country's dangers, knowing that he whi
pleased the favorite was in the light, and he who dis
pleased him, in the darkness,—for his own decline
began with a refusal on his part to appoint a follower
of Buckingham's to an office,—the wily Chief Justice
listened favorably to the renewal of a proposal of marriage between his youngest daughter and Sir John
Villiers, a brother of the favorite. The shaft struck
the mark, for he was soon at Newmarket, kissing His
Majesty's hands, and receiving assurances of employment in some capacity other than judicial.

He and Lady Hatton—for so his wife insisted on
being called, having repudiated her husband's name—
shortly before this time had engaged in litigation
respecting her property, and the two had frequently
regaled the Council-table with their bickerings. The
peace which was there patched up was broken when
she heard of her husband's proposed matrimonial disposition of her daughter. To avoid its conclusion she
eloped with the maiden. At this juncture Bacon
appeared upon the scene.

He who had suffered injustice, ill-deeds and ill-will
at the hands of Coke, who had seen his legal rival
marry the woman whom he sought, who appreciated
and feared the ability, courage and willfulness of the
disgraced Chief Justice, he who had been so instrumental in his downfall, could not be expected to look
favorably upon so close a connection with Buckingham
as this marriage would create. It implied restoration
to favor, to power, to opposition, and perhaps to supremacy in the King's Council.

When, therefore, Lady Compton, the mother of the
favorite and of the expectant bridegroom, applied to

Bacon, in the name of Coke, for a warrant to recover
his daughter, who had been so summarily and secretly
removed from his reach, Bacon refused to grant her
request, and she left him in anger, and in anger reported
his conduct to her son.   It is alleged that Bacon was
not informed that she spoke in that son's name, nor
acquainted with Buckingham's anxiety for the match.
However, his course was so opposite to what might
have been expected of him in the premises, that one
might reasonably infer that when suddenly confronted
with the alternative of either aiding Coke in his scheme
for restoration, or of offending Buckingham's mother,
he chose the latter, trusting to the future for smoothing
over matters with the favorite.   Yet he did not wait for
Buckingham's return, but wrote him a letter, from
which the following paragraphs are taken:—

"MY VERY GOOD LORD:—I shall write to Your Lordship
of a business which Your Lordship may think to concern
myself; but I do think it concerneth Your Lordship much
more.   For as for me, as my judgment is not so weak to
think it can do me any hurt, so my love to you is so strong,
as I would prefer the good of you and yours before mine
own particular.

"It seemeth that Secretary Winwood hath officiously
busied himself to make a match between your brother and
Sir Edward Coke's daughter; and, as we hear, he doth it
rather to make a faction than out of any great affection to
Your Lordship.   It is true he hath the consent of Sir Edward Coke (as we hear), upon reasonable conditions for your
brother, and yet no better than, without question, may be
found in some other matches.   But the mother's consent is
not had, nor the young gentlewoman's, who expecteth a
great fortune from her mother, which, without her consent,
is endangered.   This match, out of my faith and freedom

towards Your Lordship, I hold very inconvenient both for your brother and yourself.

"First. He shall marry into a disgraced house, which in reason of state is never held good.

"Next. He shall marry into a troubled house of man and wife, which in religion and Christian discretion is disliked.

"Thirdly. Your Lordship will go near to lose all such your friends as are adverse to Sir Edward Coke (myself only except, who, out of a pure love and thankfulness, shall ever be firm to you).

"And lastly and chiefly (believe it), it will greatly weaken and distract the King's service. For though, in regard of the King's great wisdom and depth, I am persuaded those things will not follow which they imagine, yet opinion will do a great deal of harm, and cast the King back, and make him lapse into those inconveniences which are now well on to be recovered.

"Therefore, my advice is, and Your Lordship shall do yourself great honor if, according to religion and the law of God, Your Lordship will signify unto my Lady, your mother, that your desire is that the marriage be not pressed or proceeded in without the consent of both parents; and so either break it altogether, or defer any further dealings in it till Your Lordship's return."

A thread of argument runs through this advice which connects it with Bacon's fear of, and antagonism to, Coke. It is the weakest offspring of his pen. How was the house of Coke disgraced, when the profession and the people regarded him in retirement as the champion of an independent judiciary and free constitution, as a martyr to principle? How could that be a disgraced house, when its head was receiving flattering assurances of favor from the King, and whose alliance with the favorite's family would wipe out in the minds of courtiers the stain which persecution had endeavored to put upon it?

Who, too, ever heard of an all-powerful favorite's friends (if a favorite ever had friends), deserting the distributor of honors and emoluments because he happened to restore a man to favor? And how could the marriage of a weak girl to a young fortune-hunter "distract and weaken the King's service," or create an opinion of such breadth, depth, volume and force as to "cast the King back, and make him relapse into those inconveniences which are now well on to be recovered?"

Upon hearing of Bacon's refusal to grant the warrant for restoring his daughter, Coke armed and mounted his son and a band of sturdy servants, whom he inspired with some of his own spirit, and they pursued the bone of contention. Lady Hatton had sent their daughter into the country, to be the guest of Sir Edmond Withipole. Here Coke soon arrived; and although he had a warrant, signed by Secretary Winwood, as his authority for entering the room and reclaiming his daughter, he relied on the efficacy of muscle and an impromptu battering-ram, with which he broke the door down, and transferring his daughter to a coach, he galloped off with her, surrounded by his *posse*.

When the news of the kidnapping reached Lady Hatton's ears, she enlisted "Lord Houghton, Sir Edward Sackville, Sir Rob. Rich and others, with three score of men and pistols," says a news-writer, and gave chase; but the lady's coach broke down in the highway. "They met not," says this gossip; "if they had, there had been a notable skirmish; for the Lady

Compton was with Mrs. Franch in the coach, and there was Clem Coke, my Lord's fighting son, and they all swore they would die in the place before they would part with her."

Lady Hatton, finding the fortunes of war against her, now hastened to secure the services of her old rejected lover. She reached Bacon's lodgings at an early hour, when he was enjoying his morning nap. She was permitted to occupy a room adjoining his sleeping-apartment; not, however, until she had promised to restrain her impatience and suffer her once suitor to slumber, and dream, perchance, of his early love. When she was left alone she proceeded to make enough noise to waken the seven sleepers. Bacon, suddenly aroused by this strange and violent disturbance, cried aloud for help. His servants rushed into his bedroom. Lady Hatton unceremoniously followed, apologizing to the Lord Keeper by comparing herself to "a cow who had lost her calf."

Coke's enemy and Coke's wife formed a coalition against him. The ex-Chief Justice was summoned before the Council, on the petition of his enraged spouse, for breaking the laws of England by breaking down Sir Edmond Withipole's inner door. Coke answered with counter-charges against his helpmate; and as for the "riot and force" complained of, this he justified. The Council seized upon the latter proposition, and directed the Attorney-General to file an information against Sir Edward Coke in the Court of the Star Chamber. This last proceeding was, in all probability, inspired by Bacon, who concurred in all that was done in the premises; the first act of the Council being the removal of the maiden from the custody of either

parent for the time being, and assigning her to that of
a third person until the conflict about right of possession could be settled; the second act being an issue
joined with Coke on a legal position assumed by him,
which was regarded as extravagant as some of the legal
positions in the unpurged reports, and therefore calculated to excite the animosity of the King.

Winwood had granted the warrant to Lady Hatton,
and when his coadjutors on the board drove him to the
wall, he surprised and silenced them with the information that the King was personally interested in the
match which had occupied the attention of England's
Cabinet. This news changed the situation completely.
The maiden was "sent home to Hatton House, with
orders that Lady Compton and her son should have
access to win and wear her."

Bacon now wrote to the King in reference to the
match, and endeavored to impress him with the idea
that Winwood and Coke, who had been so active in
favor of it, were not so effective as others; that he,
Bacon, in humbling Coke, had not been inspired by
personal fear or ill-will; third, that he was ready to forward the match if His Majesty were resolved that it
should go on; lastly, he endeavors to frighten the King
from espousing the match, lest it should disturb the
prerogative, lift up the humbled judges, and generally
disturb the state by Coke "coming in with the strength
of such an alliance."

This letter and its disingenuous and flimsy arguments
were treated by James as they deserved to be. Before
Bacon received the King's answer he again wrote to
Buckingham, not once only, but twice. At last he
received from the favorite a curt answer. The King's

letter had already dismayed him; the two quite disor-
ganized him. The King, in this correspondence, called
him severely to account for having indorsed a man who
was unfit to be the Queen's counsel, for the place of an
Irish baron. In reply to James, he wrote in a most
humble and propitiatory spirit, confessing that his
anger "grieved me more than any event that hath
fallen out in my life."

"I know," he continues, "that reprehensions from the
best of masters to the best of servants are necessary, and
that no chastisement is pleasant for the time, but yet worketh good effects. . . . . But since Your Majesty bid-
deth me confide in your art of empire, I have done; for as
the Scripture saith, ' *To God all things are possible,*' so cer-
tainly to wise kings much is possible."

The King had rated him for disrespect to, and insinuation against, Buckingham. He proclaims "a parent-
like" affection for the favorite, and adds: —

"I was afraid that the height of his fortune might make
him too secure, and (as the proverb is) a looker-on sometimes seeth more than a gamester. . . . It is true that
in those matters which, by Your Majesty's commandment
and reference, came before the table concerning Sir Edward
Coke, I was sometimes sharp (it may be too much). But it
was with end to have Your Majesty's will performed, or else
when he was more peremptory than became him in respect
to the honor of the table. It is true, also, that I disliked
the riot or violence, whereof we of Your Majesty's Council
gave Your Majesty advertisement by our joint letter; and I
disliked it the more because he justified it by law, which
was his old song."

After beseeching James to understand that he had
not received a letter from the favorite, he says: —

"After I had received, by a former letter of His Lordship, knowledge of his mind, I think Sir Edward Coke himself, the last time he was before the Lords, mought plainly per ceive an alteration in my carriage. And now that Your Majesty hath been pleased to open yourself to me, I shall be willing to further the match by anything that shall be desired of me, or that is in my power."

In another letter to Buckingham, he says:—

"I did fear that this alliance would go near to lose me Your Lordship, that I hold so dear, and that was the only respect particular to myself that moved me to be as I was, till I heard from you."

Was there ever a more humiliating confession and surrender of self than are here exhibited? Browbeating Coke as a law-breaker, and suddenly propitiating him as a royal favorite. Telling the King and Buckingham that the match was dangerous to the state, and damaging to the family of Villiers, and then declaring his anxiety to further it to the end. James answered the last letter to himself, and charged Bacon with disingenuousness, jealousy of, and ingratitude towards, Buckingham; justified Coke in retaking his daughter:—

"And," he says, "as for your laying the burden of your opposition upon the whole Council, we meddle not with that question; but the opposition we justly find fault with you, was a refusal to sign a warrant for the father to recover his child."

To this Bacon wrote an answer, further explaining his meaning in reference to the insinuation that the favorite's head was in danger of being turned by good fortune, and then waited with great anxiety the return of James and Buckingham to London. Coke and Yelverton went to meet them, but Bacon had not the nerve, probably. Yelverton, however, wrote him a long account of how matters were. Coke was denouncing both him and Bacon, he says. Buckingham gave him a disagreeably warm reception. Yelverton generously fought Bacon's battle as well as his own:—

"Now, my Lord," he adds, "give me leave, out of all my affections that shall ever serve you, to intimate touching yourself:—

"1st. That every courtier is acquainted that the Earl professeth openly against you as forgetful of his kindness, and unfaithful to him in your love and in your actions.

"2d. That he returneth the shame upon himself, in not listening to counsel that dissuaded his affection from you, and not to mount you so high, not forbearing in open speech as divers have told me, and this bearer, your gentleman, (hath heard, also), to tax you, as if it were an inveterate custom with you, to be unfaithful to him as you were to the Earls of Essex and Somerset.

"3d. That is too common in every man's mouth in court, that your greatness shall be abated, and as your tongue hath been as a razor to some, so shall theirs be to you.

"4th. That there is laid up for you, to make your burden the more grievous, many petitions to His Majesty against you."

After advising Bacon to meet James at Woodstock, in order to frighten some enemies by his presence, to insist upon the other Lords of the Council being equally blameable for the unpopular action, and to be undismayed, he says, "I beseech Your Lordship to burn this letter."

Bacon should have destroyed a letter inspired by friendship, but whose contents would have endangered the writer if made public. But, fortunately for us, he did not, and it is a valuable witness as to his character and career at this period. It is evident that he had made many enemies; that his behavior towards Essex was still fresh in the memories of some; that his administration of the Great Seal had given offense to some, for it must be to this that the petitions to the King, alluded to above, referred; and that his tongue, strange to say, had become an unruly member.

While pondering over this epistle, he received a short one from Buckingham, in which the latter says: —

"My Lord: — I have received so many letters lately from Your Lordship that I cannot answer them severally; but the ground of them all being only this, that Your Lordship feareth I am so incensed against you that I will hearken unto every information that is made unto me; this one letter may well make answer to them all."

Then, speaking for the King and himself, he tells Bacon they will hear his defense when they return.

A drunken fellow, about this time, having been heard to say he would kill the King, Bacon hastened to exhibit his zeal by reporting the same in a letter to James, and also suggesting the appointment of a commission to hear the suits and petitions which awaited the King's arrival.

Buckingham answered, and said the King contemned the drunken fellow's speeches, but desired an examination to be made into the man's mental condition, and that the proposition for the commission could wait his arrival. The favorite further says: —

"I do fully confess that your offer of submission unto me, and in writing (if so I would have it), battered so the unkindness that I had conceived in my heart for your behavior towards me in my absence, as out of the sparks of my old affection toward you I went to sound His Majesty's intention how he means to behave himself towards you, specially in any public meeting; where I found on the one part His Majesty so little satisfied with your late answer unto him, which he counted (for I protest I use his own terms,) confused and childish; and his rigorous resolution on the other part, so fixed that he would put some public exemplary mark upon you, as I protest the sight of his deep-conceived indignation quenched my passion."

He then says he begged James on his knees not to publicly denounce Bacon, and that the King further promised not to "disable him from the merit of future service."

How great a reaction this letter must have brought about is apparent from Bacon's answer: —

"My ever best Lord, now better than yourself. Your Lordship's pen, or rather, pencil, hath portrayed towards me such magnanimity and nobleness and true kindness, as methinkest I see the image of some ancient virtue, and not anything of these times. It is the line of my life, and not the lines of my letter, that must express my thankfulness; wherein, if I fail, then God fail me, and make me as miserable as I think myself at this time happy by this review, through His Majesty's singular clemency, and your incomparable love and favor. God preserve you, prosper you, and reward you for your kindness to

"Your raised and infinitely obliged friend and servant,

"FR. BACON, C. S.

"Sept. 22, 1617."

Thus, in this correspondence have we gone through the most melancholy chapter in Bacon's official life save one, and that is the last. If he honestly believed that this match endangered the King's prerogative and the country's peace by restoring Coke to favor, authority and aggressiveness, he should have stood by his convictions. If we are to believe his own letters to James, he sincerely held this opinion; and he claims, in his letters to the King, that his opposition to the match and his severity towards Coke were inspired by devotion to the King and to the law, whose breach Coke justified.

But we cannot accept these as his sole motives, for he assigned another to the favorite: "I did ever fear this alliance would go near to leese me Your Lordship." This inconsistency is incompatible enough with the theory of sincerity. But when we find him protesting his willingness to withdraw opposition to the dangerous match; to further it; find him claiming credit for a gentler bearing towards Coke, and apologizing for his "sharp" tongue; find him all anxiety and humility until the favorite relents, and then all submission and gratitude, we see him in the most abject of situations. A great officer of the crown, carrying the Great Seal of England in one hand, while, with the other over his mouth, he bows low at the feet of a favorite, the spirit crushed out of him, his manhood, independence, conscience, all surrendered into the hands of that favorite for the future. Bacon offended Elizabeth but once; and to propitiate her, he dedicated his life to her service, in the rôle of an unresisting, unquestioning, obedient courtier. For the first and last time he offended James; forgiveness came quickly, and subserviency never ceased.

Lady Hatton, upon being deserted by Bacon and others who followed his lead, and being opposed by the King, had to yield. Her husband was restored to the Council table; her daughter was married to Sir John Villiers, and she barely escaped prosecution for the false allegation of a pre-contract of marriage between the Earl of Oxford and that daughter, whose affections were in truth inclined towards Sir Robert Howard, with whom she subsequently eloped, leaving Sir John Villiers to reflect upon the impolicy of wooing a woman with such extraordinary instruments as a King and a King's Council.

Bacon endeavored to remove all recollection of his unpopular course in this affair by renewed diligence in the execution of his office. Buckingham indicated his forgiveness by frequent letters to Lord Keeper and Lord Chancellor Bacon, for this crowning promotion was made at a Sunday feast of the favorite, in January, 1618.

These letters were, in the main, in reference to suits pending before the Lord Chancellor, and commended to his favorable consideration one of the parties in litigation. The fact that these interfering epistles of the favorite were qualified with the expression "so far as may stand with justice and equity," has been regarded by the apologists of Bacon as a proof that the influence of Buckingham was not of a dangerous character, and that his appeals to Bacon in behalf of this or that suitor did not disturb the scales of justice. If, however, Bacon were judged by the letter of advice he once wrote to Villiers, at the beginning of his career, where he says, "By no means be you persuaded to interpose yourself either by word or letter, in any cause depending in any court of justice," he cannot be excused for receiving more than one such letter from the favorite. And when we have seen Bacon so unmanned and humiliated by the favorite's displeasure at a judicial course which Bacon protested to the King was both legal and patriotic, yet admitted to the favorite was inspired by the fear of losing his Lordship; when we see him going back in his tracks to please both James and Buckingham, we have evidence from his own acts and words that his judicial opinion and conduct were subordinated to the favors and smiles of these *arcades ambo.*

Therefore, to say that the wish of the favorite did not affect his impartiality, is to ignore the existence of the frailty which he had already exhibited. Nor is the case made stronger for Bacon by admitting that in the suits disgraced by the favorite's interference no "unjust decree" was passed. If the favorite's friends had the right of the matter, as between Buckingham and Bacon, these letters were just as disgraceful to both as if they had the wrong of the matter. It is enough to know that the man who was all-powerful with the King; whose influence had raised Bacon to the position he occupied; whose influence could degrade him; a man who notoriously sold this influence to the highest bidder, commended a litigant to his obligee's favorable consideration, and that this obliged judicial officer continued to receive promotion at the favorite's hands. For after Bacon's offer of "submission" to Buckingham, and expressed willingness to put it "in writing," as his Lordship said in a letter above quoted, he grew in favor with the now marquis, and through his instrumentality, after having been made Lord Chancellor, in July, 1617, was created Baron Verulam of Verulam.

The year that calendared this advancement will ever be remembered as that in which Sir Walter Raleigh was brought to the block in manner disgraceful to all concerned. For fifteen years this brave and brilliant Englishman had been confined in the Tower of London. Although convicted of treason, his sentence had been suspended.

His busy mind could not remain idle, even in imprisonment, and it was there that he wrote not only his "History of the World," but several brief contributions to the literature of the day.

Keeping up his interest in all that related to the new world, and not being cut off entirely from connection with kindred and adventurous spirits, who looked to that quarter for fame and fortune, he made more than one proposition to be allowed to fit out an expedition in search of gold mines, which he alleged were discoverable.

He first proposed to lead the expedition in person. This was rejected, as involving his liberty. The next was that he was to send the expedition under another, which, if successful, should secure him his freedom. These terms would seem to indicate that he had an honest belief in the probable success of his scheme. The terms of the last proposition were that he should, in person, seek the mine of gold; and that it was not near any Spanish settlement. This was accepted; and in 1616 his commission was signed, about ten years after he had originally presented the plan.

The King knew that Raleigh belonged to that generation of Englishmen who looked upon the Spaniards as their personal, political, religious and national enemies. He was as anxious to prolong peace with Spain as his subjects and some of his advisers were to hasten war with that nation. He was suspicious of Raleigh's temperament and disposition; and the Spanish envoy was suspicious of Raleigh's good faith, alleging that the mine was a pretext for a practical attack on some colonial settlement of his country. So Sir Walter was required to give security that he would not disturb a hair of a Spaniard's head, and was given to understand that if he did he would lose his own head. Under such restrictions and encouraging conditions he went forth to gather gold for himself and his royal master. It was generally understood that he had been supplied with ore from a certain mine, which he had assayed while in the Tower; and that this mine was located somewhere in the neighborhood of a Spanish settlement on the Orinoco, appears from his instructions to one of his captains.

He reached his destination; sent some of his followers to prospect; they found themselves front to front with a Spanish force; an engagement ensued; the enemy were driven into their town, then driven out of it, and it was burned. Between the Englishmen and the alleged mine were the Spaniards, who had retreated to the woods. To advance eight miles with these foes hanging about them was not deemed advisable; so they returned to their fleet, and the fleet returned home.

There Gondomar stood crying for vengeance, and James did not delay in accommodating him any further than the embarrassing surroundings necessitated. For how to judicially cut off Raleigh's head as quickly as possible was a problem for the lawyers to solve.

Lord Chancellor Bacon convened the judges at York House, his residence. After consultation they agreed that Raleigh was out of the pale of prosecution, for the law had been exhausted in his case sixteen years back, when he had been convicted of treason.   They held:—

"That Sir Walter Raleigh, having been attainted of high treason, which is the highest and last work of the law, he cannot be drawn in question judicially for any crime or offense since committed."

They recommended :—

"Either that a warrant should be immediately sent to the Lieutenant of the Tower for his immediate execution under the former sentence, or that he should be brought before the Council and principal judges, some of the nobility and gentlemen of quality being admitted to be present, and there being a recital of all his recent offenses, and then he being heard and withdrawn—without any fresh sentence, the Lords of the Council and judges should give their advice openly, whether, in respect of these offenses, the King might not, with justice and honor, give warrant for his execution on his attainder."

Execution of the sentence sixteen years old was awarded; and, to pacify Spain, more than to vindicate the law, the scholar, sailor and soldier, the patriot of one reign and the ornament of two, was beheaded. His behavior on the scaffold was that of a Christian philosopher.   Profane history has no parallel; and never died an Englishman so eloquently, if we consider either the pity and indignation which he awakened among his contemporaries, or the opinions of historians and biographers from that time to this.

Bacon shared the unpopularity of this execution as he shared that attendant upon the execution of Essex, and he was again employed in writing the "Declaration," or defense, which was to excuse the inexcusable.

The pen which performed this office turned, with comprehensive facility, to figuring in pounds, shillings and pence, and the preparation of a statement of the King's finances, as a New Year's gift to James, which, though not completed in time for presentation on that day, was promised by a letter dated January 2, 1618. This letter presents a glowing picture of a happy King and people, poetical in its conception and execution, but having one dark stroke of the pencil across its face,—the happy people would not lend or give the good King enough money to squander in extravagance, which added nothing to the "true greatness of Britain."

The subsequent pages in Bacon's official life are not of much interest until we reach the last, which is not far removed. The prosecution of the Earl of Suffolk for trafficking with the public money; the prosecution of Attorney-General Yelverton, at the instigation of Buckingham; and the prosecution of Dutch merchants for the exportation of bullion, were the prominent causes in which he appeared. When Bacon was temporarily out of favor, waiting with fear and trembling the coming of the King and favorite from Scotland, Yelverton went forth to face the anger of both, and exhibited, as we have seen, a disinterested care of Bacon, forewarning and forearming him by the friendly letter which has already been quoted. But it seems that this friendship had come to an end. "Mr. Attorney groweth pretty pert with me of late," writes the Lord Chancellor to the favorite. Yelverton was prosecuted, as Lord Campbell puts it, "on the pretext of having introduced into a charter, granted the city of London, certain clauses alleged not to be agreeable to the King's warrant, and derogatory to his honor," but in fact, because to Bacon and Buckingham he "gave great offense by refusing to pass some illegal patents." Bacon reported to Buckingham, with some pride, the vigor he displayed in the Star Chamber on this occasion : —

"I have almost killed myself," he writes, "by sitting almost eight hours. How I stirred the court I leave to others to speak. I would not for anything, but he had made his defense, for many deep parts of the charge were deeper printed by the defense."

This is small enough glorification over the fall of a man; but let us see what sentimental capital Bacon made out of the opportunity. A memorandum of what he was to say in passing sentence on Yelverton fastens hypocrisy of the worst dye upon him, when contrasted with his unsympathetic report to Buckingham : —

"Sorry for the person, being a gentleman I lived with in Gray's Inn, served with him when I was attorney, joined with him in many services, and one that ever gave me more attributes in public than I deserved; and, besides, a man of very good parts, which, with me, is friendship at first sight, much more, joined with so ancient an acquaintance. But, as judge, hold the offense very great, etc."

Chuckling with Buckingham over Yelverton's defense, congratulating himself that it unfavorably impressed the triers, then, after conviction, pretending sorrow and magnanimity in passing the sentence which followed. But all through this inglorious career, while engaged in seeking office, in executing office; while leader in the House of Commons, and in all capacities vigorously performing the legitimate and illegitimate tasks assigned him; while flattering a pedantic and conceited King, fawning around a passionate and corrupt favorite, taking sides in a family quarrel, and then deserting the cause he had espoused; while thus disgracefully occupied in public life, he, in private life, was nobly employed upon the greatest work of his pen. And now he gave to the world his "*Novum Organum.*"

The King, unworthy of its dedication, made a proper acknowledgment of the honor in a letter to Bacon. Coke wrote on the fly-leaf of the copy which Bacon was weak enough to give him, the following distich, exhibiting temper as bad as his poetry:—

> "It deserveth not to be read in schools,
>   But to be freighted in the Ship of Fooles."

The scholars, at home and abroad, who had been waiting patiently for its publication, received it with warm and flattering appreciation. To them Bacon was a philosopher; and in this character they knew him, judged him, and revered him.

PART III.

FROM PUBLICATION OF "NOVUM ORGANUM," OCT. 12, 1620, TO DEATH OF BACON, APRIL 10, 1626.

Place, power, fortune and fame,—all now seemed to be Bacon's. As Lord Chancellor and Lord Verulam, as the first lawyer, councillor and scholar in England, he celebrated his sixtieth birthday. Friends, disciples, poets and flatterers gathered around him at York House. Everything was on an extravagant and magnificent scale. And Ben Jonson was there to read an ode which the occasion inspired.

But in the midst of all this sunshine a fatal storm was brewing. The King's son-in-law, depending on English sympathy and Protestant enthusiasm, had accepted the crown of Bohemia. Instead of yielding to public sentiment and improving the opportunity of becoming the arbiter of Europe's fate, achieving popularity and glory by becoming the champion of Protestantism, James assumed the rôle of judge and mediator. While he was playing at King-craft, the Spaniards fooled him, and the Catholic coalition made his son-in-law a princely vagabond. Then it was that the duped King yielded to English and Protestant indignation, and summoned parliament to supply sinews

E

for the war, in behalf of the husband of their King's daughter; and they were of course called upon, at the same time, to relieve the necessities of James, multiplied by extravagance and mismanagement.

On the 30th of January, 1620, the two houses got earnestly at work. There were great arrears for parliamentary settlement. The people had for years been groaning under impositions. The popular branch of parliament indicated a kindly disposition toward the King, but with it a firm determination to redress the growing grievances. Coke was a member of the lower house. He had retired from the Council table because the arena was too limited; his power for independent action and leadership was cramped; and the dissatisfied ex-Chief Justice sought contentment in a wider field. Contentment with Coke meant a situation where he could successfully propose something disagreeable to somebody; or, in lieu of this, oppose anything agreeable to everybody who had given him offense.

His rôle now was that of a patriot, and his first motion was for the appointment of a committee to investigate the grievance of monopolies. Since the death of Elizabeth these wrongs had been multiplied in number and abused in execution. No one appreciated the situation better than Bacon; and he had, in the month of November, urged the favorite to anticipate parliamentary action by reform in this particular, having special reference to the patents of Sir Giles Mompesson and Sir Francis Mitchell, the "Sir Giles Overreach" and "Justice Greedy" of Massinger's great drama. These patents conferred on them respectively the licensing of taverns and the exclusive manufacture of gold and silver lace. The outrages and frauds of which both were guilty in making the most of their monopolies, so inflamed the public mind that it forced James to refer the complaints to Lord Keeper Bacon. Mompesson, *alias* "Overreach," accompanied the moralist, philosopher, lawyer and statesman to Kew, where Bacon, in society which we would suppose the least congenial, seeking recreation, combined business with pleasure, and reported "that though there were some things he would set by, he found some things he liked very well;" and in respect to the patent of Mitchell, *alias* "Greedy," he endorsed its legality.*

This was in the year 1617. Three years later the Committee of the House of Commons reported both patents to be outrageously oppressive on the people. The patentees were proceeded against vigorously and successfully. Sir Edward Villiers, half-brother of the favorite, was interested in the ale-house patent; and in order to save him from prosecution and punishment, an honorable retirement beyond the seas in a diplomatic capacity was thought of by the Dean of Westminster, who was the first to suggest foreign service as the Botany Bay of dishonest servants at home.

Having worked this mischief to the favorite's favorite, the next movement in the house was an inquiry into the abuses of Courts of Justice. The investigation exposed channels of corruption centering in the Court of Chancery, and exhibited the Lord Chancellor as the recipient of gifts of money from first one party litigant, then another; and lastly, even from both. Bacon's want of suspicion was akin to innocence, or his moral sensibilities were so blunted that, as is often the case, he ceased to see things through the same moral atmosphere through which lookers-on saw them.

* Lord Campbell's Life. 383.

When Christopher Aubrey's relation to the committee of how he had presented the Lord Chancellor with a sum of money to despatch a suit reached Bacon's ears, he wrote to Buckingham : —

" I know I have clean hands and a clean heart, and I hope a clean house for friends and servants. But Job himself, or whosoever was the justest judge, by such hunting for matters against him as hath been used against me, may for a time seem foul, specially in a time when greatness is the mark and accusation is the game. And if this is to be a Chancellor, I think if the Great Seal lay upon Hounslow Heath, nobody would take it up. But the King and Your Lordship will, I hope, put an end to these miseries one way or other."

The inference from this letter is that he was acquainted with the activity of Coke and others, and was keenly affected by their pointed attack, but relied on the King and favorite to protect him by "putting an end to these miseries." On the heel of Aubrey's case came another charge, also involving a gift of money. Now followed the report of the committee, charging corruption to the account of the Lord Chancellor. As the proceeding ripened, Bacon became too ill to attend the session of the House of Lords, and on March 19, 1620, he addressed a letter to that body, explaining and excusing his absence : —

" MY VERY GOOD LORDS : — I humbly pray Your Lordships all to make a favorable and true construction of my absence. It is no feigning nor fainting, but sickness both of my heart and of my back, though joined with that comfort of mind that persuadeth me that I am not far from heaven, whereof I feel the first fruits ; and because, whether I live or die, I would be glad to preserve my honor and fame, as far as I am worthy, hearing that some complaints of base bribing are come before Your Lordships, my requests unto Your Lordships are: First, that you will maintain me in your good opinion, without prejudice, until my cause be heard; secondly, that in regard I have sequestered my mind at this time in great part from worldly matters, thinking of my account and answer in a higher court, Your Lordships would give me some convenient time, according to the course of other courts, to advise with my counsel, and to make my answer; wherein, nevertheless, my counsel's part will be the least, for I shall not, by the grace of God, trick up an innocency with cavillations, but plainly and ingenuously (as Your Lordships know my manner is) declare what I know or remember; thirdly, that according to the course of justice, I may be allowed to except to the witnesses brought against me, and to move questions to Your Lordships for their cross-examination, and likewise to produce my own witnesses for discovery of the truth; and lastly, if there come any more petitions of like nature, that Your Lordships would be pleased not to take any prejudice or apprehension of any number or muster of them, especially against a judge that makes two thousand decrees and orders in a year (not to speak of the courses that have been taken in hunting out complaints against me); but that I may answer them, according to the rules of justice, severally and respectively. These requests, I hope, appear to Your Lordships no other than just. And so, thinking myself happy to have so noble peers and reverend prelates to discern of my cause, and desiring no privilege of greatness for subterfuge of guiltiness, but meaning, as I said, to deal fairly and plainly with Your Lordships, and to put myself upon your honors and favors, I pray God to bless your counsels and your persons, and rest

"Your Lordships' humble servant,

"Fr. St. Alban.

"19th March, 1620."

This letter, which every reader will dissect for himself, presents Bacon as either a man ill unto death, or
as endeavoring to awaken sympathy by representing
himself in this condition, and to secure for his assertions the credibility due a dying declaration.

Yet, after the representation of himself and mind as
sequestered from worldly matters, dwelling upon a
speedy summons to a higher court, we find him
asking time for the preparation of a defense which
necessarily contemplated a considerable prolongation
of life. And the demand, in its details, shows the
possession of a clear head and judgment, a thorough
appreciation of the situation and of his legal rights in
the premises. Therefore, the least that can be said
about the letter is, that it is disingenuous. The
endorsement of the court which was to try his cause
may have been sincerely made.

Although James was desirous of appointing a special
tribunal for the occasion, Buckingham presented this
letter to the Lords, and supplemented it with a report
that he had visited the Lord Chancellor twice, at the
instance of the King; that he found him at first "very
sick and heavy," but at the second visit much cheered
by the assurance that the House of Lords was to be
his judge and jury. A verbal answer to this letter was
sent, the substance of which was that they "intended
to proceed in the cause according to the right rule of
justice; and they shall be glad if his Lordship shall
clear his honor therein; to which end they pray his
Lordship to provide for his defense."

The King and favorite were, it is asserted, now
acting under the advice of Williams, Dean of Winchester, who was soon to be made Lord Chancellor.

He had undertaken to guide their craft through the shoals, and his method was to lighten it by throwing, occasionally, one of the crew overboard. There was a disposition on the part of James and his favorite to save Bacon; but when it was evident that any exertion in his favor involved angering the two Houses, they deserted him and left him to his fate. The one effort that the King made was to propose a commission to examine into the charges; but he did not press it when it became apparent that both Houses were too earnest in the prosecution to confide it to other hands.

The committees proceeded to examine witnesses, one of the Learned Counsel being in attendance to conduct the cause in a legal channel. It does not appear that Bacon was present, or represented by counsel; nor does it appear that the Lords acted upon his request for this privilege, or that he persisted in it, or presented himself for admission.

The 24th of March being the anniversary of the King's accession, the busy wheels of investigation were stopped. On the 25th, Bacon wrote to Buckingham, and enclosed a letter to the King:—

" MY VERY GOOD LORD:—Yesterday, I know, was no day; now I hope I shall hear from Your Lordship, who are my anchor in these floods. Meanwhile, to ease my heart a little, I have written to His Majesty the enclosed, which I pray Your Lordship to read advisedly, and to deliver it, or not to deliver it, as you think best. God ever prosper Your Lordship.

"Yours ever what I am,

" FR. ST. ALBAN, Cauc.

"March 25, 1621."

To the King he said : —

"It may please Your Most Excellent Majesty, time hath been when I have brought unto you *gemitum columbæ* from others; now I bring it from myself. I fly unto Your Majesty with the wings of a dove, which once within these seven days I thought would have carried me a higher flight.

"When I enter into myself I find not the materials of such a tempest as is comen upon me. I have been, as Your Majesty knoweth best, never author of any immoderate counsel, but always desired to have things carried *suavibus modis.* I have been no avaricious oppressor of the people. I have been no haughty, or intolerable, or hateful man in my conversation or carriage. I have inherited no hatred from my father, but am a good patriot born. Whence should this be? For these are the things that used to raise dislikes abroad.

"For the House of Commons, I began my credit there, and now it must be the place of the sepulture thereof; and yet this parliament, upon the message touching religion, the old love revived, and they said I was the same man still, only that honesty was turned into honor.

"For the Upper House, even in those days before these troubles, they seemed as to take me into their arms, finding in me ingenuity, which they took to be the true, straight line of nobleness, without crooks or angles.

"And for the briberies and gifts wherewith I am charged, when the books of hearts be opened I hope I shall not be found to have the troubled fountain of a corrupt heart in a depraved habit of taking rewards to pervert justice; howsoever I may be frail and partake of the abuses of the times. And therefore I am resolved, when I come to my answer, not to trick up my innocency, as I writ to the Lords, by cavillations or voidances, but to speak to them the language my heart speaketh to me, in excusing, extenuating, or ingenuous confession, praying to God to give me the grace to see to the bottom of my faults, and that no hardness of heart do steal upon me, under show of more neatness of conscience than is cause.

"But not to trouble Your Majesty longer, craving pardon for this long mourning letter; that which I thirst after as the hart after the streams, is that I may know, by the matchless friend that presenteth to you this letter, Your Majesty's heart (which is an *abyssus* of goodness, as I am an *abyssus* of misery) toward me. I have been ever your man, and counted myself but an usufructuary of myself, the property being yours. And now, making myself an oblation, to do with me as may best conduce to the honor of your justice, the honor of your mercy, and the use of your service, resting as clay in Your Majesty's gracious hands,

"FR. ST. ALBAN, Cauc.

"March 25, 1621."

Of this letter it will be seen that the important passages are Bacon's denial of a "depraved *habit* of taking rewards to pervert justice;" an admission that he might "be frail and partake of the abuses of the times;" and a disposition to hope in and rely upon the mercy of the King. But on the next day James addressed the House of Lords as the "Highest Court of Justice," expressed himself ready to execute their sentence, and promised, of his own will, to revoke the inns, ale-houses, and gold and silver thread patents. Never had he exhibited such a spirit of acquiescence, such an obliging disposition; and the parliament was both gratified and encouraged to proceed with the work in hand.

Bacon retired to the country, where Prince Charles, returning from hunting, "espied a coach, attended with a goodly troop of horsemen, who, it seems, were gathered together to wait upon the Chancellor to his house at Gorhambury, at the time of his declension. At which the Prince smiled: "Well, do we what we can," said he, "this man scorns to go out like a snuff."

This anecdote seems to be generally accepted as authentic by Bacon's biographers; but Mr. Spedding is the only one who assigns the event to this particular time. The moral it points is that either the Lord Chancellor's pride of place and love of show were not chastened by the serious situation of his affairs, or he did not fully appreciate that situation, or he retained a blind confidence in the disposition and power of the King to interpose in his behalf. Yet not the least inconsistency of this problematical character is exhibited by a comparison between this story and the solemnity of the will which he executed about this time, April 10, 1621, or of the "prayer, or psalm," which he then wrote. The one he thus begins:—

"I bequeathe my soul to God above, by the oblation of my Saviour.

"My body to be buried obscurely.

"My name to next ages and foreign nations."

The other he thus ends:—

"And now, when I have thought most of place and honor, Thy hand is heavy upon me, and hath humbled me according to Thy loving-kindness. . . . Besides my innumerable sins, I confess before Thee that I am a debtor to Thee for the gracious talent of Thy gifts and graces, which I have neither put into a napkin, nor put it, as I ought, to exchangers, where it might have made best profit, but misspent it in things for which I was least fit; so as I may truly say my soul hath been a stranger in the course of my pilgrimage."

Too late did he now acknowledge to himself and his

God that his great gifts had indeed been misused, those
talents buried in the mire of a low ambition for political
place and power which should have been entirely
absorbed in glorifying God and advancing his fellow-
man.

While Bacon remained apparently inactive, his prosecutors were busy in examining new witnesses upon
new accusations, which were brought to the front when
the doors were thrown open. Before he even decided
upon a course of conduct, he deemed it essential to
have a private interview with the King. A remarkable
change had taken place in the behavior of James
toward parliamentary reformers. The arrogant pedant
had grown almost obsequiously considerate of their
opinions and wishes. He would not consent to an
interview with Bacon until he had consulted the Lords
who were of his Council. In the meantime the Lord
Chancellor prepared the following notes of the matters
to which he desired to call the King's attention:—

"There be three degrees or cases of bribery charged or
supposed in a judge:—

"1. The first, of bargain or contract for reward to prevent justice, *pendente lite*.

"2. The second, when the judge conceives the cause to
be at an end by the information of the party, or otherwise,
and useth not such as he ought to inquire of it.

"3. And the third, when the cause is really ended, and it
is *sine fraude*, without relation to any precedent promise.

"Now if I might see the particulars of my charge, I should
deal plainly with Your Majesty, in whether of these degrees
every particular case falls.

"But for the first of them, I take myself to be as innocent
as any born upon St. Innocent's Day, in my heart.

"For the second, I doubt in some particulars I may be faulty.

"And for the last, I conceived it to be no fault; but therein I desire to be better informed, that I may be twice penitent,—once for the fact, and again for the error; for I had rather be a briber than a defender of bribes.

"I must likewise confess to Your Majesty that at New Year's tides, and likewise at my first coming in (which was, as it were, my wedding), I did not so precisely as perhaps I ought examine whether those that presented me had causes before me, yea or no.

"And this is simply all that I can say for the present concerning my charge, until I may receive it more particularly. And all this, while I do not fly to that as to say that these things are *vitia temporis* and not *vitia hominis*. For my fortune, *summa summarum* with me is, that I may not be made altogether unprofitable to do Your Majesty service or honor. If Your Majesty continue me as I am, I hope I shall be a new man, and shall reform things out of feeling, more than another can do out of example. If I cast part of my burden I shall be more strong and *delivré* to bear the rest. And to tell Your Majesty what my thoughts run upon, I think of writing a story of England, and of re-compiling of your laws into a better digest. But, to conclude, I most humbly pray Your Majesty's direction and advice. For as Your Majesty hath used to give me the attribute of care of your business, so I must now cast the care of myself upon God and you."

The tone of this paper evinces the remarkable elasticity of spirit which characterized Bacon. We have seen how disappointment, or threatened disgrace, plunged him into the depth of dejection; how often he resolved and threatened to retire into privacy and dedicate himself to the pursuits of "a sorry book-maker;" and how sudden was the reaction, the recovery of lightheartedness, and the return to the arena of active life.

When the petition of Aubrey was presented to the House of Commons, Bacon's first letter to Buckingham opened with: "Your Lordship spoke of purgatory. I am now in it, but my mind is calm." But was it calm? Hardly; for he adds:—

"And if this be to be a Chancellor, I think if the Great Seal lay upon Hounslow Heath nobody would take it up. But the King and your Lordship will, I hope, put an end to these miseries one way or other."

When additional accusations were brought against him he became ill, and apologized to the Lords for his non-attendance by a letter whose pitiful beginning presented him as contemplating speedy death. In his next letter to Buckingham he calls the favorite his "anchor in these floods" which threatened to overwhelm him. He then presents himself to the King in the plaintive and helpless rôle of a sighing dove, who had expected to be "carried a higher flight." Shortly after these sad epistles he is seen in pomp at his country retreat. Then follow his sad will and solemn prayer,—the one confiding his fame to posterity and strangers, who might forget, if not forgive, the Lord Chancellor when conversing with the philosopher; the other confiding his penitential soul to the mercy of his Maker. And lastly, his notes of his proposed interview with the King exhibit the cool, calm lawyer discussing the legal points of the case; the unsuspicious frankness of a faithful servant in private conversation with a presumably kindly-disposed king.

But the remarkable features of these notes are those

which indicate that Bacon had no idea that the most serious outcome of the investigation would deprive him of the political capacity to hold office; and the only evidence that a doubt troubled him is that he offers inducements to the King to interpose his prerogative, should the worst come to the worst. He says: "If Your Majesty continue me as I am," that is, as Lord Chancellor, or one of the Council, " I shall be reformed," he adds in substance, "into a reformer; my past moral weakness shall supply future moral strength, and then I will write you a history of England, and re-compile your laws." It is a pitiful picture, — this blind trust in James, and this appeal for continuation in office.

Whether it moved the King for the moment to change his posture and shield the too subservient courtier, whom he and his favorite had contributed to place in this melancholy situation, is not known. But after the painful interview was over James reported to the Lords, through the Lord Treasurer, that the Lord Chancellor desired the particulars of the charges; that where he could refute them he would, and where he could not he would ingenuously confess and put himself on their mercy. And the King further gave the Lords to understand that he had declined to interfere in Bacon's behalf.

It would require some time and labor to furnish the Lord Chancellor with the particulars he desired, so they set about the preparation of those already examined and included in the allegations to be presented, at the same time provided for receiving other complaints against Bacon, and examining the witnesses produced to sustain them, for "the floods" were being swollen by many streams.

These things took place about the 19th of April, 1621, and on the 20th Bacon wrote the following letter to the King:—

"It may please Your Most Excellent Majesty, I think myself infinitely bounden to Your Majesty for vouchsafing me access to Your Royal Person, and to touch the hem of your garment. I see Your Majesty imitateth Him that would not break the broken reed nor quench the smoking flax. And as Your Majesty imitateth Christ, so I hope, assuredly, my Lords of the Upper House will imitate you; and unto Your Majesty's grace and mercy, and next to my Lords, I recommend myself.

"It is not possible, nor it were not safe, for me to answer particulars till I have my charge, which, when I shall receive, I shall, without fig-leaves or disguise, excuse what I can excuse, extenuate what I can extenuate, and ingenuously confess what I can neither clear nor extenuate. And if there be anything which I mought conceive to be no offense, and yet is, I desire to be informed, that I may be twice penitent,—once for my fault, and the second time for my error. And so submitting all that I am to Your Majesty's grace, I rest,—

"20th April, 1621."

The latter part of this letter is substantially what Bacon had already said to the King, and which had been reported to the Lords, together with the assurance that James would not interpose. The first part, with its grateful humility, on being permitted to touch the hem of James' garment, its profane comparison, and its recommendation of himself to the mercy of King and Lords, is somewhat inconsistent with his reiterated demand of particulars, since there are, side by side, an apparent abandonment of defense, and a determination to answer, and justify or excuse, where either course would be available.

On the day following he again wrote to the King:—

"It may please Your Majesty, it hath pleased God for these three days past to visit me with such extremity of headache upon the hinder part of my head, fixed in one place, that I thought verily it had been some imposthumation. And then the little physic that I have told me that either it must grow to a congealation, and so to a lethargy, or to break, and so to a mortal fever or sudden death, which apprehension, and chiefly the anguish of the pain, made me unable to think of any business. But now that the pain itself is assuaged to be tolerable, I resume the care of my business, and therein prostrate myself again, by my letter, at Your Majesty's feet.

"Your Majesty can bear me witness that at my last so comfortable access, I did not so much as move Your Majesty, by your absolute power of pardon, or otherwise, to take my cause into your hands, and interpose between the sentence of the House; and according to mine own desire, Your Majesty left it to the sentence of the House, and so was reported by the Lord Treasurer.

"But now, if not *per omnipotentiam*, as the divines speak, but *per potestatem suaviter disponentem*, Your Majesty will graciously save me from a sentence, with the good liking of the House, and that cup may pass from me; it is the utmost of my desires.

"This I move with the more belief, because I assure myself that if it be reformation that be sought, the very taking away the Seal, upon my general submission, will be as much an example for these four hundred years as any furder severity.

"The means of this I most humbly leave unto Your Majesty. But surely I conceive that Your Majesty opening yourself in this kind to the Lords Counsellors, and a motion from the Prince after my submission, and my Lord Marquis using his interest with his friends in the House, may effect the sparing of a sentence, I making my humble suit to the House for that purpose, joined with the delivery of the Seal into Your Majesty's hands.

"This is the last suit I shall make to Your Majesty in this business, prostrating myself at your mercy-seat, after fifteen years of service, wherein I have served Your Majesty in my poor endeavors with an entire heart, and as I presumed to say unto Your Majesty, am still a virgin for matters that concern your person and crown; and now, only craving that after eight steps of honor, I be not precipitated altogether.

"But because he that hath taken bribes is apt to give bribes, I will go furder and present Your Majesty with a bribe. For if Your Majesty give me peace and leisure, and God give me life, I will present Your Majesty with a good history of England and a better digest of your laws. And so concluding with my prayers, I rest,

"Your Majesty's afflicted
"but ever devoted servant,
"Fr. St. Alban, Cauc.
"21st April, 1621."

Heretofore we have found Bacon vibrating between a demand for particulars of the charges against him and a disposition to rely upon the mercy of King and Lords. A characteristic indecision seems to have prevented him from settling upon any definite course; and although yesterday exhibited him as contemplating a defense, to-day he presents himself before the mercy-seat. Is this letter to the King the letter of an innocent man? Would a guiltless Lord Chancellor have, by implication, admitted a single charge of bribery, and been content to surrender character and Great Seal without a struggle, upon a compromise which secured him the surplus of honors and possessions? The conditions Bacon offered were the retention of his seat in the Council and House of Lords, security against fine and imprisonment, and the other probable incidents to conviction and sentence.

His argument that his frailty and this punishment would be a warning for four hundred years to come was sound, for does his name not now serve to point a moral? His appeal to the King's gratitude was based upon fact, for he had been only too faithful to the "person and crown" of James. Was he a coward, whose very faculties had been paralyzed by fear? Had his devotion to the Court been such as to alienate his fellow-countrymen and fellow-Lords? It does not appear that he had any warm defender or advocate among his peers. He confesses that his sole dependence are the King, Buckingham and Prince Charles; and how inexplicable is his playful allusion to bribing the King with future service of his pen,—an offer which we have seen him make seriously in his notes touching his speech at the interview, notes which have already been quoted. All that we know is that on the 20th he reiterated his demand for the indictment, and on the 21st asked for mercy. Of the same date was his letter to the Lords, entitled "The Humble Submission and Supplication of the Lord Chancellor," which he conveyed to them before they had even formulated the several counts of their indictment: —

"It may please your Lordships, I shall humbly crave, at your Lordships' hands, a benign interpretation of that which I shall now write. For words that come from wasted spirits and an oppressed mind are more safe in being deposited in a noble construction, than being circled in any reserved caution.

"This being moved, and, as I hope, obtained, in the nature of a protection to all that I shall say, I shall now make into the rest of that wherewith I shall at this time trouble your Lordships, a very strange entrance. For in the midst of a state of as great affliction as I think a mortal man can endure, honor being above life, I shall begin with the professing of gladness in some things.

"The first is, that hereafter the greatness of a judge or magistrate shall be no sanctuary or protection of guiltiness, which, in few words, is the beginning of a golden world.

"The next, that after this example, it is like that judges will fly from anything that is in the likeness of corruption, though it were at a great distance, as from a serpent; which tendeth to the purging of the courts of justice, and reducing them to their true honor and splendor.

"And in these two points God is my witness that, though it be my fortune to be the anvil whereupon these good effects are beaten and wrought, I take no small comfort.

"But to pass from the motions of my heart, whereof God is only judge, to the merits of my cause, whereof your Lordships are judges, under God and his lieutenant: I do understand that there hath been heretofore expected from me some justification; and therefore I have chosen one only justification, instead of all other, out of the justifications of Job. For after the clear submission and confession which I shall now make unto your Lordships, I hope I may say and justify with Job in these words: 'I have not hid my sin, as did Adam, nor concealed my faults in my bosom.' This is the only justification which I will use.

"It resteth, therefore, that, without fig-leaves, I do ingenuously confess and acknowledge that, having understood the particulars of the charge, not formally from the House, but enough to inform my conscience and memory, I find matter sufficient and full, both to move me to desert the defense, and to move your Lordships to condemn and censure me.

"Neither will I trouble your Lordships by singling those particulars which I think may fall off.

"*Quid te exempta juvat spinis de pluribus una?* Neither
will I prompt your Lordships to observe upon the proofs,
where they come not home, or the scruples, touching the
credits of the witnesses. Neither will I represent unto your
Lordships how far a defense might, in divers things, extenuate the offense, in respect of the time or manner of the
gift, or the like circumstances, but only leave these things
to spring out of your own noble thoughts and observations
of the evidence and examinations themselves, and charitably
to wind about the particulars of the charge, here and there,
as God shall put into your mind; and so submit myself
wholly to your piety and grace.

"And now that I have spoken to your Lordships as
judges, I shall say a few words to you as peers and prelates,
humbly commending my cause to your noble minds and
magnanimous affections.

"Your Lordships are not simple judges, but parliamentary
judges. You have a further extent of arbitrary power than
other courts; and if your Lordships be not tied by the
ordinary course of courts or precedents in points of strict-
ness and severity, much more in points of mercy and
mitigation.

"And yet, if anything I shall move might be contrary to
your honorable and worthy ends to introduce a reformation,
I should not seek it. But herein I beseech your Lordships
to give me leave to tell you a story: Titus Manlius took his
son's life for giving battle against the prohibition of his
general. Not many years after, the like severity was pursued by Papirius Cursor, the Dictator, against Quintus
Maximus, who, being upon the point to be sentenced, by
the intercession of some principal persons of the Senate,
was spared; whereupon Livy maketh this grave and gracious
observation: '*Neque minus firmata est disciplina militaris
periculo Quinti Maximi, quam miserabili supplicio Titi
Manlii.*' The discipline of war was no less established by
the questioning of Quintus Maximus than by the punishment of Titus Manlius. And the same reason is of the

reformation of justice; for the questioning of men of eminent place hath the same terror, though not the same rigor,
with the punishment.

"But my case standeth not there.   For my humble desire
is that His Majesty would take the Seal into his hands,
which is a great downfall, and may serve, I hope, in itself,
for an expiation of my faults.

"Therefore, if mercy and mitigation be in your power,
and do no ways cross your ends, why should I not hope of
your Lordships' favor and commiseration?

"Your Lordships will be pleased to behold your chief
pattern, the King, our Sovereign, a King of incomparable
clemency, and whose heart is inscrutable for wisdom and
goodness.   Your Lordships will remember there sat not
these hundred years before a Prince in your House, and
never such a Prince, whose presence deserveth to be made
memorable by records and acts mixed of mercy and justice.
Yourselves are either nobles—and compassion ever beateth
in the veins of noble blood—or reverend prelates, who are
the servants of Him that would not 'break the bruised reed
nor quench the smoking flax.'   You all sit upon one high
stage, and therefore cannot but be more sensible of the
changes of the world, and of the fall of any of high place.

"Neither will your Lordships forget that there are *vitia
temporis* as well as *vitia hominis*, and that the beginning of
reformations hath the contrary power of the pool of Bethesda,
for that had strength to cure only him that was first cast
in, and this hast commonly strength to hurt him only that is
first cast in.   And for my part I wish it may stay there and
go no further.

"Lastly, I assure myself your Lordships have a noble
feeling of me, as a member of your own body, and one that,
in this very session, had some taste of your loving affections,
which I hope was not a lightning before the death of them,
but rather a spark of that grace which now, in the conclusion, will more appear.

"And therefore my humble suit to your Lordships is, that

my penitent submission may be my sentence, and the loss of the Seal my punishment; and that your Lordships will spare any further sentence, but recommend me to His Majesty's grace and pardon for all that is past. God's Holy Spirit be amongst you.

"Your Lordships' humble
"servant and suppliant,
"Fr. St. Alban, Cauc.

"April 22, 1621."

On the 24th of April the House of Lords met to hear the report of the committees that had been engaged in the work assigned them. Prince Charles arose and announced that the Lord Chancellor had confessed and submitted, and delivered the paper, which was twice read in the midst of probably a profound silence, not unmingled with surprise. We are told that some time elapsed before any one addressed the House. Finally the Lord Chamberlain said: "The question is whether this submission be sufficient to ground your Lordships' judgment for a censure, without further examination."

Certainly it was irregular, to say the least, for a general confession to be made, in qualified terms, to a charge which had not been formally presented to the accused, who had urged this formality as a necessary precedent to the making of either a submission or defense; so the House went into a committee of the whole, and the twenty-three charges were read.

Prince Charles and the favorite stood together and alone in making a feeble effort in Bacon's behalf. They threw out a tentative suggestion, which received no encouragement, that the submission should be accepted, and formal sentence avoided. Suffolk said :—

"The confession is not sufficient, for he desireth to be a judge,—to lose his Seal, and that to be the sentence; wherefore it is far short of that we expect."

The Lord Chamberlain said:—

"It is not sufficient; for the confession is grounded upon a rumor. . . . He neither speaks of the particular charge, nor confesseth anything particular."

Southampton said:—

"He is charged by the Commons with corruption; and no word of confession of any corruption in his submission. It stands with the justice and honour of this House not to proceed without the parties' particular confession; or to have the parties hear the charge, and we to hear the parties' answer."

The next question was whether Bacon should be brought to the bar, and there be confronted with the charges. The result of the vote which saved him from this trying ordeal indicates that the temper of a majority of his judges was mercifully inclined. So the "collection of corruptions" were sent to Bacon, "without the proofs," the Lords accepting his willingness to confess to be established, but not accepting his form of confession as satisfactory. With the charges they sent this message:—

"That the Lord Chancellor's confession is not fully set down by his Lordship in the said submission, for three causes: 1. His Lordship confesseth not any particular bribe nor corruption. 2. Nor showeth how his Lordship heard of the charge thereof. 3. The confession, such as it is, is afterwards extenuated in the same submission; and therefore the Lords have sent him a particular of the charge, and do expect his answer to the same with all convenient expedition."

A comparison of the straightforward action of the House of Lords—legal in form and considerate in spirit—with Bacon's letter, reflects no honor upon the Lord Chancellor.

He begins by putting upon the Lords the burden of an "interpretation" of what he writes. He pretends to rejoice in the reflection that he is to be the offering upon the shrine of judicial integrity, and that his example and fate will regenerate the bench. He declines to justify his conduct, and compares himself to Job, at the expense of Adam. He protests his sincerity; yet, after so earnest an introduction, treats the charge so lightly as to accept it on hearsay, the same as if presented in writing; and this, too, when the charge is one involving that "honor above life." He admits that his knowledge is such as moves him to desert his defense, yet insinuates defenses while disclaiming them. The paragraph beginning "Neither will I prompt your Lordships to observe upon the proofs, where they come not home, or the scruples touching the credits of the witnesses, etc.," catalogues and suggests the possible or probable defenses against acts of injustice with which he is threatened. He appeals to the fraternal feeling of the peers, the pious Godlikeness of the prelates; he enlists classic anecdote; he becomes his own judge and names the penalty; he hints at the King's disposition toward him; he adroitly suggests to their Lordships that their own day to be as he is may come; he burdens the times with half the vices of the man, and ends with a "penitent submission," limited in its effect to the loss of the

Great Seal, and the retention of everything else worth having, especially after losing the Lord Chancellorship for corruption, the capacity to hold other offices of honor and trust.

It would seem that, after the frank and friendly action of the House of Lords in the premises, Bacon would have pursued a strictly straightforward course. But he wrote a private letter to the Chief Justice, which excited the suspicions of, and irritated, the Lords. It was not regarded as official, and therefore not presented to the House; but it was known to contain a reference to an extension of time. Even his influential friend, the Prince, could not brook this trifling, and it was on his motion that the House demanded of Bacon a plain and positive answer to the question whether or not he was going to confess or defend. If, as he had protested, he was going to confess, the plea of "guilty" required no consideration. He had already said:—

"I do ingenuously confess and acknowledge that, having understood the particulars of the charge, not formally from the House, but enough to inform my conscience and memory, I find matter sufficient and full, both to move me to desert the defense and to move your Lordships to condemn and censure me."

But now, when the message of the Lords reached him, demanding, in a peremptory tone, definite action on his part, he replied:—

"The Lord Chancellor will make no manner of defense to the charge; but meaneth to acknowledge corruption, and to make a particular confession to every point, and after that an humble submission. But humbly craves liberty, that where the charge is more full than he finds the truth of the fact, he may make declaration of the truth in such particulars, the charge being brief and containing not all the circumstances."

Driven to the wall, he reiterates his intention of avowing his corruption, which avowal, previously made, had already influenced the Lords to understand that he required only of them the indictment, so to speak; and although he had also before declared that "he understood the particulars of the charge, enough to inform his conscience and memory," he now hints that this informed conscience and memory is prepared to submit explanations which, if not absolute defenses, would amount to mitigating circumstances; or, in other words, he returns to the position which he assumed in the letter of the 21st of April, when he wrote the King that he would excuse and extenuate where he could, and where he could do neither, would "ingenuously confess."

The Lords took him at his word, and sent him the particulars of the charge without the proofs derived from the examination of witnesses, without even furnishing him with the names of the witnesses. His apologists picture his position as a hard one. But when he claimed to be sufficiently informed of "the particulars," as the basis of his first confession, which was rejected on account of its equivocations; and when the Lords, for the first and only time during the investigation, exhibited some impatience, and somewhat sharply said, defend yourself if you have any defense, confess if you are going to confess, and he replied that he would confess, there was nothing for them to do but oblige him with a copy of the particulars.

It is evident that Bacon had, to some extent, kept

pace with the inquiry, and had derived information touching the proceedings sufficient enough to at least refresh his memory; for his final confession deals with the charges *seriatim*, and abounds in particulars of his own, extenuating and excusing when he does not, "without fig-leaves, ingenuously confess."

"TO THE RIGHT HONORABLE THE LORDS SPIRITUAL AND TEMPORAL IN THE HIGH COURT OF PARLIAMENT ASSEMBLED.

"*The Confession and Humble Submission of me, Lord Chancellor :*—

"Upon advised consideration of the charge, descending into my own conscience, and calling my memory to account so far as I am able," [Here the reader will recall the assertion in his previous "ingenuous" confession of an unqualifiedly informed memory, "having understood the particulars of the charge enough to inform my conscience and memory,"] "I do plainly and ingenuously confess that I am guilty of corruption, and do renounce all defense, and put myself upon the grace and mercy of your Lordships."

If the English language is capable of conveying an idea, the uninitiated would certainly accept this as conclusive of Bacon's guilt. No excuses or extenuations could, it would be presumed, qualify this fact. Yet the industrious and eloquent pens of the editors of the two fullest and best editions of the works of Lord Bacon have followed him through his answers to the twenty-eight distinct charges of corruption, and have expended the subtlety of logic, the refinement of casuistry, the ardor of partisanship, the devotion of disciples, to prove that Bacon was innocent of corruption,— or rather to disprove Bacon's confession of corruption. It were better that every line he had written were blotted out of existence, and that the human race were deprived of the benefits which those writings have conferred upon it, than that honesty, truth and justice should be compromised. Why propose this sacrifice, as needless as it is dreadful? Cannot we bow before the majesty of his intellect without enslaving our moral instincts? If the great mind was linked to a small nature, must we condone his desertion of Essex, his flattering the living and abusing the dead Salisbury, his subserviency to James, his disgraceful propitiation of the angry favorite, his justification of torture, his vindictiveness toward the more vindictive Coke, his diversion of great gifts from philosophical pursuits to place-hunting, his puerile passion for pomp, to which he sacrificed his honor, his defense of the prerogative, to which he was ready to sacrifice the liberties of England, his support of monopolies, whose execution resulted in the robbery of the poor and the outraging of the helpless, and lastly, his official corruption? Must we condone all these incidents and elements in his career and character because admiration and awe of his brilliant intellect seem irreconcilable with the contempt which this long list merits, just as his writings are irreconcilable with his actions, his lessons of life with his mode of life, his advice to judges with his judicial conduct?

In the Appendix at the end of this volume the reader will find the confession, which, after the introductory, unqualified admission, separately admits each charge, with, however, qualifications and explanations, such as that he received the money or presents of the litigants before or after the passage of a final decree; that one litigant gave him money before the decision, the other

party to the same suit gave it after the decision. He
dwells with some self-gratulation upon his unsuccessful
attempt to return one present, and with unction upon
the fact of his having taken money openly and above
board in another instance, from three parties litigant:
"If I had taken it in the nature of a corrupt bribe, I
knew it could not be concealed." In conclusion, by
presents of gold buttons to beautify his coat, a diamond
to glitter in his hat, suits of hangings for his walls, and
cash received, the Lord Chancellor's one hand closed
upon about £12,320, or $61,600, while the other hand
held the Great Seal of England for the brief period of
two years.

To the last charge, that of passing decrees at the
request of corrupt servants, he says: "I confess it was
a great fault of neglect in me that I looked no better
to my servants."

All argument in this branch of charge and confession
can be dismissed by applying the touchstone which
Bacon has applied to those who sit in judgment on
official corruption, or to those who contemplate such
laxity, their consciences being lulled to sleep by the
subtle casuistry of the philosopher's apologists. In his
"Essay on Great Place" he says:—

"For corruption do not only bind thine own hands or thy
servants' hands from taking, but bind the hands of suitors
from offering. For integrity used doth the one, but integrity professed, and with a manifest detestation of bribery,
doth the other; and avoid not only the fault, but the
suspicion."

This appeal from "Philip drunk" to "Philip sober"
ends the present consideration of Bacon's moral and

legal responsibility, and concludes all question of his moral and legal guilt in respect to his abuse of power and confidence at the instigation of his subordinates.

Not the least remarkable feature of this confession and ear-mark of Bacon's characteristic inconsistency is, that after excuses and extenuations which have furnished texts upon which his apologists have expatiated at large, he himself deprives them of all weight and worthiness by admitting a possibility of error in fact on his part; or, if he should be correct in his facts, he is still "guilty as indicted."

"This declaration," continues the confession, after the last particular answer, "I have made to your Lordships with a sincere mind, humbly craving that, *if there should be any mistaking,* your Lordships would impute it to want of memory, and not to any desire of mine to obscure truth or palliate anything; for *I do again confess that in the points charged upon me, although they should be taken as myself have declared them, there is a great deal of corruption and neglect;* for which I am heartily and penitently sorry, and submit myself to the judgment, grace and mercy of the court."

The prosecutors and court of Bacon were merciful and tender. He was not brought in the rôle of a great criminal to face his accusers and judges, to be browbeaten by a Coke and misrepresented by a once bosom friend,—Southampton,—whom, twenty years before, he had confronted and prosecuted, whose slender thread of hope he had cut with the sharp edge of his legal sword, as it whirled about the heads of the two young earls who were faithful unto death. Southampton was now one of his judges. Perhaps he recalled the scene where, when he pleaded that the intention of the actor gave color to the act, Bacon said : —

"Neither is it any point of law, as my Lord of Southampton would have it believed, that condemns them of treason. To take secret counsel, etc.! Will any simple man take this to be less than treason?"

The earl was, however, as considerate as any of those who pitied a Lord Chancellor whose frailty crowned his old age with dishonor. Bacon's confession might well have challenged the credulity of his peers, whether it was that it presented no substantial extenuation of the charge, and was so entirely, in its introduction and close, an admission of guilt; or whether they regarded his explanations with suspicion, and, in view of his first unsatisfactory and disingenuous confession, as a kind of reservation; or whether they deemed it essential to regularity of legal procedure for him to be confronted by at least some of his judges, they decided to send a committee of twelve to wait upon him. This committee found him bowed in spirit and sick in body. They approached fallen greatness with the delicacy of gentlemen and the charity of Christians. They even attempted to console the inconsolable by the assurance that "the Lords conceived it to be an ingenuous and full confession," as they extended the paper to him and inquired if the signature was genuine, and if he was still of the same mind.

With anguish of soul and voice which we can well imagine, he replied: "My Lords, it is my act, my hand, my heart. I beseech your Lordships, be merciful to a . broken reed."

They quickly retired from the sad scene and reported

their interview to the House of Lords. The King was moved to sequester the Great Seal. He immediately appointed a commission to receive it. These three gentlemen found Bacon, as the previous messengers had left him, sick in mind and body. They, too, indulged in kindly speech, and on their wishing "it had been better with him," he replied: "The worse the better. By the King's great favor I received the Great Seal; by my own great fault I have lost it."

Nothing now was left but to proceed to judgment and sentence.

On the 2d of May the House of Lords met, and it was decided to summon Bacon to appear and receive sentence on the morrow. But Bacon was found, and reported to be sick in bed. His excuse for his non-appearance was accepted, and the case proceeded with. The vote was taken, and "they all agreed that the Lord Chancellor is guilty of the matters wherewith he is charged, *nemine dissentiente.*"

Sentence followed. A fine of £40,000, imprisonment in the Tower during the King's pleasure, incapacity for office and banishment from court, closed Bacon's official life and public career.

On the 3d of May, 1621, final judgment was pronounced, and the last of the month found him paying a portion of his heavy penalty as a prisoner in the Tower of London.

The King and favorite are charged with having offered up Bacon as a pledge to the people of England that the spirit of reform, which spared neither a greedy Lord Chancellor nor a greedy Justice of the Peace, was earnest and sincere; they are credited with placing themselves under the guidance of that wily Welshman,

Dean Williams, who advised his being cast into the whirlpool of popular and virtuous indignation as a tub is thrown to a whale; but as far as they dared, they stood by their too accommodating servant. They were too cautious to run any risks. Buckingham voted that he was guilty, but was the only dissentient to the sentence. To him Bacon turned, ere he had been imprisoned two days, according to one account; according to all, but a few days:—

"GOOD MY LORD:—Procure the warrant for my discharge this day. Death, I thank God, is so far from being unwelcome to me as I have called for it (as a Christian resolution would permit) any time these two months. But to die before the time of His Majesty's grace, and in this disgraceful place, is even the worst that could be. And when I am dead, he is gone that was always in one tenor, a true and perfect servant to his master, and one that was never author of any immoderate, no, nor unsafe, no, I will say it, nor unfortunate counsel; and one that no temptation could ever make other than a trusty, an honest and thrice-loving friend to your Lordship; and howsoever I acknowledge the sentence just, and for reformation sake fit, the justest Chancellor that hath been in the five changes since Sir Nicholas Bacon's time. God bless and prosper your Lordship, whatsoever become of me.

"Your Lordship's true friend, living and dying,
"FR. ST. ALBAN.
"Tower, 31st May, 1621."

It cannot be gainsaid that he was a true and perfect servant to James and his service, and fate suggests the sad soliloquy of Wolsey, fitter far for the lips of the Lord Chancellor than of the Lord Cardinal. Nor did he ever swerve from the service of the favorite but once; but that departure he redeemed by deserting his

F

principles and his co-conspirator, Lady Hatton; therefore they both might well be appealed to for the exercise of clemency, which was in the power of the King
and at the bidding of the favorite.   But what Bacon
means by calling himself the justest among five Chancellors, after his confession of corruption, is a problem
which Lord Campbell solves by saying :—

"He tries to delude himself into some sort of self-
complacency, from the thought that his decrees were sound
in spite of all the bribes he had accepted, and that he sold
justice, not injustice." *

His sentence of imprisonment was during the King's
pleasure; and it was Buckingham's as well as James'
pleasure that he should not linger long.   On the 4th of
June we find him thanking the favorite for his release,
and, strange being! complaining that his mind would
be still in prison until he could be on his feet to do to
His Majesty and His Majesty's favorite faithful service.   Out of prison, but not in office.   Liberty, but
not license.   Time for philosophy, but no stage for
politics.   And what an exhibition of self-rehabilitation,
of elasticity, does this note of gratitude present!

"I heartily thank your Lordship," he writes, "for getting
me out of prison; and now my body is out, my mind, nevertheless, will be still in prison till I may be on my feet to do
His Majesty and your Lordship faithful service, wherein
your Lordship, by the grace of God, shall find that my
adversity hath neither spent nor pent my spirits."

A letter of thanks was written to Prince Charles,
who completed the friendly trio.   To him, too, he
touches on the subject of future employment.

* Campbell's Lives.   Vol. II., 416 p.

Abruptly ending his imprisonment was releasing but one penalty. There were others to be paid. So in his letter of thanks to the King he says:—

"But Your Majesty, that did shed tears in the beginning of my trouble, will, I hope, shed the dew of your grace and goodness upon me in the end. Let me live to serve you, else life is but the shadow of death to Your Majesty's most devoted servant."

This petition, too, was favorably answered, for ere the end of June, James invited the judge, who was convicted of corruption, and who countenanced monopolies, to advise how best to set about reforming courts of justice and redressing grievances; and the ex-Lord Chancellor resumed his pen and responded promptly and ably to the demand.

It is strange that one who, in the bitterness of his heart, when the storm first broke upon him, exclaimed that the symbol of the highest employment would not be picked up on Hounslow Heath, for it was also the symbol of the deepest misery; who, as the storm increased in anger, turned his eyes toward heaven and protested that death would soon take him by the hand and lead him into that haven where "the wicked cease from troubling and the weary be at rest"; that one who had confessed his utter unworthiness; one whom Southampton urged his peers to spare from the sentence of degradation, "though worthy"; one of whom this merciful but just judge said, "Shall he whom this House thinks unfit to be a constable come to the parliament?"— it is more than strange that such an one should, ere the ink was dry on the record of his confession, his guilt, his exile from court, his incapacitation for service, hope for employment, seek employment, receive employment.

London was almost as dear to the heart of Bacon as to that of Dr. Johnson. But his sentence excluded him from so near an approach to the court. He appealed to the King and favorite. They listened favorably to his prayer; but the politic Dean, now Lord Keeper, and Bacon's successor in the confidence of James and Buckingham, interposed, and represented that parliament would resent this second nullification of the entirety of the sentence. He advised the post-ponement of further favor until after the adjournment; so Bacon was compelled to retire to Gorhambury, his rural retreat, where extravagance of adornment had contributed to the corruption of which he had been guilty.

He reluctantly accepted the inevitable, after lament-ing his separation from James and the favorite, and begging for permission to stay in London until the last of July, "to take some present order for the debts that press me most."

But even this request, made June 20th, 1621, had to be refused; and by a second letter to Buckingham, written on the 22d, he says he is content to go forthwith to Gorhambury, as "His Majesty's instructions" indi-cate. His arrival there he announces to Buckingham, and adds : —

"My Lord, I wish myself by you in this stirring world; not for any love to place or business, for that is almost gone with me, but for my love to yourself."

Was that all? His postscript is the answer : —

"Being now out of use and out of sight, I recommend myself to your Lordship's favor, to maintain me in His Majesty's grace and good intention."

Another letter to Buckingham indignantly denies the accusation made to the favorite, who contemplated devising some means to relieve Bacon's straightened circumstances, that the ex-Lord Chancellor had received "an hundred thousand pounds gifts" while he held the Great Seal; and then follows this earnest protest:—

"I praise God for it, I never took penny for any benefice or ecclesiastical living; I never took penny for releasing anything I stopped at the Seal; I never took penny for any commission, or things of that nature; I never shared with any servant for any second or inferior profit."

These are the corruptions he was not guilty of. Is it a subject of self-gratulation that he did not run up and down the gamut of judicial frailty? Do we measure innocence by the quantity which a thief has taken, or the number of blows the murderer has given his victim? The fair statue of Justice lay shattered at the feet of the Lord Chancellor as soon as the first guinea crossed his palm. Some scruples about this self-laudation arose while he was presenting himself as one outraged by the tongue of slander, for he continues:—

"My offenses I have myself recorded, wherein I studied, as a good confessant, guiltiness and not excuse; and therefore I hope it leaves me fair to the King's grace, and will turn many men's hearts to me."

A letter to the King ascribes Bacon's "New Birth" to the joint work upon him of God and James the First. "This '*Nova Creatura*' is the work of God's pardon and the King's," he writes, and then enumerates the Roman and Grecian philosophers and patriots who, like himself, had been guilty of corruption, had been disgraced and banished, but who had been recalled and restored to place and power. He disclaims the self-evident application of the comparison:—

"This, if it please Your Majesty," he says, "I do not say for appetite of employment, but for hope that if I do by myself as is fit, Your Majesty will never suffer me to die in want or dishonor."

This letter he enclosed with one to Buckingham, which contains this gloomy picture of his affairs:—

"I have lived hitherto on the scraps of my former fortunes, and I shall not be able to hold out longer. . . . I am much fallen in love with a private life; but yet I shall so spend my time as shall not decay my abilities for use;"— [*i. e.* when he should be recalled to public life.]

Another letter on the same subject is sent to the King. In this he catalogues the sources of his revenue in the past, the surrender of profitable employments for those which were more honorable, and thus expresses what many a great office-holder has thought and felt in retirement, though never so forcibly uttered, when similarly situated:—

"The honors which Your Majesty hath done me have put me above the means to get my living; and the misery I am fallen into hath put me below the means to subsist as I am."

This letter is supplemented by still another to the Prince, on the same subject.

These repeated efforts were crowned with a release of the £40,000 fine, or rather its assignment by the King, to whom it was due, to persons named by Bacon himself, in trust for Bacon, which was a protection against his other creditors, since the King's claim had preference; and thus were the debtor's prison and the tip-staff banished from Bacon's dreams by night, and fears by day.

This favor was conferred as well upon literature, science, philosophy. the living and the unborn; for it gave some liberty and leisure to the great faculties hitherto dedicated to unworthy objects, to devote themselves to pursuits the most fitting, and, too, the most congenial, when unrivalled by "the last infirmity of noble minds."

The noble and beautiful segment of Bacon's life is confined to the brief period which succeeded his political, and preceded his natural, death.

This golden twilight of the stormy day was ushered in by the publication of his "History of Henry VII.," for he had resumed his sceptre — the pen.

Occasionally, in the midst of comparative poverty, his old love of display would exhibit itself, as in the instance of his refusing to sell the woods about Gorhambury to relieve his necessities, giving, as one excuse, "I will not be stripped of my feathers," and upon the heel of full pardon temporarily revived the old love of political activity; but he must be regarded as one who now acquiesced gracefully, and gave the first proof of that wisdom and virtue which he commended to others in such profound and persuasive lessons.

Though in his old age disgrace and dishonor drove him into retirement, philosophy and religion supported him on either side. The shattered bark rested in the peaceful harbor, the dimmed lamp of his youth shone brightly again, and the old man's eyes "dwelt upon the bright countenance of Truth, in the quiet and still air of delightful studies."

The "Advancement of Learning" was translated into Latin, and enlarged into his "*De Augmentis Scientiarum;*" yet the former has not been swallowed up entirely, but remains to be read and admired for its individual merits of style and expression, as well as of the thought which the greater work further develops.

His tireless pen next produced the "History of Life and Death," and a new revised and enlarged edition of the "Essays;" the one the lesson of man's physical, the other the lesson of man's moral, nature. Then followed his several contributory chapters to his "Great Instauration," whose title remains unfilled, because the life of one man could not have possibly accomplished the design; the "Discourse of a War with Spain," "A Dialogue Touching on Holy War," both political pamphlets for the times, the "New Atlantis," the incompleted undertaking of digesting the laws of England, of writing the "History of Henry VIII.," translations of certain of the Psalms into English verse, "*Sylva Sylvarum;* or the Natural History," scientific tracts, and translations of certain of his works, originally in English, into Latin, for he had no faith in the immortality of the English tongue. "These modern languages will some day," he says, "play the bankrupts with books." And, lastly, among his contributions was his "Apothegms; or Jest-Book," which is, in parts, annually rehashed in the footnotes of American almanacs and the humorous columns of rural newspapers.

And of all these labors, not one of them is there, save the political pamphlets, which was not inspired by the wish and hope of making future generations happier, wiser and better than himself and his fellow-men about him.

The reader is familiar with how, in the midst of these labors, he fell a victim to his beloved experimental philosophy, exposing himself to extreme cold and damp while trying whether meat could not be artificially preserved by being packed in snow, — an experiment whose present application is a profitable branch of trade between nations separated by oceans. He was away from home at the time, and being taken with a chill, was driven to the house of the Earl of Arundel, for he had descended from his coach, and the wayside was his laboratory. There the housekeeper assigned him to a damp room and bed; he grew rapidly worse, and died on Easter morning, April 9th, 1626.

He died under a strange roof, in the arms of Sir Julius Cæsar. No ministering hands of feminine love soothed his fevered brow, moistened his parched lips; no gentle woman's voice, modulated by sympathy and sorrow, fell upon his ear. He was worse than wifeless, for the alderman's daughter, the "handsome maiden to his liking," had not shared his sorrows; she was gone from him, living upon an allowance spared with difficulty from his narrow means. It is said she was faithless; at any rate, she honored the memory of the great philosopher by marrying "her gentleman-usher" ere the funeral baked meats grew cold.

Bacon was not only worse than wifeless; he was without children —

"To rock the cradle of reposing age,
    With lenient hands extend a father's breath,
    Make languor smile, and smooth the bed of death,
    Explore the thought, explain the asking eye,
    And keep awhile that father from the sky."

Little or nothing is known of his funeral. A few friends, faithful among the faithless, enthusiastic young disciples, among whom was Hobbes, the then budding philosopher of Malmesbury, Sir Thomas Meawtys, his devoted chaplain, Rawley, and servants whom adversity could not alienate, composed the train which followed fallen greatness to its last resting-place.

As a mother's face is the first which the infant's eyes recognize, so is it probably the last image of the dying man's vision; and the great philosopher, in solemn contemplation of the future and reflective retrospection of the past, recalled his mother's tender care of his childhood, her affecting reception on his return to a fatherless home, her devotion to his material and spiritual advancement, her unwavering loyalty until her own troubles, darkened by religious fanaticism, clouded her once vigorous and self-reliant intellect.

It was in the midst of such reflections that, in his old age, he bethought himself of the mother who had been his only disinterested friend, and in his will directed that his worn-out body should be laid beside her in St. Michael's Church. There he is represented, on his monument, in a contemplative posture, his head resting on his hand. This tribute to his memory was erected by his ardent admirer, Sir Thomas Meawtys, his secretary, who found a resting-place after death at the feet of his beloved master. A Latin inscription, written by Sir Henry Wotton, is carved upon the stone.

The executors of his will neglected to qualify, and Buckingham, who was to have supervised the execution of his testamentary wishes, was, at the time of Bacon's death, too much occupied in the matter of his own impeachment to do anything but study how to escape long-merited and long-postponed punishment.

Letters of administration with the will annexed were granted to two of his creditors, who proceeded to settle the estate.

Allusion has been made to the suspected faithlessness of Lady Bacon. This opinion rests upon the following extract from his will, the inferences of his biographers, and, perhaps, traditional gossip : —

"Whatsoever I have given, granted, confirmed or appointed to my wife, in the former part of this will, I do now for *just and great* causes utterly revoke and make void, and leave her to her right only."

The large indebtedness of Bacon made a sale of everything necessary. The sum realized was comparatively insignificant, especially from the real estate. The lands brought about £6,000, while the personal property produced about £7,000. His debts were nearly double the total, or about £23,371. His library was scattered, probably, for few traces of it remain. His manuscripts fell into the hands of his devoted chaplain, Dr. Rawley, and his friend, Sir William Boswell. The former held far the larger share, which he jealously guarded and edited; those bequeathed to the latter were not so well cared for, and many of them were lost.

The first edition of Bacon's works noticed by Lowndes was "published by John Blackbourne, London, 1730. Folio, 4 vols., with portrait by Vertue." This may be considered the beginning of the Baconian revival. His writings published in his lifetime had been advertised during preparation through the channel of that correspondence which was general among the scholars of his time, who formed a close corporation of brains. His greater works were waited for impatiently, for they were delayed and their completion prevented by his other pursuits. When written in English they were translated into Latin, and many of them further translated into Continental tongues, so that his essays and the lighter fruits of his pen were placed in the hands of those who did not belong to the Senate of that age's Republic of Letters. In this way the name and fame of Bacon crossed the channel, and he became the best and widest known and admired of all Englishmen. " Eminent foreigners crossed the seas on purpose to see and discourse with him." We are told that the Marquis D'Effrat, when attending Henrietta Maria from France, visited him, and he found the philosopher confined to his bed. There Bacon received him, and oddly enough conversed with him from behind the drawn curtains of his couch. What the Frenchman thought he perhaps did not say, but he is credited with this speech : —

"You resemble the angels; we hear those beings constantly talked of, we believe them superior to mankind, and we never have the consolation to see them."

Bacon replied : —

" If the charity of others compared him to an angel, his own infirmities told him he was a man."

After this first attempted collection of Bacon's writings and their publication in 1730, there followed another with a life, by David Mallet, in 1740, and then came a succession of editions of his then extant writings. His essays were his only writings from which he himself could be said to have derived any pecuniary profit.

Their popularity was unprecedented at home and hardly paralleled abroad. They circulated on the Continent and among the American colonists. They are said to have been the first book published in Philadelphia, or rather a part of this first book, which was entitled "The Temple of Wisdom," and was printed by William Bradford, Philadelphia, 1688.

At last, Basil Montagu, Esq., a scholarly lawyer, accomplished the grateful task of editing a nearly perfect collection of "The Works of Francis Bacon, Lord Chancellor of England," which were supplemented by a life of the lawyer, statesman and philosopher; the persistent place-hunter, the elastic moralist and the corrupt judge. Published in 1825-1834, it was reviewed by Macaulay in 1837, in the *Edinburgh*. Mr. Montagu, instead of throwing the veil of charity over the man, demanded entire veneration for the writer. He defended dishonesty with such honesty, hypocrisy with such sincerity, deceit with such frankness, and cowardice with such courage, that if his mission had been to overthrow the decalogue, destroy all distinctions between right and wrong, and degrade manhood, he could not have better fulfilled it than by becoming the biographer of Bacon. The reader is familiar with the essay of Macaulay. It is an honest and eloquent appeal in behalf of the principles of morality that are eternal and universal. Lord Campbell, in his lives of the Lord Chancellors, wrote the life of Bacon from a professional and narrower standpoint; and he stands on Lord Macaulay's platform, as the champion of judicial integrity. But since Mr. Montagu undertook to offer "extenuations and excuses" for Bacon, which he himself, in "all ingenuousness, without fig-leaves," could

not submit to his judges, the Ex-Chancellor has been a
problematical character. Sides have been taken, and
critics and apologists have been arrayed against one another. Hence it is impossible to talk about him without discussion or write about him without argument.
Within a comparatively recent period a new edition of
his writings, supplemented by a life, has been ably and
conscientiously edited, but his biographer, as blinded
as Mr. Montagu, has walked the same path the latter
trod.

The aim of this sketch has been to point out with
particularity the frailty of the man, in order to avoid
confusing his intellectual excellence with his moral
weakness.

"There is scarcely any delusion which has a better claim
to be indulgently treated than that," says Macaulay, "under
the influence of which a man ascribes every moral excellence
to those who have left imperishable monuments of their
genius."

It is against this tendency towards a blind partiality
that the reader of Bacon's works is to fortify himself.
Without reviewing the details of his conduct preceding
his promotion to the Lord Keepership, it is proposed to
dwell briefly upon the moral quality of his conduct
which involved his trial and conviction on the charge
of corruption.

The defense of Bacon, as is well known, was originally advanced by Mr. Montagu on the ground that
the acceptance of presents was a very common thing
in those days, not regarded as wrong by public opinion ;
and secondly, that the gifts he received were not bribes,
but friendly or grateful gratuities. His later apologist

finds consolation and excuse in the reflection that the oath administered to the judges of England not to receive anything from suitors, even after final judgment,* was not taken by the Lord Chancellor, and that therefore he stood in a different relation in the premises than the ordinary judges occupied. To argue against extravagant defenses such as these, seems, at first blush, to be a work of supererogation. But what has been seriously submitted should be seriously considered. It is true, as Mr. Spedding says, that the Lord Chancellor did not take the oath which the ordinary judges took. But the statute imposing it must be regarded as declaratory of the Common Law. Its aim was to more particularly define bribery, and throw additional safeguards around judicial purity and integrity. In cataloguing crimes, Blackstone says : —

"Bribery is the next species of offense against public justice; which is when a judge, *or other person concerned in the administration of justice,* takes any undue reward to influence his behavior in office. In the East it is the custom never to petition any superior for justice, not excepting their Kings, without a present. This is calculated for the genius of despotic countries, where the true principles of government are never understood, and it is imagined there is no obligation from the superior to the inferior, no relative duty owing from the governor to the governed. The Roman law, though it contained many severe judgments against bribery, as well as for selling a man's vote in the Senate or other public assembly, as for the bartering of common justice, yet by a strange indulgence in one instance it tacitly encouraged this practice; allowing the magistrates to receive small presents, provided they did not in the whole

* Spedding's Life, vol. II., p. 455. Am. ed.

exceed a hundred pounds in the year; not considering the insinuating nature and gigantic practice of this vice when once admitted. * * * In England, in judges, especially the superior ones, it hath been always looked upon as so heinous an offense that the Chief-Justice Thorpe was hanged for it in the reign of Edward III."*

We have the offense of bribery referable to any person concerned in the administration of justice. This, though, is a limited view, for there are others who are susceptible to the temptation and crime, such, for instance, as legislative or executive servants of a government.

But the next question is, was a Lord Chancellor a judge? If the reader will turn to the preceding pages, and refer to the correspondence of Bacon, and to his notes touching his proposed interview with the King, it will be found that the Lord Chancellor used the word "judge" as applicable to himself in the rôle of a defendant.

"The High Court of Chancery," says Blackstone, treating of the judicial system of England, which was the same in Bacon's day, "is, in matters of civil property, by much the most important of any of the King's superior and original courts of justice." †

Notwithstanding the distinction attempted to be drawn by the latest enthusiastic defender of Bacon, the conclusion is inevitable that chancery was a court, and the Lord Chancellor a judge, and these, too, in fact, in law, and in the opinion of Bacon, as he referred to him-

* Blk. Com. Bk. IV., p. 139.
† Bl. Com. Bk. III., p. 47.

self as a judge in his writings touching the charge and defense.

The next point is, was the custom of receiving presents from suitors so general, so established by precedent, and so sustained by public opinion, as to be venial?

Sir Thomas More was the ornament of the reign of Henry VIII. He was, too, a scholar with whose life and writings Bacon must have been familiar. As Lord Chancellor he was the embodiment of a just judge and honest man. He, too, was once tempted with gifts by a suitor; but how he met the incipient bribe and rebuked him who offered it, Bacon himself informs us, for among his "Apothegms" is this story:—

"Sir Thomas More had sent him, by a suitor in chancery, two silver flagons. When they were presented by the gentleman's servant he said to one of his men: 'Have him to the cellar, and let him have of my best wine.' And turning to the servant he said: 'Tell thy master, friend, if he like it let him not spare it.'"

Other anecdotes of the same character are told of this predecessor of Bacon on the wool-sack. He was accused of taking a bribe from one Vaughn, and admitted that the man's wife had offered him a silver cup, which he took and filled with wine, which he drank to her health, then returned the cup, telling her to restore it to her husband:—

"As freely as your husband hath given this cup to me, even so freely give I the same to you again, to give to your husband for his New Year's gift."

A lady presented him with a pair of gloves stuffed with angels, to the amount of £40. He said:—

"Mistress, since it were against good manners to refuse your New Year's gift, I am content to take your gloves, but as for the lining, I utterly refuse it."

Both Lords Macaulay and Campbell refer to the public sentiment which enthusiastically reciprocated Hugh Latimer's philippics against the offering and taking of the so-called "gifts," whose acceptance brought disgrace and dishonor upon Bacon.

Burton, born in the year 1576, who published the first edition of his "Anatomy of Melancholy" in 1621, and subsequent editions in 1624 and later, is a contemporaneous authority on public sentiment. Referring to Old Verulam, the place suggests the fallen Chancellor, and he says, "Near St. Albans, which must not now be whispered in the ear,"—his only special allusion to Bacon; yet he will be found to indulge in moralizings on the evils of his day, some of which may have been suggested by the frailty of Bacon himself.

"To see so much difference," he lamentingly says, "betwixt words and deeds, so many parasangs betwixt tongue and heart. . . . Men give good precepts to others, soar aloft, while they themselves grovel on the ground. . . . To see a man bend all his forces, means, time, fortune, to be a favorite's favorite's favorite."

Then, in painting his model commonwealth, he protests against such patents as those which Bacon, as the first law officer of the crown, did not at least protest against, nor try and reform until their existence became so obnoxious to the people as to become dangerous to the King, the favorite, their advisers, agents and friends. "I will have no private monopolies to enrich one man and beggar a multitude," exclaims old Burton. Yet

Bacon apologetically saying, "I may be frail and partake of the abuses of the times," before admitting his guilt, suggests this defense; and his apologists assume that public sentiment regarded his acceptance of gifts as the customary thing, and as venial.

His own opinion and precepts answer and refute these apologists. He could not have been ignorant of the virtues or vices of his predecessors. We have seen how he was acquainted with the integrity of Sir Thomas More. In his "Essay on Great Place" he thus advises:—

"In the discharge of the place set before thee the best examples, for imitation is a globe of precepts; and after a time set before thee thine own example, and examine thyself strictly, whether thou dost not best at first. Neglect not, also, the examples of those that have carried themselves ill in the same place; not to set off thyself by taxing their memory, but to direct thyself what to avoid."

Let us compare this precept with a paragraph from one of his letters to Buckingham,—the one from the Tower, dated May 31st, 1621, in which he refers to his service to King and favorite, and says of himself further that:—

"Howsoever, I acknowledge the sentence just, and for reformation sake, fit, the justest chancellor that hath been in the five changes since Sir Nicholas Bacon's time."

Did he really follow the honest example of his honest father? His confession says no. Did he shun the evil examples of his five immediate predecessors? The same voice gives the same answer. Does he set off himself by taxing their memory? He assuredly does in

the very face of his precept.   Again, the moral quality
of an official, be he Lord Chancellor or a constable,
which office Southampton declared Bacon to be unfit to
fill,—not in the spirit of anger or revenge, but in that
of honorable, righteous indignation,—the moral quality
of a servant of a government, a trustee of a people,
accepting gifts from persons who have private interests
depending on their official action, is well defined by
Bacon in his "model commonwealth," the "New
Atlantis."

An imaginary voyage is made by Bacon and others,
and they were driven by storm into an unknown part of
the South Sea.   They came upon a land peopled by a
strange race, in an advanced stage of moral and material civilization.   Their ship was visited by officials, one
of whom came aboard with a servant.   They conversed
in the Spanish tongue with the officer.   He came to
inquire into and relieve their necessities, and went away,
leaving the servant behind : —

"We offered some reward in pistolets unto the servant,
and a piece of crimson velvet to be presented to the officer;
but the servant took them not, nor would scarce look upon
them."

Subsequently another official visited their ship: —

"When we offered him some pistolets he smilingly said
he 'must not be twice paid for one labor,' meaning, as I take
it, that he had a salary sufficient of the State for his service.
For as I afterwards learned, they called *an officer that taketh
rewards, Twice-paid.*"

Are we to believe that Bacon ever meant to maintain
that a bad example made a good imitator; that multi-

plying official corruption purified it; that he was the less guilty because many before him and around him were equally so?

Indeed, he does not deserve as broad a charity as they merit. He was a profound thinker and writer upon moral, social and political subjects. He was a historian, and well informed as to the lives of England's kings, their favorites, advisers and servants. He was a teacher of kings, favorites, advisers and subjects. Truth and honesty belong to no age. Morality and its precepts were as familiar to Bacon as they are to us. He was the exponent of them with his pen to his own age, as he is to our age. Summon him to the bar of his own immortal sayings and teachings, and he must be condemned out of his own mouth. Where is there a segment upon which an apologist can stand in this sentence, which is the circle he draws around a public servant?

"For corruption do not only bind thine own hands or thy servant's hands from taking, but bind the hands of suitors from offering; for integrity used doth the one, but integrity professed, and with a manifest detestation of bribery, doth the other; and avoid not only the fault, but the suspicion."

But, after having frankly admitted that, in the pursuit of office, and in the execution of one office as a stepping-stone to another, he was guilty of offenses which would have degraded an ordinary man, which were doubly degrading in his case, there is enough of the true, the good, the beautiful, the strong, about him and his works to command our admiration and veneration.

In private life he was gentle and unselfish. Generosity to his immediate friends and followers, and an

indulgence in his taste for building, landscape garden-
ing, ornamentation of his homes, dress, pomp and hos-
pitality, crippled his fortunes and opened the channel
to corruption.

In public affairs he was laborious, progressive, broad-
minded and patriotic, when his moral and intellectual
vision was not blinded by a place or the prospect of a
place.

Of his eloquence, Ben Jonson has left this flattering
account: "The fear of every man that heard him was
lest he should make an end." Living in an age of
church controversy, he was conservative in his opinions
and charitable in his judgments.

James Howell, whose bright and clever letters have
probably entertained the reader, was a contemporary,
and a great Church of England man. He illustrates
the prevailing sectarian sentiment of the time:—

"Difference of opinion," he says, "may work a disaffec-
tion in me, but not a detestation. I rather pity than hate
Turk or infidel. If I hate any, it is those schismatics who
puzzle the sweet peace of our church, so that I would be
content to see an Anabaptist go to hell on a Brownist's
back."

In striking contrast are Bacon's sentiments:—

"God grant," he exclaims, "that we may contend with
other churches, as the vine with the olive, which of us shall
bear the first fruit; and not as the briar with the thistle,
which of us is most unprofitable."

The lawyers of that day were as bigoted as the
churchmen. Littleton was their god and Coke was his
prophet. Here is a picture of the mass, drawn by the

pen of a contemporary, to which, however, neither Coke
nor Bacon belonged:—

"A purse-milking nation, a clamorous company, gowned
vultures; they take upon them to make peace, but are indeed
the very disturbers of our peace. I mean our common
hungry pettifoggers. I love and honor, in the meantime, all
good laws and worthy lawyers, that are so many oracles and
pilots of a well-governed commonwealth."*

It was the narrow-mindedness of the legal profession
which made it distasteful to Bacon. It distributed its
rewards too often to ignorance and impudence, and the
forum was an arena of wild beasts, of whom Sir Edward
Coke was king, because he towered so far above them.
His antipathy and antagonism towards Bacon were due,
probably, to the fact that he recognized in the timid
philosopher the germ of a lawyer far greater than
himself.

To Bacon, law was not a system of unchangeable
rules, but a science capable of beneficent development. He contracted his vision to the smallness
of its details, and dilated it to embrace its great possibilities. To his mind "precedents," as was said by his
favorite disciple, Hobbes, "showed only what was done,
not what was well done." And this spirit of investigation and independence made him the first great reformer
of English jurisprudence.

As a statesman he was eminently progressive, in wish
and intention. Reference has been made to reforms
which he espoused, but which were not accomplished
for centuries.

"The knowledge of a lawyer is one and of a law-

* Democritus to the Reader.

maker is another," he says; and while Coke and others were clinging to what was, whose only excuse for being was that it had been, he was contemplating, digesting and improving the whole system.   Among his greatest efforts and most earnest schemes were the union of England and Scotland, and the assimilation or absorption of the ever-unhappy Irishmen, always vibrating between misgovernment and rebellion, suffering from tyranny or famine, who then, as now, deemed "Boycotting" the only efficient method to insure political freedom and good potato crops.

"The harp of Ireland," says Bacon, "is not tuned to harmony.   Blessed with the dowries of nature, it is a desolate and neglected country."   And he suggested measures, which, had they been adopted, would have centuries ago assured prosperity to a land and people who have so long been in the slough of adversity.

Called upon to solve the problem which Bacon's character presents, to account for actions which cannot be reconciled with the expressed sentiments of the man, the mind is embarrassed by the inconsistencies presented.

In the light of his writings he had one great aim — the good of mankind; in the light of his career one little aim — the good of Francis Bacon.

He was at one and the same time the most selfish and the most philanthropic of men, the most timid and most fearless.   His selfishness inspired him to prosecute a benefactor and defame his memory, to flatter a pedantic king and serve a corrupt favorite.

His philanthropy inspired him to confront the errors of centuries, to drag idols from shrines guarded by a militant priesthood, to emancipate from intellectual stagnation the Anglo-Saxon mind, and to lead it from its metaphysical monastery into the highways of life, into the fields of busy and fruitful investigation and experiment. Bacon was not the inventor of the inductive method, he was the missionary of its application; he accomplished nothing with it himself, but he liberated the English mind from a fruitless school, a narrow path, a limited horizon, and suggested possibilities to the disciples of free thought and original investigation. His good intentions were marred by making his theory one of "Idols," which he deprecates. He condemned Aristotle, Copernicus, and all philosophers, methods and theories, but himself and his own scheme. He is not credited by moderns with a philosophy, or with carrying out his theory to a successful issue. He treats of the reform and progress of science, and the classification of knowledge, with a view to systemization. But he accomplished no practical result as a scientist and philosopher in any special department of science and philosophy. What he did effect was this: he enlisted other minds in the great field of practical science. At a critical period in the intellectual movement of his age he appeared as the missionary of the great idea that God has clothed men with powers whose proper exercise contributes to the social and material well-being of the human race. He said to men, there are a thousand channels which lead to the paradise of your hopes; if you will only bend your faculties to the discovery, you will find them.

There are two sentences in his writings which define what Bacon aimed at and accomplished. In the introduction to his "Great Instauration" he says:—

"It appears to me that men know not either their acquirements or powers, and trust too much to the former and too little to the latter."

And in his "Advancement of Learning" he says:—

"Disciples do owe unto masters a temporary belief, and a suspension of their judgments until they be fully instructed, and not an absolute resignation and perpetual captivity."

If there is a Baconian philosophy, these are the *Alpha* and *Omega* of it. They mean intellectual emancipation, free thought, free inquiry. And for his example and teachings in this respect we cannot be too grateful. For any man who leads the human mind into new paths, or from an old path, is a benefactor; for out of the very errors of courageous inquirers come enlightenment, truth and benefit.

Yet Dr. Draper, in his "Intellectual Development of Europe," says:—

"It is true that the sacred name of philosophy should be severed from its long connection with that of one who was a pretender in science, a time-serving politician, an insidious lawyer, a corrupt judge, a treacherous friend, a bad man."

But the lawyer who reads his law tracts must acknowledge that the English-speaking profession of this last quarter of the 19th century are indebted to him for much that is good in our jurisprudence, while they cannot also help recognizing him as having possessed the wisdom and the true spirit of a reformer. The statesman and politician cannot lay aside his political tracts without being confirmed in the opinion that he understood the philosophy of government, and interpreted its vital principles with the clearness of sunlight.

Judges can sit at his feet and learn to perform their functions as all should, and few do, perform them. The sectarian can learn from his controversial tracts the lesson of charity.

And no man can read his popular works without meeting with some thought which is worth preserving, some lesson worth learning. In accounting for his moral frailty we should not forget that he was the favorite son of an influential father; was reared in comparative affluence; was encouraged to cultivate his great natural gifts for enlistment in the advancement of knowledge and the agreeable service of his country.

His father's intention to secure him a competency was known; his father's ability to secure him preferment was undoubted; employment by the State seemed a hereditary right. But that father's death substituted a hopeless blank in the place of brilliant prospects, and the sanguine youth was confronted not only with comparative poverty, but with powerful friends transformed into oppressors. He was panic-stricken when he failed to receive the support and patronage which he had a right to expect; yet having fastened his gaze on a place at court, his eyes rarely turned from the anxious prospect.

While waiting for preferment he wasted his small patrimony, extravagant tastes became habits, his profession was distasteful, and he kept borrowing and spending, until he began to trade his manhood for office. At last

> " He was cursed and stigmatized by power, '
> And raised to be exposed."

The rest has been related. If we pay to his memory

the tribute of respect, we are compelled to shut out that part of his life which preceded his retirement from public service, and follow him after his re-assumption of the student's and writer's mantle. If we confine our judgments to his writings, then must we bow before the scholar, lawyer, reformer, statesman, moralist and philosopher.

FRANCIS BACON.

ESSAYS AND EXTRACTS.

ESSAYS.*

OF TRUTH.†

What is truth? said jesting Pilate; and would not stay for an answer. Certainly there be that delight in giddiness; and count it a bondage to fix a belief; ‡ affecting § free-will in thinking, as well as in acting. And though the sects of philosophers of that kind be gone, yet there remain certain discoursing ‖ wits, which are of the same veins, though there be not so much blood in them as was in those of the ancients. But it is not only the difficulty and labour which men take in finding out of truth, nor again, that when it is

* "Bacon's *Essays* are the best-known and most popular of all his works. It is also one of those where the superiority of his genius appears to the greatest advantage; the novelty and depth of his reflections often receiving a strong relief from the triteness of the subject. It may be read from beginning to end in a few hours; and yet, after the twentieth perusal, one seldom fails to remark in it something unobserved before. This indeed is a characteristic of all Bacon's writings, and only to be accounted for by the inexhaustible aliment they furnish to our own thoughts, and the sympathetic activity they impart to our torpid faculties." —*Dugald Stewart.*

† "What is truth?" — St. John, xviii., 38.

This essay embraces in its scope theological, philosophical and civil, or social, truth.

‡ The sects referred to are probably those skeptical schools founded by Heraclitus and his followers.

§ *Affect.* To love, be fond of.

‖ *Discoursing.* Some commentators say this word is used in the sense of *discursive; i. e. roving, unsettled.* It may also mean *discussing, debating, arguing.*

found, it imposeth upon men's thoughts, that doth bring lies in favor, but a natural though corrupt love of the lie itself. One of the later schools of the Grecians examineth the matter, and is at a stand to think what should be in it, that men should love lies ; where neither they make for pleasure, as with poets ;* nor for advantage, as with the merchant, but for the lie's sake. But I cannot tell : this same truth is a naked and open daylight, that doth not show the masques, and mummeries, and triumphs of the world, half so stately and daintily as candle-lights. Truth may perhaps come to the price of a pearl, that showeth best by day, but it will not rise to the price of a diamond or carbuncle, that showeth best in varied lights. A mixture of a lie † doth ever add pleasure. Doth any man doubt, that if there were taken out of men's minds, vain opinions, flattering hopes, false valuations, imaginations as one would, ‡ and the like, but it would leave the minds of a number of men, poor shrunken things, full of melancholy and indisposition, and unpleasing to themselves ? One of the fathers, in great severity, called poesy " *vinum dæmonum*," § because it filleth the imagination, and yet it is but with the shadow of a lie. But it is not the lie that passeth through the mind, but the lie that sinketh in, and settleth in it, that doth the hurt, such as we spake of before. But howsoever these things are thus in men's depraved judgments and affections, yet truth, which only doth judge itself, teacheth, that the inquiry of truth, which

* Byron thinks that " there should always be some foundation for the most airy fabric," and adds that " pure invention is but the talent of a liar." — *Letter to Mr. Murray. 1817.*

† Bacon uses the word *lie* with its two meanings : 1st. As a culpable breach of truth. 2d. As the embodiment of a poet's imagination.

"The truth is moral, though the tale's a lie." — *Dryden.*

‡ *As one would.* Used for *wish.*

§ " Wine of demons," used by St. Augustine, Bishop of Hippo, North Africa. A. D. 4th cent.

is the love-making, or wooing of it, the knowledge of truth, which is the presence of it, and the belief of truth, which is the enjoying of it, is the sovereign good of human nature. The first creature of God, in the works of the days, was the light of the sense: the last was the light of reason; and His Sabbath work ever since, is the illumination of His Spirit. First, He breathed light upon the face of the matter, or chaos; then He breathed light into the face of man; and still He breatheth and inspireth light into the face of His chosen. The poet that beautified the sect, * that was otherwise inferior to the rest, saith yet excellently well: " It is a pleasure to stand upon the shore, and to see ships tossed upon the sea: a pleasure to stand in the window of a castle, and to see a battle, and the adventures thereof below: but no pleasure is comparable to the standing upon the vantage ground of truth," (a hill not to be commanded, and where the air is always clear and serene,) "and to see the errors, and wanderings, and mists, and tempests, in the vale below," † so always that this prospect be with pity, and not with swelling or pride. Certainly, it is Heaven upon Earth, to have a man's mind move in charity, rest in Providence, and turn upon the poles of truth.

To pass from theological and philosophical truth, to the truth of civil business, it will be acknowledged even by those that practice it not, that clean and round dealing is the honour of man's nature, and that mixture of falsehood is like alloy in coin of gold and silver, which may make the metal work the better, but it embaseth it. For these winding and crooked courses are the goings of the serpent; which goeth

* The poet meant is Lucretius; the sect the Epicureans.

† This is not the literal translation. Bacon rarely confines himself closely to the original text, adopting Boileau's rule that "a good writer will rather imitate than translate, and rather emulate than imitate."

"The basis of all excellence is truth."—*Dr. Johnson's Life of Cowley.*

G

basely upon the belly, and not upon the feet. There is no vice that doth so cover a man with shame as to be found false and perfidious ; and therefore Montaigne saith prettily, when he inquired the reason, why the word of the lie should be such a disgrace, and such an odious charge, saith he, " If it be well weighed, to say that a man lieth, is as much as to say, that he is brave towards God, and a coward towards men. For a lie faces God, and shrinks from man." Surely the wickedness of falsehood, and breach of faith cannot possibly be so highly expressed, as in that it shall be the last peal to call the judgments of God upon the generations of men : it being foretold, that when " Christ cometh," He shall not " find faith upon the earth."

OF DEATH. *

Men fear death, as children fear to go in the dark ; and as that natural fear in children is increased with tales, so is the other. Certainly, the contemplation of death, as the wages

* Death is the inevitable lot of fool and philosopher, and nothing distinguishes the one from the other more clearly than their respective ways of contemplating the end of life. The approach of death is in the majority of cases cognizable ; but whether or no, in instances other than those of death by violence or necessarily painful symptoms, the experience of dying is accompanied by physical anguish, no man can say ; whether or no there is even mental consciousness contemporaneous with the act of dying is a problem. Who can tell what is seen, felt or heard during the minutes or moments preceding dissolution ? The organs of sensation grow duller and duller as the end approaches ; the placid face does not reflect the grief-tortured countenances surrounding it ; the silent lips do not echo the sighs of sorrow ; the nerveless and cold-growing hand does not return the warm pressure of affec-

of sin, and passage to another world, is holy and religious; but the fear of it, as a tribute due unto Nature, is weak. Yet in religious meditations, there is sometimes mixture of

tion's lingering farewell; no response is made to the anxious gaze, as

> "Unto dying eyes
> The casement slowly grows a glimmering square."
> — *Tennyson, " The Princess."*

To the God-loving, to Virtue's votary who feels, as Shelley beautifully expresses it, the ecstatic and exultant throb when he sums up the thoughts and actions of well-spent days,

> "There is no death; what seems so is transition.
> This life of mortal-breath
> Is but a suburb of the life elysian,
> Whose portal we call death."
> — *Longfellow.*

"I thank God I never was afraid of hell. I have so fixed my contemplation on Heaven that I have almost forgot the idea of hell, and am afraid rather to lose the joys of one than endure the misery of the other. I fear God, yet am not afraid of Him; His mercies make me ashamed of my sins, before His judgments afraid thereof. I can hardly think there was ever any scared into Heaven; they go the fairest way to Heaven that would serve God without hell." — *Religio Medici. LII.*

The essay points to the surroundings of death as giving it an artificial terror, and as more dreadful to confront than death itself; hence we find Rochefoucauld saying, "Let us hope more from our constitutions than from those feeble reasonings which would make us believe that we can approach death with indifference." Byron, who was evidently an admirer, and to some extent a disciple, of the French philosopher, writes to Moore that "a death-bed is a matter of nerves and constitution, and not of religion;" and in "Mazeppa" he gives the thought poetic form:—

> "Save the future, which is viewed
> Not quite as men are bad or good,
> But as their nerves may be endued."

"The preservation of life," says Addison, "should be only a

vanity and of superstition. You shall read in some of the friars' books of mortification, that a man should think with himself, what the pain is, if he have but his finger's end pressed or tortured; and thereby imagine what the pains of death are, when the whole body is corrupted and dissolved; when many times death passeth with less pain than the torture of a limb: for the most vital parts are not the quickest of sense. And by him that spake only as a philosopher, and natural man, it was well said, "*Pompa mortis magis terret, quam mors ipsa.*" * Groans and convulsions, and a discolored face, and friends weeping, and blacks and obsequies, and the like, show death terrible. It is worthy the observing, that there is no passion in the mind of man so weak, but it mates and masters the fear of death; and therefore death is no such terrible enemy when a man hath so many attendants about him that can win the combat of him. Revenge triumphs over death; love slights it; honor aspireth to it; grief flieth to it; fear preoccupateth it: nay, we read, after Otho the emperor had slain himself, pity (which is the tenderest of affections) provoked many to die out of mere compassion to their sovereign, and as the truest sort of followers. Nay, Seneca adds, niceness and satiety: "*Cogita quamdiu eadem feceris; mori velle, non tantum fortis, aut miser, sed etiam fastidiosus potest.*" † A man would die, though he were neither valiant nor miserable, only upon a weariness to do the same thing so oft over and

secondary concern, and the direction of it our principal. If we have this frame of mind, we shall take the best means to preserve life, without being over-solicitous about the event, and shall arrive at the point of felicity which Martial has mentioned as the perfection of happiness, of neither fearing nor wishing for death." — *Spectator.*

* "The surroundings of a death-bed strike more terror than death itself." — *Seneca.*

† "Consider how often you do the same things. A man may be willing to die, not because he is brave or miserable, but simply because he is tired of living."

over. * It is no less worthy to observe, how little alteration in good spirits the approaches of death make: for they appear to be the same men till the last instant. Augustus Cæsar died in a compliment; "*Livia, conjugii nostri memor, vive et vale.*" † Tiberius in dissimulation, as Tacitus saith of him, "*Jam Tiberium vires et corpus, non dissimulatio, deserebant:*" ‡ Vespasian in a jest, sitting upon the stool, "*Ut puto Deus fio:*" § Galba with a sentence, "*Feri, si ex re sit populi Romani,*" ‖ holding forth his neck: Septimus Severus in despatch: "*Adeste, si quid mihi restat agendum*" ¶ and the like. Certainly the Stoics bestowed too much cost upon death, and by their great preparations made it appear more fearful. Better, saith he, "*qui finem vitæ extremum inter munera ponit naturæ.*" ** It is as natural to die as to be born; and to a little infant, perhaps, the one is as painful as the other. He that dies in an earnest pursuit, is like one that is wounded in hot blood; who, for the time, scarce feels the hurt; and therefore a mind fixed and bent upon somewhat that is good, doth avert the dolours of death;

* "When all the blandishments of life are gone,
  The coward sneaks to death, the brave live on."
  — *Dr. Jno. Sewell, from Martial.*

"It is a brave act of valour to contemn death; but when life is more terrible than death, it is then the truest valour to dare to live." — *Religio Medici.*

† "Livia, mindful of our union, live on, and farewell;" *i. e.* I dwell in my last moments on our harmonious married life, and wish you a long life, and bid you an affectionate good bye.

"'Cæsar Augustus died in a compliment.' 'I hope it was a sincere one,' said my Uncle Toby. ''Twas to his wife,' replied my father." — *Tristram Shandy. V. 4.*

‡ "His strength and vitality were now leaving Tiberius, but not his duplicity."

§ "I am becoming a god, I suspect," said he, in a rebuking sneer to his flatterers.

‖ "Strike, if it is for the good of the Roman people."

¶ "Hurry, if anything remains for me to do."

** "Who looks upon death as one of nature's blessings."

but, above all, believe it, the sweetest canticle is "*Nunc
dimittis*" * when a man hath obtained worthy ends and
expectations.   Death hath this also, that it openeth the
gate to good fame, and extinguisheth envy: "*Extinctus
amabitur idem.*" †

OF REVENGE.

Revenge is a kind of wild justice, which the more man's
nature runs to, the more ought law to weed it out: for as
for the first wrong, it doth but offend the law, but the
revenge of that wrong putteth the law out of office. ‡ Certainly, in taking revenge, a man is but even with his enemy;
but in passing it over, he is superior; for it is a prince's part
to pardon: and Solomon, I am sure, saith, "It is the glory

* " Now, dismiss us," or "me."

† "The same man will be loved, though dead."
One of the fathers saith "that there is but this difference
between the death of old men and young men: that old men go
to death, and death comes to young men." — *Bacon's Apothegms.*

‡ "The use of the law," says Bacon, in his treatise on that subject, " consisteth principally in these three things: 1. To secure
men's persons from death and violence. 2. To dispose the property of their goods and lands. 3. For preservation of their good
names from shame and infamy." Until law was enacted and
enforced, there was no settled society or established government.
Each man was a law unto himself, and according to his ability
secured for himself the benefits which society and government
secure for us. ʃThe law protects a right or redresses a wrong; but
before there was law, a man redressed his wrong by inflicting an
equal or greater injury upon one who wronged him. In society
and under government this kind of setting things to rights, this
individual assumption of the authority of government, is very forcibly credited with an offense greater than law-breaking, *i. e.* putting the law out of office, which if practiced unchecked in any
society would result in anarchy and reduce that society back to a
state of nature.

of a man to pass by an offense." That which is past is gone and irrecoverable, and wise men have enough to do with things present and to come; therefore they do but trifle with themselves, that labour in past matters. There is no man doth a wrong for the wrong's sake, but thereby to purchase himself profit, or pleasure, or honour, or the like; therefore why should I be angry with a man for loving himself better than me? And if any man should do wrong, merely out of ill-nature, why, yet it is but like the thorn or briar, which prick and scratch, because they can do no other. The most tolerable sort of revenge is for those wrongs which there is no law to remedy; but then, let a man take heed the revenge be such as there is no law to punish, else a man's enemy is still beforehand, and it is two for one. Some, when they take revenge, are desirous the party should know whence it cometh: this is the more generous; for the delight seemeth to be not so much in doing the hurt as in making the party repent: but base and crafty cowards are like the arrow that flieth in the dark. Cosmus, * Duke of Florence, had a desperate saying against perfidious or neglecting friends, as if those wrongs were unpardonable. "You shall read," saith he, "that we are commanded to forgive our enemies, but you never read that we are commanded to forgive our friends." But yet the spirit of Job was in a better tune: "Shall we," saith he, "take good at God's hands, and not be content to take evil also?" and so of friends in a proportion. This is certain, that a man that studieth revenge, keeps his own wounds green, which otherwise would heal

---

* Cosmo de Medici, patron of art and literature at Florence, head of the Florentine Republic, A. D., 1389–1464. Sidney Smith takes a wiser and more charitable stand towards neglecting friends when he says: "True, it is most painful not to meet the kindness and affection you feel you have deserved and have a right to expect from others; but it is a mistake to complain of it, for it is of no use; you cannot extort friendship with a cocked pistol." — *Memoirs.*

and do well.   Public revenges * are for the most part fortunate; as that for the death of Cæsar; † for the death of
Pertinax; for the death of Henry the Third of France; and
many more.   But in private revenges it is not so; nay,
rather vindictive persons live the life of witches; who, as
they are mischievous, so end they unfortunate.

OF ADVERSITY. ‡

It was a high speech of Seneca (after the manner of the
Stoics), that the good things which belong to prosperity
are to be wished, but the good things that belong to adversity are to be admired: — "*Bona rerum secundarum opta-
bilia, adversarum mirabilia.*"   Certainly, if miracles be the

---

* The spirit of resentment is commoner than that of revenge;
the one is a sudden passion, the other a prolonged enmity. A
French philosopher says that men are as prone to forget injuries
as they are to forget benefits, because the constant study to either
avenge evil or recompense good appears to them a slavery, to
which they find it difficult to submit.

† Revenges here mean vindications by punishment.

"Thus the whirligig of Time brings in his revenges."
—*Shakespeare's* "*Twelfth Night.*" *Act. v., sc. I.*

Revenge is the earmark of savage condition and nature, as
magnanimity of soul or gentleness of heart is that of culture, piety
and civilization.   Revenge is the nurse of anarchy in the State,
forgiveness the bond of harmony in the family.

"How happy might we be, and end our time with blessed days
and sweet content, if we could contain ourselves, and, as we
ought to do, put up injuries, learn humility, meekness, patience,
forget and forgive." — *Burton's* "*Anatomy of Melancholy.*"

‡ This essay first appeared in the edition of 1625.   The author
had experienced the extremes of good and bad fortune.   He had
sinned, suffered and repented, and wrote as much from the heart
as from the head.

command over nature, they appear most in adversity. It is yet a higher speech of his than the other (much too high for a heathen, *) "It is true greatness to have in one the frailty of a man, and the security of a god; "— " *Vere magnum habere fragilitatem hominis, securitatem dei.*" This would have done better in poesy, where transcendencies are more allowed; and the poets, indeed, have been busy with it; for it is in effect the thing which is figured in that strange fiction of the ancient poets, which seemeth not to be without mystery; nay, and to have some approach to the state of a Christian, "that Hercules, when he went to unbind Prometheus (by whom human nature is represented), sailed the length of the great ocean in an earthen pot or pitcher, lively describing Christian resolution, that saileth in the frail bark of the flesh through the waves of the world."

* " Much too high for a heathen." This parenthetical sneer is surprising, coming from Bacon, who was so familiar with the far-reaching thoughts and lofty aspirations of philosophers, to whom neither the light of the law — the Old Testament, — nor the light of the promise — the New Testament, — had come.

St. Paul, Romans ii., 14, 15, regarded the heathen with different eyes, and confronts the Gentile with the light of nature and its corollary, moral responsibility. "For when the Gentiles, which have not the law, do by nature the things contained in the law, those having not the law are a law unto themselves; which show the work of the law written in their hearts." It was the bigoted theologian who summarily disposed of those to whom Moses and the prophets never spoke — to whom the promise of the cross never came.

Old Sir Thomas Brown quaintly, plaintively yet dubiously appeals from the narrowness of man's judgment to the broadness of God's justice: "There is no salvation to those that believe not in Christ; that is, say some, since his nativity, and, as divinity affirmeth, before, also; which makes me much apprehend the end of those honest worthies and philosophers which died before his incarnation. It is hard to place those souls in hell whose worthy lives do teach us virtue on earth. Methinks among those many subdivisions there might have been some limbo left for them."

But, to speak in a mean, the virtue of prosperity is temper-
ance, the virtue of adversity is fortitude, which in morals is
the more heroical virtue.   Prosperity is the blessing of the
Old Testament, adversity is the blessing of the New, which
carrieth the greater benediction, and the clearer revelation
of God's favour.   Yet even in the Old Testament, if you
listen to David's harp, you shall hear as many hearse-like
airs as carols; and the pencil of the Holy Ghost hath
labored more in describing the afflictions of Job than the
felicities of Solomon.   Prosperity is not without many fears
and distastes; and adversity is not without comforts and
hopes.   We see in needleworks and embroideries, it is more
pleasing to have a lively work upon a sad and solemn
ground, than to have a dark and melancholy work upon a
lightsome ground : judge, therefore, of the pleasure of the
heart by the pleasure of the eye.   Certainly virtue is like
precious odours, most fragrant when they are incensed, *
or crushed : for prosperity doth best discover vice, but
adversity doth best discover virtue.

OF PARENTS AND CHILDREN.

The joys of parents are secret, and so are their griefs and
fears ; they cannot utter the one, nor they will not utter the
other.   Children sweeten labours, but they make misfor-
tunes more bitter : they increase the cares of life, but they
mitigate the remembrance of † death.   The perpetuity by

* Among Bacon's " Apothegms " we find the following : " Mr.
Bettenham said that virtuous men were like herbs and spices that
give not their sweet smell till they be broken and crushed."

† Bacon was himself childless, and does not speak with the
same authority on this subject as on those where his experience
supplemented observation.   When, in this essay, he extends his
observation beyond the close relation of parent and child, and
generalizes, his opinions, in all probability, meet with less antago-

generation is common to beasts; but memory, merit, and
noble works, are proper to men: and surely a man shall
see the noblest works and foundations * have proceeded
from childless men, which have sought to express the
images of their minds, where those of their bodies have
failed; so the care of posterity is most in them that have
no posterity. They that are the first raisers of their houses
are most indulgent towards their children, beholding them
as the continuance, not only of their kind, but of their work;
and so both children and creatures.

The difference in affection of parents towards their several children, is many times unequal, and sometimes unworthy, especially in the mother; as Solomon saith, "A wise
son rejoiceth the father, but an ungracious son shames the
mother." A man shall see, where there is a house full of
children, one or two of the eldest respected, and the youngest made wantons; † but in the midst some that are as it

nism. Thus, when he deprecates the breeding of jealous emulation, he addresses himself to the relation of brothers and sisters;
the same sound doctrine is applicable to the relation of school-
mates; and when he advises the parent to determine for the child
its life pursuit, he enters the arena of the social philosopher and
pedagogue.

Remembrance here means the notice of something absent.

"Let your remembrance still apply to Banquo." — *Shakespeare.*

Probably its use is explained in the last sentence of this paragraph. The first raisers of houses, *i. e.* families of rank, do not
look upon their inevitable death as destructive of their life-work;
and although, while indulging in self-gratulation, they recall or
remember that they, too, shall surely die, the idea is softened by
beholding in their children their successors who will perpetuate
their name.

* *Foundations,* meaning establishments of a charitable kind.
Pope speaks of the wealth of the childish miser : —

"Or wanders, heaven-directed, to the poor."

† *Wantons, i. e.* spoiled children.

were forgotten, who, many times, nevertheless, prove the best. The illiberality of parents, in allowance towards their children, is an harmful error, and makes them base; acquaints them with shifts; makes them sort* with mean company; and makes them surfeit more when they come to plenty: and therefore the proof is best when men keep their authority towards their children, but not their purse. Men have a foolish manner (both parents, and schoolmasters, and servants), in creating and breeding an emulation between brothers during childhood, which many times sorteth to discord when they are men, and disturbeth families. The Italians make little difference between children and nephews, or near kinsfolk; but, so they be of the lump, they care not, though they pass not through their own body; and, to say truth, in nature it is much a like matter; insomuch that we see a nephew sometimes resembleth an uncle, or a kinsman, more than his own parent, as the blood happens. Let parents choose betimes the vocations and courses they mean their children should take, for then they are most flexible; and let them not too much apply themselves to the disposition of their children, as thinking they will take best to that which they have most mind to. † It is true, that if the affection, or aptness of the children be extraordinary, then it is good not to cross it; but generally the precept is

---

* This doctrine will be thought heterodox by some, and perhaps comes as much from the heart as the head. Bacon, when on the threshold of manhood, was in straightened circumstances, soon made the acquaintance of money-lenders, and the aid which he asked of his mother was promised with conditions incompatible with his self-esteem.

The word *sort* means associate; the word *sorteth*, further on, means *happen, come to.*

† The tendency of modern education is to encourage the natural bent of the mind.

> " No profit grows where is no pleasure ta'en ;
> In brief, sir, study what you most affect."
>
> — *Shakespeare.*

good, "*Optimum elige, suave et facile illud faciet consue-tudo.*" *—Younger brothers are commonly fortunate, but seldom or never where the elder are disinherited. †

OF MARRIAGE AND SINGLE LIFE.

He that hath wife and children hath given hostages to fortune; for they are impediments to great enterprises, either of virtue or mischief. Certainly the best works, and of greatest merit for the public, have proceeded from the unmarried or childless men; which, both in affection and means, have married and endowed the public. Yet it were great reason that those that have children should have greatest care of future times, unto which they know they must transmit their dearest pledges. Some there are, who, though they lead a single life, yet their thoughts do end with themselves, and account future times impertinences; ‡ nay, there are some other that account wife and children but as bills of charges; nay more, there are some foolish rich covetous men, that take a pride in having no children, because § they may be thought so much the richer; for, perhaps, they have heard some talk, "Such an one is a great

* "Select the career which seems best; habit will make it practicable and pleasant."

† According to the English law of primogeniture the oldest son got the lion's share of the father's estate at the latter's death. Sometimes the estate was entailed, *i. e.* so fixed that it could not be divided up among all the children, or disposed of by sale or by last will, but descended from father to the oldest son, through succeeding generations. When not entailed, the owner could dispose of it by last will, as he might see fit. In the United States the power to entail property has been abolished; if not devised, all children share alike.

‡ *Impertinences.* A word used in equity pleadings, meaning things irrelevant.

§ *Because.* In order that.

rich man," and another except to it, "Yea, but he hath a
great charge of children;" as if it were an abatement to his
riches: but the most ordinary cause of a single life is
liberty, especially in certain self-pleasing and humorous *
minds, which are so sensible of every restraint, as they will
go near to think their girdles and garters to be bonds and
shackles.   Unmarried men are best friends, best masters,
best servants; but not always best subjects; for they are
light to run away; and almost all fugitives are of that condition.   A single life doth well with churchmen, for charity
will hardly water the ground where it must first fill a pool. †
It is indifferent for judges and magistrates; for if they be
facile and corrupt, you shall have a servant five times worse
than a wife.   For soldiers, I find the generals commonly,
in their hortatives, ‡ put men in mind of their wives and
children; and I think the despising of marriage among

* *Humorous.*   Whimsical.

† The celibacy of the priesthood was based upon other grounds.
It was a part of the Roman Catholic policy, and necessary to its
hierarchy.   Its missionary orders could not, it was thought, wed
and work.   Its monastic orders could not people their cells with
wives and children; a nunnery would not resemble its heathen
prototype — the temple of vestal virgins — if the sisters in the
church took husbands from the world.   In a word, the theory
was that every religious, from pope to begging friar, from abbess
to nun, was wedded to the church and loosed from all family and
worldly ties.   In the primitive church, when the priesthood of one
day might be made the martyrs of the next, when the conversion
of Greek and Roman, philosopher and barbarian, was the life-
mission of each, marriage and domestic duties were incompatible
with the fulfillment of the higher mission; but when Luther revolutionized a part of the priesthood by his example and writings,
the face of society and state of the church had undergone a
change.   Yet it was some time before the English Church followed
in the footsteps of the Lutheran.

‡ " Strike — for your altars and your fires;
    Strike — for the green graves of your sires,
       God and your native land."— *Marco Bozzaris.*

the Turks maketh the vulgar soldier more base. Certainly wife and children are a kind of discipline of humanity; and single men, though they be many times more charitable, because their means are less exhaust, * yet, on the other side, they are more cruel and hard-hearted (good to make severe inquisitors), because their tenderness is not so oft called upon. Grave natures, led by custom, and therefore constant, are commonly loving husbands, as was said of Ulysses, "*Vetulam suam prætulit immortalitati.*" † Chaste women are often proud and froward as presuming upon the merit of their chastity. It is one of the best bonds, both of chastity and obedience, in the wife, if she think her husband wise; which she will never do if she find him jealous. ‡ Wives are young men's mistresses, companions for middle age, and old men's nurses; so as a man may have a quarrel §

* *Exhaust.* Exhausted.

† He preferred his aged wife (Penelope) to immortality.

‡ Jealousy is a natural and universal weakness, which is not base, like envy, but is a source of sorrow to its possessor, and if not restrained by reason it becomes an evil passion. In the Song of Solomon it is described as being "cruel as the grave." Shakespeare points the moral of its indulgence in Othello. Milton calls it "the injured lover's hell." Rochefoucauld and Goldsmith defend or apologize for it. The former says: "Jealousy is in some sort just and reasonable, since it only has for its object the preservation of a good which belongs, or which we fancy belongs, to ourselves; while envy, on the contrary, is madness which cannot endure the good of others." — *Maxim 29.*

Goldsmith, in "The Good-natured Man," thus defends it: "It is natural to suppose that merit which has made an impression on one's own heart may be powerful over that of another." — *Act I., scene I.*

§ *Quarrel.* Excuse or ground.

In an old scrap-book there are the following lines, said to be inscribed on a tombstone in an old English graveyard: —

> "Tho' marriage by some is counted a curse,
> Three wives did I marry for better or worse:
> The first for her person, the second her purse,
> The third for warming-pan, doctress and nurse."

to marry when he will: but yet he was reputed one of the wise men, that made answer to the question when a man should marry:—"A young man not yet, an elder man not at all." *   It is often seen, that bad husbands have very good wives; whether it be that it raiseth the price of their husbands' kindness when it comes, or that the wives take a pride in their patience; but this never fails, if the bad husbands were of their own choosing, against their friends' consent, for then they will be sure to make good their own folly. †

* The answer of the reputed wise man has been put into verse by some disciple:—

> "I would advise a man to pause
> Before he take a wife;
> Indeed, I own I see no cause
> He should not pause for life."

† The poet Thompson thus describes the transition from lover to husband:—

> "First a kneeling slave, and then a tyrant."
> — *Tancred and Sigismundi.*

Horace Walpole writes to Sir Horace Mann that Lady Boyle's portrait bore the inscription, "Died of a cruel husband."

Unhappy marriages seem to result oftenest from hasty unions, where the shortest cut has been taken to the altar, or where romantic women, knowing the weaknesses or vices of their lovers, are silly enough to think that they can make good husbands out of bad men.

"The universal reception that marriage has had in the world is enough to fix it for a public good, and to draw everybody into the common cause; but there are some constitutions, like some instruments, so peculiarly singular that they make tolerable music by themselves, but never do well in concert."—*Farquar's " The Inconstant."*

"Courtship to marriage is a very witty prologue to a very dull play."—*Congreve's " The Old Bachelor." Act v., sc. 2.*

> "O cursed state!
> How wide we err when apprehensive of the load

OF GREAT PLACE. *

Men in great place are thrice servants; servants of the sovereign or State, servants of fame, and servants of business; so as they have no freedom, neither in their persons, nor in their actions, nor in their times. It is a strange desire to seek power and to lose liberty; or to seek power over others, and to lose power over a man's self. The rising unto place is laborious, and by pains men come to

Of life.   *   *   *   *

We hope to find
That help which nature meant in womankind!
To man that supplemental self designed." — *Ibid.*

The following attractive picture of married life will be found in Farquar's "Sir Harry Wildair": —

"There was never such a pattern of unity. Her wants were still prevented by my supplies; my own heart whispered me her desires, because she herself was there. No contention ever arose but the dear strife of who should most oblige. No noise about authority; for neither would stoop to command, because both thought it glory to obey."

Byron characterizes matrimony as the finger-post of Doctors-Commons. "Not a divorce stirring," he writes to the poet Moore, "but a good many in embryo in the shape of marriages."

And Peter Pindar compares it to Jeremiah's figs: —

"Ah! matrimony! thou art like
To Jeremiah's figs;
The good were very good, the bad
Too sour to give the pigs."

"'Alack-a-day!' replied the corporal, brightening up his face; 'your honour knows I have neither wife nor child. I can have no sorrows in this world.'" — *Tristram Shandy.*

* No man's experience comprised more of the vicissitudes of place-hunting than Bacon's. His career began with disappointment and ended in disgrace. "If this be to be a Lord Chancellor," he said, "I think if the Great Seal lay upon Hounslow Heath, nobody would take it up."

greater pains; and it is sometimes base, and by indignities *
men come to dignities. The standing is slippery, and the
regress is either a downfall, or at least an eclipse, which is
a melancholy thing: "*Cum non sis qui fueris, non esse cur
velis vivere.*" † Nay, retire men cannot when they would,
neither will they when it were reason; but are impatient of
privateness even in age and sickness, which require the
shadow; ‡ like old townsmen, that will be still sitting at
their street-door, though thereby they offer age to scorn.
Certainly great persons had need to borrow other men's
opinions to think themselves happy; for if they judge by
their own feeling, they cannot find it: but if they think with
themselves what other men think of them, and that other
men would fain be as they are, then they are happy as it
were by report, when, perhaps, they find the contrary

---

* *Indignities, i. e.* those slights and snubs which the place-
hunter submits to in order to attain his end.

"Whoever is apt to hope good from others is diligent to please
them; but he that believes his powers strong enough to force their
own way commonly tries only to please himself."— *Dr. Johnson,
"Life of Gay."*

> "So many a winter, many a summer ran
> Calm and unclouded o'er the pliant man."
> — *Juvenal, IV Satire.*

Sir Pertinax Macsycophant: "I naver in my life could stand
straight i' th' presence of a great man; but always boowed and
boowed and boowed, as if it were by instinct."

Egerton: "How do you mean by instinct, sir?"

Sir Pertinax: "I mean by the instinct of interest, which is the
universal interest of mankind."— *Mackiln's "Man of the World,"
Act III., sc. 1.*

† *Cum sis, etc.* Since you are not what you were, why do you
care to live as a nobody?

‡ *Shadow.* Retirement.

> "Old politicians chew on wisdom past,
> And totter on in business to the last."
> — *Pope, Moral Essay.*

within:* for they are the first that find their own griefs, though they be the last that find their own faults. Certainly men in great fortunes are strangers to themselves, and while they are in the puzzle of business they have no time to tend their health either of body or mind: "*Illi mors gravis incubat, qui notus nimis omnibus, ignotus moritur sibi.*"† In place there is license to do good and evil; whereof the latter is a curse: for in evil the best condition is not to will: the second not to can. But power to do good is the true and lawful end of aspiring; for good thoughts (though God accept them), yet towards men are little better than good dreams, except they be put in act; and that cannot be without power and place, as the vantage and commanding ground. Merit and good works is the end of man's motion; and conscience ‡ of the same is the accomplishment of man's rest: for if a man can be partaker of God's theater, he shall likewise be partaker of God's rest: "*Et conversus Deus, ut aspiceret opera, quæ fecerunt manus suæ, vidit quod omnia essent bona nimis;*" § and then the Sabbath.

In the discharge of the place set before thee the best

---

* Bacon here alludes to the disposition in most of us which inspires us to make ourselves miserable in order to be thought happy, or at least enviable, by our neighbors. This is most apparent in the social ambition of both men and women, who, to lift themselves a grade higher in the social scale, sacrifice self-respect and the tangible enjoyments which are within their reach in the class to which they belong by natural selection.

"He who looks for applause from without leaves his happiness in other men's keeping." — *Goldsmith, " The Good-natured Man."*

"Happiness lies in the taste, not in the things, and it is from having what we desire that we are happy, not from having what others think desirable." — *Rochefoucauld.*

† Death weighs heavily upon him who, too well known by others, dies self-ignorant.

‡ *Conscience* means consciousness.

§ And God having turned to behold the works which His hands had done, saw that all things were very good.

examples; for imitation is a globe * of precepts; and after a time set before thee thine own example; and examine thyself strictly whether thou didst not best at first. Neglect not also the examples of those that have carried themselves ill in the same place; not to set off thyself by taxing their memory, but to direct thyself what to avoid. Reform, therefore, without bravery † or scandal of former times and persons; but yet set it down to thyself, as well to create good precedents as to follow them. Reduce things to the first institution, and observe wherein and how they have degenerated; but yet ask counsel of both times; of the ancient time what is best; and of the later time what is fittest. Seek to make thy course regular, that men may know beforehand what they may expect; but be not too positive and peremptory; and express thyself well when thou digressest from thy lure. Preserve the right of thy place, but stir not questions of jurisdiction; and rather assume thy right in silence, and "*de facto*," ‡ than voice it with claims and challenges. Preserve likewise the rights of inferior places; and think it more honour to direct in chief than to be busy in all. Embrace and invite helps § and advices touching the execution of thy place; and do not drive away such as bring thee information as meddlers, but accept of them in good part.

The vices of authority are chiefly four; delays, corruption, roughness, and facility. For delays give easy access; keep times appointed; go through with that which is in hand, and interlace not business but of necessity. For corruption, do not only bind thine own hands or thy servants' hands from taking, but bind the hands of suitors also from offering; for integrity used doth the one; but integrity

---

* *Globe, i. e.* circle.

† *Bravery, i. e.* rashness, pride, arrogance.

‡ *De facto, i. e.* as a matter of fact; as admitted on all sides.

§ "He who calls in the aid of an equal understanding doubles his own." — *Burke's reply to Fox, debate on French Revolution.*

professed, and with a manifest detestation of bribery, doth the other; and avoid not only the fault, but the suspicion. Whosoever is found variable, and changeth manifestly without manifest cause, giveth suspicion of corruption: therefore, always when thou changest thine opinion or course, profess it plainly, and declare it, together with the reasons that move thee to change, and do not think to steal it. * A servant or a favourite, if he be inward, † and no other apparent cause of esteem, is commonly thought but a by-way to close corruption. For roughness, it is a needless cause of discontent: severity breedeth fear, but roughness breedeth hate. Even reproofs from authority ought to be grave, and not taunting. As for facility—it is worse than bribery; for bribes come but now and then; but if importunity or idle respects ‡ lead a man, he shall never be without; as Solomon saith, "To respect persons is not good, for such a man will transgress for a piece of bread."

It is most true that was anciently spoken, "A place showeth the man; and it showeth some to the better and some to the worse." "*Omnium consensu capax imperii, nisi imperasset,*" § saith Tacitus of Galba; but of Vespasian

---

* "*Steal it,*" *i. e.* conceal it or lie about it.

"When a man owns himself to have been in error, he does but tell you, in other words, that he is wiser than he was."— *Pope, letter to Hon. J. C., June 15, 1711.*

† *Inward, i. e.* intimate.

Close, i. e. secret.

‡ *Facility,* that is accessibility to, and persuadability too, by the few, and indifference to the many, is the too common characteristic of the public servant, whether king, president, judge, legislator, or even the petty chief of some petty bureau.

"No man," says Macaulay, in speaking of Charles II., "is fit to govern great societies who hesitates about disobliging the few who have access to him for the sake of the many whom he will never see."

§ If he had not governed, all would have said that he was capable of governing.

he saith, "*Solus imperantium, Vespasianus mutatus in melius;*" * though the one was meant of sufficiency, the other of manners and affection. It is an assured sign of a worthy and generous spirit, whom honour amends; for honour is, or should be, the place of virtue; and as in nature things move violently to their place, and calmly in their place, so virtue in ambition is violent, in authority settled and calm. † All rising to great place is by a winding stair; and if there be factions, it is good to side a man's self whilst he is in the rising, and to balance himself when he is placed. Use the memory of thy predecessor fairly and tenderly; for if thou dost not, it is a debt will sure be paid when thou art gone. If thou have colleagues, respect them; and rather call them when they look not for it, than exclude them when they have reason to look to be called. Be not too sensible or too remembering of thy place in conversation and private answers to suitors; but let it rather be said, " When he sits in place he is another man."

* Of the emperors, Vespasian alone changed for the better.

† Bacon seems to recognize but one road to place, a path which begins in the mire and leads up to the mountain. Self-respect, honor, independence, individuality, must all be sacrificed in the beginning, and great place will finally compensate. He does not state it as a fact; he announces it as a principle, that "stooping to points of necessity and convenience cannot be disallowed; for though they may have some outward baseness, yet in judgment truly made, they are to be accounted submissions to the occasion and not the person." — "*Advancement of Learning.*"

He preaches the orthodoxy of party as a means to place when he points out the benefits of being a partisan, when one is in the rising, and advises a course which few men follow, when they succeed, in suggesting that they should "balance" themselves, *i. e.* be impartial when placed. "If a man so tempers his action as in some one of them, he doth content every faction or combination of people," he says in an "Essay on Honor and Reputation," "the music will be the fuller."

OF BOLDNESS. *

It is a trivial grammar-school text, but yet worthy a wise man's consideration. Question was asked of Demosthenes what was the chief part of an orator? he answered, action: what next? action: what next again? action. He said it that knew it best, and had by nature himself no advantage in that he commended. A strange thing, that that part of an orator which is but superficial, and rather the virtue of a player, should be placed so high above those other noble parts of invention, elocution, and the rest; nay almost alone, as if it were all in all. But the reason is plain. There is in human nature generally more of the fool than of the wise; and therefore those faculties by which the foolish part of men's minds is taken, are most potent. Wonderful like is the case of boldness in civil business; what first? boldness: what second and third? boldness. † And yet boldness is a child of ignorance and baseness, far inferior

---

* This essay comes very appropriately after the one "Of Great Place," for both are dedicated to the consideration of the one subject which so occupied the mind of Bacon, *i. e.* success in life.

† Lady Mary Wortley Montagu, writing to Mr. Wortley Montagu, says: "Riches being another word for power, to the obtaining of which the first necessary qualification is impudence, and (as Demosthenes said of pronunciation [*sic*] in oratory) the second is impudence, and the third still impudence, no modest man ever did or ever will make his fortune." — *Memoirs and Letters. Vol. I., 215.*

The coin of this impudence and boldness is current in a vicious market, where there "is generally more of the fool than the wise." The more a community advances in culture the less influence, power or success have the unblushing pretenders to merit. Bacon was himself of a timid nature, and was often embarrassed by the rude, overbearing boldness of Coke and others, and probably

to other parts : but nevertheless, it doth fascinate, and bind
hand and foot those that are either shallow in judgment or
weak in courage, which are the greatest part : yea, and pre-
vaileth with wise men at weak times : therefore we see it
hath done wonders in popular States, but with senates and
princes less ; and more, ever upon the first entrance of bold
persons into action than soon after; for boldness is an ill
keeper of promise.   Surely as there are mountebanks for
the natural body, so are there mountebanks for the politic
body; men that undertake great cures, and perhaps have
been lucky in two or three experiments, but want the
grounds of science, and therefore cannot hold out : nay, you
shall see a bold fellow many times do Mahomet's miracle.
Mahomet made the people believe that he would call a hill
to him, and from the top of it offer up his prayers for the
observers of his law.   The people assembled : Mahomet
called the hill to come to him again and again; and when
the hill stood still, he was never a whit abashed, but said,
" If the hill will not come to Mahomet, Mahomet will go to
the hill."   So these men, when they have promised great
matters and failed most shamefully, yet (if they have the
perfection of boldness) they will but slight it over, and make
a turn, and no more ado.   Certainly to men of great judgment, bold persons are a sport to behold; nay, and to the
vulgar also boldness hath somewhat of the ridiculous : for
if absurdity be the subject of laughter, doubt you not but
great boldness is seldom without some absurdity ; especially

assigned to impudence more power as an aid to success than it
possessed.   Elsewhere he says : —

" Ostentation is rather a vice in manners than in policy.   . . .
Not a few solid natures that want this ventosity are not without
some prejudice and disadvantage." — "*Advancement of Learning.*"

> " Win power with craft, wear it with ostentation,
>   For confidence is half security;
>   Deluded men think boldness conscious strength,
>   And grow the slaves of their own want of doubt."
> — *Walpole,* "*Mysterious Mother,*" *Act I., sc. 3.*

it is a sport to see when a bold fellow is out of countenance, for that puts his face into a most shrunken and wooden posture as needs it must; for in bashfulness the spirits do a little go and come; but with bold men, upon like occasion, they stand at a stay; like a stale at chess, where it is no mate, but yet the game cannot stir: but this last were fitter for a satire than for a serious observation. This is well to be weighed, that boldness is ever blind; for it seeth not dangers and inconveniences: therefore it is ill in counsel, good in execution; so that the right use of bold persons is, that they never command in chief, but be seconds and under the direction of others; for in counsel it is good to see dangers, and in execution not to see them except they be very great.

OF GOODNESS, AND GOODNESS OF NATURE.

I take goodness in this sense, the affecting of the weal of men, which is that the Grecians call *Philanthropia;* and the word humanity (as it is used), is a little too light to express it. Goodness I call the habit, and goodness of nature the inclination. This of all virtues and dignities of the mind, is the greatest, being the character of the Deity: and without it man is a busy, mischievous, wretched thing, no better than a kind of vermin. Goodness answers to the theological virtue charity, and admits no excess but error. The desire of power in excess caused the angels to fall; the desire of knowledge in excess caused man to fall: but in charity there is no excess, neither can angel or man come in danger by it. The inclination to goodness is imprinted deeply in the nature of man; insomuch, that if it issue not towards men, it will take unto other living creatures; as it is seen in the Turks, a cruel people, who nevertheless are kind to beasts, and give alms to dogs and birds; insomuch, as Busbechius * reporteth, a Christian boy in Constantinople had like to have been stoned for gagging in a waggishness a long-billed fowl. Errors indeed, in this virtue, of goodness or charity, may be committed. The Italians have an ungracious proverb, " *Tanto buon che val niente;*" " so good, that he is good for nothing;" and one of the doctors of Italy, Nicholas Machiavel, † had the confidence to put in writing, almost in plain terms, "That the Christian faith had given up good men in prey to those that are tyrannical and unjust;" which he spake, because, indeed, there was never law or sect or opinion did so much magnify goodness as the Christian religion doth: therefore, to avoid the scandal and the danger both, it is good to take knowledge of the errors of a habit so excellent. Seek the good of other men, but be not in bondage to their faces or fancies; for that is but facility or softness, which taketh an honest mind prisoner. Neither give thou Æsop's cock a gem, who would be better pleased and happier if he had had a barley-corn. The example of God teacheth the lesson truly: "He sendeth His rain, and maketh His sun to shine upon the just and the unjust;" but He doth not rain wealth, nor shine honour and virtues upon men equally: common benefits are to be communicated with all, but peculiar benefits with choice. And beware how in making the portraiture thou breakest the pattern: for divinity maketh the love of ourselves the pattern; the love of our neighbours but the portraiture: "Sell all thou hast and give it to the poor, and follow Me:" but sell not all thou hast except thou come and follow Me; that is, except thou have a vocation wherein thou mayest do as much good with little means as with great; for otherwise, in feeding the streams, thou driest the fountain.

Neither is there only a habit of goodness directed by

* Native of Flanders, born 1522; was a great traveller.

† A Florentine, author of "The Prince," and protégé of Cæsar Borgia.

right reason; but there is in some men, even in nature, a disposition towards it; as, on the other side, there is a natural malignity: for there be that in their nature do not affect the good of others. The lighter sort of malignity turneth but to a crossness, or frowardness, or aptness to oppose, or difficileness,* or the like; but the deeper sort to envy, and mere mischief. Such men in other men's calamities, are, as it were, in season, and are ever on the loading part: not so good as the dogs that licked Lazarus' sores, but like flies that are still buzzing upon anything that is raw; misanthropi, that maketh it their practice to bring men to the bough, and yet have never a tree for the purpose in their gardens, as Timon† had: such dispositions are the very errors of human nature, and yet they are the fittest timber to make great politics of; like to knee-timber, ‡ that is good for ships that are ordained to be tossed, but not for building houses that shall stand firm.

The parts and signs of goodness are many. § If a man be gracious and courteous to strangers, it shows he is a citizen of the world, and that his heart is no island cut off from other lands, but a continent that joins to them: if he be compassionate towards the afflictions of others, it shows that his heart is like the noble tree that is wounded itself when it gives the balm: ‖ if he easily pardons and remits

* *Difficileness, i. e.* stubbornness.

† Timon of Athens, a typical misanthrope.

‡ Timber used in ship-building; so called because of its angular shape.

§ " Wealth may be courted, wisdom be revered,
    And beauty praised, and brutal strength be feared;
    But goodness only can affection move."
                                                — *Mrs. Barbauld.*

‖ This is the nature of gratitude and true thankfulness; for time, which knaws and diminisheth all things else, augments and increases benefits, because a noble action of liberality done to a man of reason doth grow continually by his generous thinking of it and remembering it." — *Rabelais, Bk. I., ch. L.*

offenses, it shows that his mind is planted above injuries, so that he cannot be shot: if he be thankful for small benefits, it shows that he weighs men's minds, and not their trash: but, above all, if he have St. Paul's perfection, that he would wish to be an anathema from Christ for the salvation of his brethren, it shows much of a divine nature, and a kind of conformity with Christ himself.

OF ATHEISM.

I had rather believe all the fables in the Legend,* and the Talmud,† and the Alcoran, than that this universal frame is without a mind; and, therefore, God never wrought miracles to convince atheism, because His ordinary works convince it. It is true, that a little philosophy inclineth man's mind to atheism, but depth in philosophy bringeth men's minds about to religion; for while the mind of man looketh upon second causes scattered, it may sometimes rest in them, and go no further; but when it beholdeth the chain of them confederate, and linked together, it must needs fly to Providence and Deity: nay, even that school which is most accused of atheism doth most demonstrate religion; that is the school of Leucippus,‡ and Democritus, and Epicurus, for it is a thousand times more credible that four mutable elements, and one immutable fifth essence, duly and eternally placed, need no God, than that an army of infinite small portions, or seeds unplaced, should have produced this order or beauty without a divine marshal. The Scripture saith, "The fool hath said in his heart, there

* A collection of miraculous stories.

† A book composed of Jewish traditions and Rabbinical commentaries.

‡ Leucippus, a philosopher of Abdera, author of the atomic theory, which was adopted and taught by his disciples, Democritus and Epicurus.

is no God ; " it is not said, " The fool hath thought in his heart ; " so as he rather saith it by rote to himself, as that he would have, than that he can thoroughly believe it, or be persuaded of it ; for none deny there is a God, but those for whom it maketh * that there were no God.   It appeareth

* *Maketh*, *i. e.* it is profitable; *e. g.* a popular lecturer who receives so much a night for saying with his tongue, " There is no God," who, like Shelley, " robs the wretched of a hope which, even if false, is worth all this world's best truths."

" For myself," says Byron, " I would not give up the poetry of religion for all the wisest results that philosophy has ever arrived at." — *Moore's " Life of Byron," Vol. II., 412.*

" A sceptike in religion is one that hangs in the balance with all sorts of opinions, whereof not one but stirres him and none swayes him, — a man guiltier of credulity than he is taken to bee, for it is out of his beleefe of everything that hee fully beleeves nothing. Hee would be wholy a Christian but that he is something of an atheist, and wholy an atheist but that he is partly a Christian ; and a perfect heretic, but that there are so many to distract him. He finds reason in all opinions, truth in none ; indeed, the least reason perplexes him and the best will not satisfy him. His learning is too much for his brayne, and his judgment too little for his learning, and his own opinion of both spoyls all. He cannot think so many wise men should be in error, nor so many honest men out of the way, and his wonder is doubled when he sees these oppose one another. His whole life is a question, and his salvation a greater, which death only concludes, and then he is resolved." — *John Earle's " Micro-Cosmographic."*

" There is more faith in honest doubt,
Believe me, than in half the creeds."
— *Tennyson.*

The fact that we have reason and apply it to the examination of our world and ourselves, and reach certain results which we call conclusive, makes us turn this mental microscope upon infinity of time, space, power, mercy, justice and wisdom ; and because we, by unassisted reason, cannot reach certain results, we deny the possibility of conclusions.

in nothing more, that atheism is rather in the lip than in the heart of man, than by this, that atheists will ever be talking of that their opinion, as if they fainted in it within themselves, and would be glad to be strengthened by the consent of others : nay more, you shall have atheists strive to get disciples, as it fareth with other sects; and, which is most of all, you shall have of them that will suffer for atheism, and not recant; whereas, if they did truly think that there were no such thing as God, why should they trouble themselves ?   Epicurus is charged, that he did but dissemble for his credit's sake, when he affirmed there were blessed natures, but such as enjoyed themselves without having respect to the government of the world; wherein they say he did temporize, though in secret he thought there was no God : but certainly he is traduced, for his words are noble and divine : *"Non Deos vulgi negare profanum; sed vulgi opiniones Diis applicare profanum."* *   Plato could have said no more; and, although he had the confidence to deny the administration, he had not the power to deny the nature. The Indians of the West have names for their particular gods, though they have no name for God : as if the heathens

> " Dim as the beam of moon and stars,
>   To lonely, weary travellers, is reason
>   To the soul."
>
> — *Dryden's Religio-Laici.*

But reason, which is like a proud, unbridled steed, roaming through every field, constantly demands for faith similar proofs that it demands for physical phenomena; hence doubt follows faith as one's shadow follows,

> "And like the shadow, proves the substance true."

For the exclamation of the father in St. Mark is ever on the honest lips of the sincere believer who cannot see with his understanding into the mystery of Creator, creation, death and the life to come, and so exclaims: "I believe; help thou my unbelief."

* "It is not profane to deny the gods of the multitude; but to apply to the gods the opinions of the multitude is profane."

should have had the names Jupiter, Apollo, Mars, etc., but not the word *Deus*, which shows that even those barbarous people have the notion, though they have not the latitude and extent of it : so that against atheists the very savages take part with the very subtilest philosophers. The contemplative atheist is rare, a Diagoras, a Bion, a Lucian perhaps, and some others ; and yet they seem to be more than they are ; for that all that impugn a received religion, or superstition, are, by the adverse part, branded with the name of atheists : but the great atheists indeed are hypocrites, which are ever handling holy things, but without feeling ; so as they must needs be cauterized in the end.

The causes of atheism are, divisions in religion, if there be many ; for any one main division addeth zeal to both sides, but many divisions introduce atheism : another is, scandal of priests, when it is come to that which St. Bernard saith, "*Non est Jam dicere, ut populus, sic sacerdos ; quia nec sic populus, ut sacerdos :*"* a third is, custom of profane scoffing in holy matters, which doth by little and little deface the reverence of religion ; and, lastly, learned times, especially with peace and prosperity ; for troubles and adversities do more bow men's minds to religion. They that deny a God destroy man's nobility ; for certainly man is of kin to the beasts by his body ; and, if he be not of kin to God by his spirit, he is a base and ignoble creature. It destroys likewise magnanimity, and the raising of human nature ; for take an example of a dog, and mark what a generosity and courage he will put on when he finds himself maintained by man, who to him is instead of a God, or "*melior natura;*" † which courage is manifestly such as that creature, without that confidence of a better nature than his own, could never attain. So man, when he resteth and assureth himself upon divine protection and favour, gathereth a force and faith,

---

* "It cannot now be said 'Like priest, like people,' because the people are not like the priest."
† Superior nature.

which human nature in itself could not obtain; therefore, as atheism is in all respects hateful, so in this, that it depriveth human nature of the means to exalt itself above human frailty. * As it is in particular persons, so it is in nations: never was there such a State for magnanimity as Rome; of this State hear what Cicero saith, "*Quam volumus, licet, Patres conscripti, nos amemus, tamen nec numero Hispanos, nec robore Gallos, nec calliditate Pœnos, nec artibus Grœcos, nec denique hoc ipso hujus gentis et terræ domestico nativoque sensu Italos ipso et Latinos; sed pietate, ac religione, atque hac una sapientia, quod Deorum immortalium numine omnia regi, gubernarique perspeximus omnes, gentes nationesque superavimus.*" †

OF SUPERSTITION.

It were better to have no opinion of God at all, than such an opinion as is unworthy of Him; for the one is unbelief, the other is contumely: and certainly superstition is the reproach of the Deity. Plutarch saith well to that purpose: "Surely," said he, "I had rather a great deal men should say there was no such man at all as Plutarch, than that they should say that there was one Plutarch that would eat his children as soon as they were born; " as the poets speak of Saturn: and, as the contumely is greater towards God, so

* "If it is a dream let me enjoy it, since it makes me both a happier and a better man." — *Addison, Spectator, No. 186.*

† Let us be ever so self-complacent, conscript fathers, still we have not surpassed the Spaniards in number, nor the Gauls in strength, nor the Carthagenians in cunning, nor, finally, the Latins and Italians of this nation and land in natural intelligence about home affairs; but we have excelled all nations and people in piety and religion, and this one wisdom of fully recognizing that all things are ordered and governed by the power of the immortal gods.

the danger is greater towards men. Atheism leaves a man to sense, to philosophy, to natural piety, * to laws, to reputation: all which may be guides to an outward moral virtue, though religion were not; but superstition dismounts all these, and erecteth an absolute monarchy in the minds of men: † therefore atheism did never perturb States; for it makes men wary of themselves, as looking no further, and we see the times inclined to atheism (as the time of Augustus Cæsar) were civil times : ‡ but superstition hath been the confusion of many States, and bringeth in a new "*primum mobile*," § that ravisheth all the spheres of government. The master of superstition is the people, and in all superstition wise men follow fools; and arguments are fitted to practice, in a reversed order. It was gravely said, by some of the prelates in the Council of Trent, where the doctrine of the schoolmen bare great sway, that the schoolmen were like astronomers, which did feign eccentrics and epicycles, and such engines of orbs to save the phenomena, though they knew there were no such things ; and, in like manner, that the schoolmen had framed a number of subtile and intricate axioms and theorems, to save the practice of the church.

The causes of superstition are, pleasing and sensual rites and ceremonies; excess of outward and pharisaical holiness; over-great reverence of traditions, which cannot but load the church; the stratagems of prelates for their own ambition and lucre; the favouring too much of good intentions, which openeth the gate to conceits and novelties; the tak-

* *Natural piety, i. e.* morality.

† "Sickness and sorrow come and go, but a superstitious soul hath no rest." — *Burton, "Anatomy of Melancholy."*

‡ The profligacy of luxury and the preponderance of atheism were then sapping the foundations of Roman virtue, valour and power. So the spirit of unbelief reigned as twin demon with that of the murder of the innocents, which stamped the French Revolution as a godless revolution.

§ The central body attracting all others.

H

ing an aim at divine matters by human, which cannot but breed mixture of imaginations: and, lastly, barbarous times, especially joined with calamities and disasters. Superstition, without a veil, is a deformed thing; for as it addeth deformity to an ape to be so like a man, so the similitude of superstition to religion makes it the more deformed: and, as wholesome meat corrupteth to little worms, so good forms and orders corrupt into a number of petty observances. There is a superstition in avoiding superstition, when men think to do best if they go farthest from the superstition formerly received; therefore care would * be had that (as it fareth in ill purgings) the good not be taken away with the bad, which commonly is done when the people is the reformer.

OF TRAVEL.

Travel, in the younger sort, is a part of education; in the elder, a part of experience. He that travelleth into a country, before he hath some entrance into the language, goeth to school, and not to travel. That young men travel under some tutor, or grave servant, I allow † well; so that he be such a one that hath the language, and hath been in the country before; whereby he may be able to tell them what things are worthy to be seen in the country where they go, what acquaintances they are to seek, what exercises or discipline the place yieldeth; for else young men shall go hooded, and look abroad little. It is a strange thing that, in sea voyages, where there is nothing to be seen but sky and sea, men should make diaries; but in land-travel, wherein so much is to be observed, for the most part they omit it; as if chance were fitter to be registered than observation: let diaries, therefore, be brought in use. The

* *Would* is used here for *should.*
† *Allow, i. e.* approve.

things to be seen and observed are, the courts of princes, especially when they give audience to ambassadors; the courts of justice, while they sit and hear causes; and so of consistories ecclesiastic; the churches and monasteries, with the monuments which are therein extant; the walls and fortifications of cities and towns; and so the havens and harbours, antiquities and ruins, libraries, colleges, disputations, and lectures, where any are; shipping and navies; houses and gardens of state and pleasure, near great cities: armories, arsenals, magazines, exchanges, bourses, * warehouses, exercises of horsemanship, fencing, training of soldiers, and the like: comedies, such whereunto the better sort of persons do resort; treasuries of jewelries and robes; cabinets and rarities; and, to conclude, whatsoever is memorable in the places where they go: after all which the tutors or servants ought to make diligent inquiry. As for triumphs, † masques, feasts, weddings, funerals, capital executions, and such shows, men need not be put in mind of them: yet they are not to be neglected. If you will have a young man to put his travels into a little room, and in short time to gather much, this you must do; first, as was said, he must have some entrance into the language before he goeth; then he must have such a servant, or tutor, as knoweth the country, as was likewise said: let him carry with him also some card, or book, describing the country where he travelleth, which will be a good key to his inquiry; let him keep also a diary; let him not stay long in one city or town, more or less as the place deserveth, but not long; nay, when he stayeth in one city or town, let him change his lodging from one end and part of the town to another, which is a great adamant ‡ of acquaintance; let him sequester himself from the company of his countrymen, and diet in such places where there

---

* *Bourses.* French word *bourse* means purse, and this was sign of the merchants' place of meeting for their money dealings.

† *Triumphs, i. e.* shows of a public character.

‡ *Adamant, i. e.* loadstone.

is good company of the nation where he travelleth : let him, upon his removes from one place to another, procure recommendation to some person of quality residing in the place whither he removeth, that he may use his favour in those things he desireth to see or know; thus he may abridge his travel with much profit.

As for the acquaintance which is to be sought in travel, that which is most of all profitable, is acquaintance with the secretaries and employed men of ambassadors: for so in travelling in one country he shall suck the experience of many : let him also see and visit eminent persons in all kinds, which are of great name abroad, that he may be able to tell how the life agreeth with the fame ; for quarrels, they are with care and discretion to be avoided; they are commonly for mistresses, healths, * place, and words ; and let a man beware how he keepeth company with choleric and quarrelsome persons, for they will engage him into their own quarrels. When a traveller returneth home, let him not leave the countries where he hath travelled altogether behind him; but maintain a correspondence by letters with those of his acquaintance which are of most worth ; and let his travel appear rather in his discourse than in his apparel or gesture ; † and in his discourse let him be rather advised ‡ in his answers than forward to tell stories : and let it appear that he doth not change his country manners for those of foreign parts; but only prick in some flowers of that he hath learned abroad into the customs of his own country.

* Healths of absent lady-loves were commonly proposed, also of friend, patron, king or country; a refusal to pledge in wine was considered and treated as an insult when men wore, and were so ready with, their swords.

† Sir Richard Steele says that "a general trader (*i. e.* merchant who travels) of good sense is pleasanter company than a general scholar."

‡ *Advised.* Circumspect.

OF WISDOM FOR A MAN'S SELF.

An ant is a wise creature for itself, but it is a shrewd *
thing in an orchard or garden; and certainly men that are
great lovers of themselves waste the public. Divide with
reason between self-love and society; and be so true to thyself, as thou be not false to others, † specially to thy king
and country. It is a poor center of a man's actions, himself.
It is right earth; for that only stands fast upon his own
center; ‡ whereas all things that have affinity with the
heavens, move upon the center of another, which they benefit. The referring of all to a man's self, is more tolerable
in a sovereign prince, because themselves are not only
themselves, but their good and evil is at the peril of the
public fortune : but it is a desperate evil in a servant to a
prince, or a citizen in a republic; § for whatsoever affairs
pass such a man's hands, he crooketh them to his own
ends, which must needs be often eccentric, to the ends of
his master or State: therefore let princes, or States, choose
such servants as have not this mark; except they mean their
service should be made but the accessary. That which
maketh the effect more pernicious is, that all proportion is
lost; it were disproportion enough for the servant's good
to be preferred before the master's; but yet it is a greater
extreme, when a little good of the servant shall carry things

* *Shrewd, i. e.* mischievous.

† This suggests a line in the address of Polonius to Laertes.
Hamlet, act i., sc. 3.
In the "Advancement of Learning" Bacon says : " The sum of
behavior is to retain a man's own dignity without intruding on the
dignity of others."

‡ Bacon did not accept the Copernician system, for which he
has been much maligned by moderns.

§ Bacon describes such men elsewhere as "never caring, in all
tempests, what becomes of the ship of State so they save themselves in the cock-boat of their own fortune."

against a great good of the master's: and yet that is the
case of bad officers, treasurers, ambassadors, generals, and
other false and corrupt servants; which set a bias upon
their bowl, of their own petty ends and envies, to the overthrow of their master's great and important affairs: and,
for the most part, the good such servants receive is after
the model of their own fortune; but the hurt they sell for
that good is after the model of their master's fortune: and
certainly it is the nature of extreme self-lovers, as they will
set a house on fire, an * it were but to roast their eggs; and
yet these men many times hold credit with their masters,
because their study is but to please them, and profit themselves; and for either respect they will abandon the good of
their affairs.

Wisdom for a man's self is, in many branches thereof, a
depraved thing: it is the wisdom of rats, that will be sure
to leave a house somewhat before it fall: it is the wisdom
of the fox, that thrusts out the badger, who digged and made
room for him: it is the wisdom of crocodiles, that shed tears
when they would devour. But that which is specially to be
noted is, that those which (as Cicero says of Pompey) are,
"*sui amantes, sine rivali,*" † are many times unfortunate;
and whereas they have all their time sacrificed to themselves,
they become in the end themselves sacrifices to the incon-
stancy of fortune, whose wings they thought by their self-
wisdom to have pinioned.

OF INNOVATIONS.

As the births of living creatures at first are ill-shapen, so
are all innovations, which are the births of time; yet notwithstanding, as those that first bring honour into their

* *An, i. e.* if.
† Lovers of themselves, without a rival.

family are commonly more worthy than most that succeed,
so the first precedent (if it be good) is seldom attained by
imitation; for ill to man's nature as it stands perverted,
hath a natural motion strongest in continuance; but good,
as a forced motion, strongest at first. Surely every medicine * is an innovation, and he that will not apply new
remedies must expect new evils; for time is the greatest
innovator; and if time of course alter things to the worse,
and wisdom and counsel shall not alter them to the better,
what shall be the end? It is true, that what is settled by
custom, though it be not good, yet at least it is fit; and
those things which have long gone together, are, as it were,
confederate within themselves; whereas new things piece
not so well; but, though they help by their utility, yet they
trouble by their inconformity: besides, they are like strangers, more admired, and less favoured. All this is true, if
time stood still; which, contrariwise, moveth so round, that
a froward retention of custom is as turbulent a thing as an
innovation; and they that reverence too much old times, are
but a scorn to the new. It were good, therefore, that men
in their innovations, would follow the example of time itself,
which indeed innovateth greatly, but quietly, and by degrees
scarce to be perceived; † for otherwise, whatsoever is new
is unlooked for; and ever it mends some, and pairs ‡ other;
and he that is holpen § takes it for a fortune, and thanks the
time; and he that is hurt, for a wrong, and imputeth it to
the author. It is good also not to try experiments in States,
except the necessity be urgent, or the utility evident; and
well to beware that it be the reformation that draweth on
the change, and not the desire of change that pretendeth

* *Medicine, i. e.* remedy.

† Elsewhere Bacon lays down this rule for reformers: "Let a
living spring flow into the stagnant waters."

‡ *Pairs, i. e.* harms.

§ *Holpen, i. e.* old preterite of *help.*

the reformation ; * and lastly, that the novelty, though it be
not rejected, yet be held for a suspect; † and, as the Scripture saith, "That we make a stand upon the ancient way,
and then look about us, and discover what is the straight
and right way, and so to walk in it."

OF SEEMING WISE.

It hath been an opinion, that the French are wiser
than they seem, and the Spaniards seem wiser than they
are ; but, howsoever it be between nations, certainly it is so
between man and man ; for as the apostle saith of godliness, "Having a show of godliness, but denying the power
thereof ;" so certainly there are in points of wisdom and
sufficiency, that do nothing or little very solemnly : "*magno
conatu nugas.*" ‡   It is a ridiculous thing, and fit for a satire

---

* "New interests beget new maxims of government and new
methods of conduct.   These, in their turn, beget new manners,
new habits, new customs." — *Bolingbroke*, "*Study of History*,"
Letter VI.

It is only when new interests become general that old laws,
which interfere with their enjoyment, should be repealed, or new
laws, which may better secure their enjoyment and development,
should be enacted.   A people can suffer no greater curse than a
meddling legislature, which leads instead of following public
opinion.   Every good law is moulded in the hearts of the people
by their wants and necessities before it is ready to be embodied
into a statute.   It is a response to their requirements when
passed.   The theorist who thinks he can make a people of average intelligence happier by the enactment of laws which they
have not in some way acknowledged the need of, is a reformer
who threatens more harm than war or pestilence.

† *Suspect, i. e.* suspicion.

‡ *Achieve nothing with great labor, i. e.* the mountains labor and
give birth to an insignificant mouse.

to persons of judgment, to see what shifts these formalists
have, and what prospectives * to make superficies to seem
body that hath depth and bulk. Some are so close and
reserved, as they will not show their wares but by a dark
light, and seem always to keep back somewhat; and when
they know within themselves they speak of that they do not
well know, would nevertheless seem to others to know of
that which they may not well speak. † Some help themselves with countenance and gesture, and are wise by signs;
as Cicero saith of Piso, that when he answered him he
fetched one of his brows up to his forehead, and bent the
other down to his chin; "*Respondes, altero ad frontem sub-
lato, altero ad mentum depresso supercilio, crudelitatem
tibi non placere.*" ‡ Some think to bear it by speaking a
great word, and being peremptory; and go on, and take by
admittance that which they cannot make good. Some,
whatsoever is beyond their reach, will seem to despise, or
make light of it as impertinent or curious : § and so would
have their ignorance seem judgment. Some are never without a difference, ‖ and commonly by amusing men with a
subtilty, blanch ¶ the matter; of whom A. Gellius saith,
"*Hominem delirum, qui verborum, minutiis rerum frangit*

* *Prospective, i. e.* perspective glass, which presented an object
in a false light.

† "Mystery, the wisdom of blockheads, may be allowed in a
foreign minister."—*Horace Walpole, Correspondence. 2d Series,
IV.*

A French philosopher says: "Gravity is a mysterious carriage
of the body to cover the defects of the mind."—*Rochefoucauld's
Maxims.*

‡ "With one brow raised to your forehead, the other bent toward your chin, you reply that cruelty does not delight you."

§ *Impertinent, i. e.* irrelevant. *Curious, i. e.* over-nice.

‖ *Difference, i. e.* fine distinction.

¶ *Blanch, i. e.* elude.

pondera." * Of which kind also Plato, in his *Protagoras*, bringeth in Prodicus in scorn, and maketh him make a speech that consisteth of distinctions from the beginning to the end. Generally such men, in all deliberations, find ease to be of the negative side, and affect a credit to object and foretell difficulties; for when propositions are denied, there is an end of them; but if they be allowed, it requireth a new work; which false point of wisdom is the bane of business. To conclude, there is no decaying merchant, or inward beggar, hath so many tricks to uphold the credit of their wealth, as these empty persons have to maintain the credit of their sufficiency. Seeming wise men may make shift to get opinion; but let no man choose them for employment; for certainly, you were better take for business a man somewhat absurd than over-formal.

OF FRIENDSHIP.

It had been hard for him that spake it to have put more truth and untruth together in few words than in that speech, " Whosoever is delighted in solitude, is either a wild beast or a god : " † for it is most true, that a natural and secret hatred and aversation towards ‡ society, in any man, hath somewhat of the savage beast; but it is most untrue, that it should have any character at all of the divine nature, except it proceed, not out of a pleasure in solitude, but out of a love and desire to sequester a man's self for a higher conversation: such as is found to have been falsely and

---

* A foolish man who fritters away matters of importance by silly words, *i. e.* a trifler.

"It is better to be doing nothing than be doing of nothing," says an old philosopher.

† Aristotle.

"He who loves not others lives unblest."— *Home's " Douglas."*

‡ *Aversation, i. e.* aversion.

feignedly in some of the heathen; as Epimenides, the
Candian; Numa, the Roman; Empedocles, the Sicilian;
and Apollonius of Tyana; and truly and really in divers of
the ancient hermits and holy fathers of the church. But
little do men perceive what solitude is, and how far it
extendeth; for a crowd is not company, and faces are but
a gallery of pictures, and talk but a tinkling cymbal where
there is no love. The Latin adage meeteth with it a little:
"*Magna civitas, magna solitudo;*" * because in a great town
friends are scattered, so that there is not that fellowship,
for the most part, which is in less neighbourhoods: but we
may go farther, and affirm most truly, that it is a mere † and
miserable solitude to want true friends, without which the
world is but a wilderness; and even in this sense also of
solitude, whosoever in the frame of his nature and affections
is unfit for friendship, he taketh it of the beast, and not
from humanity.

A principal fruit of friendship is the ease and discharge
of the fullness and swellings of the heart, which passions of
all kinds do cause and induce. We know diseases of stop-
pings and suffocations are the most dangerous in the body;
and it is not much otherwise in the mind; you may take
sarza ‡ to open the liver, steel to open the spleen, flower of
sulphur for the lungs, castoreum for the brain; but no
receipt openeth the heart but a true friend, to whom you
may impart griefs, joys, fears, hopes, suspicions, counsels,
and whatsoever lieth upon the heart to oppress it, in a kind
of civil shrift or confession.

---

* "A great city is a great desert."

† *Mere, i. e.* utter.

"Life without a friend is death without a witness," says a
Spanish proverb; and in "Gray's Elegy" is a parallel thought, or
the proverb paraphrased:—

> "On some fond breast the parting soul relies,
> Some pious drops the closing eye requires."

‡ *Sarza, i. e.* sarsaparilla.

It is a strange thing to observe how high a rate great kings and monarchs do set upon this fruit of friendship whereof we speak: so great, as they purchase it many times at the hazard of their own safety and greatness: for princes, in regard of the distance of their fortune from that of their subjects and servants, cannot gather this fruit, except (to make themselves capable thereof) they raise some persons to be as it were companions, and almost equals to themselves, which many times sorteth to inconvenience. The modern languages give unto such persons the name of favourites, or privadoes, as if it were matter of grace, or conversation; but the Roman name attaineth the true use and cause thereof, naming them "*participes curarum;*" * for it is that which tieth the knot: and we see plainly that this hath been done, not by weak and passionate princes only, but by the wisest and most politic that ever reigned, who have oftentimes joined to themselves some of their servants, whom both themselves have called friends, and allowed others likewise to call them in the same manner, using the word which is received between private men.

L. Sulla, when he commanded Rome, raised Pompey (after surnamed The Great) to that height, that Pompey vaunted himself for Sulla's overmatch; for when he had carried the Consulship for a friend of his, against the pursuit of Sulla, and that Sulla did a little resent thereat, and began to speak great, Pompey turned upon him again, and in effect bade him be quiet; for that more men adored the sun rising than the sun setting. With Julius Cæsar, Decimus Brutus had obtained that interest, as he set him down in his testament for heir in remainder after his nephew; and this was the man that had power with him to draw him forth to his death: for when Cæsar would have discharged the Senate, in regard of some ill presages, and specially a dream of Calphurnia, this man lifted him gently by the arm out of his chair, telling him he hoped he would not dismiss

* Partners of our sorrows.

the Senate till his wife had dreamt a better dream; and it seemed his favour was so great, as Antonius, in a letter which is recited verbatim in one of Cicero's *Philippics*, calleth him "*vernifica*," "witch;" as if he had enchanted Cæsar. Augustus raised Agrippa, (though of mean birth,) to that height, as, when he consulted with Macænas about the marriage of his daughter Julia, Macænas took the liberty to tell him, that he must either marry his daughter to Agrippa, or take away his life: there was no third way, he had made him so great. With Tiberius Cæsar, Sejanus had ascended to that height as they two were termed and reckoned as a pair of friends. Tiberius, in a letter to him, saith, "*Hæc pro amicitia nostra non occultavi;*"* and the whole Senate dedicated an altar to friendship, as to a goddess, in respect of the great dearness of friendship between them two. The like, or more, was between Septimius Severus and Plautianus; for he forced his eldest son to marry the daughter of Plautianus, and would often maintain Plautianus in doing affronts to his son; and did write also, in a letter to the Senate, by these words: " I love the man so well, as I wish he may over-live me." Now, if these princes had been as a Trajan, or a Marcus Aurelius, a man might have thought that this had proceeded of an abundant goodness of nature; but being men so wise, of such strength and severity of mind, and so extreme lovers of themselves, as all these were, it proveth most plainly, that they found their own felicity, (though as great as ever happened to mortal men,) but as an half-piece, except they might have a friend to make it entire; and yet, which is more, they were princes that had wives, sons, nephews; yet all these could not supply the comfort of friendship.

It is not to be forgotten what Comineus observeth of his first master, Duke Charles the Hardy, namely, that he would communicate his secrets with none; and least of all,

---

* "Because of our friendship I have not concealed these things."

those secrets which troubled him most. Whereupon he
goeth on, and saith that towards his latter time that closeness did impair and a little perish his understanding.
Surely Comineus might have made the same judgment also,
if it had pleased him, of his second master, Louis the
Eleventh, whose closeness was indeed his tormentor.   The
parable of Pythagoras is dark, but true, " *Cor ne edito*," " Eat
not the heart." Certainly, if a man would give it a hard
phrase, those that want friends to open themselves unto are
cannibals of their own hearts: but one thing is most admirable (wherewith I will conclude this first fruit of friendship),
which is, that this communicating of a man's self to his
friend works two contrary effects, for it redoubleth joys,
and cutteth grief in halves; for there is no man that
imparteth his joys to his friend, but he joyeth the more:
and no man that imparteth his griefs to his friend, but he
grieveth the less.   So that it is, in truth, of e; 'ration upon
a man's mind of like virtue as the alchymists used to attribute to their stone for man's body, that it worketh all contrary effects, but still to the good and benefit of nature:
but yet, without praying in aid of alchymists, there is a
manifest image of this in the ordinary course of nature;
for, in bodies, union strengtheneth and cherisheth any natural action; and, on the other side, weakeneth and dulleth
any violent impression ; and even so it is of minds.

   The second fruit of friendship is healthful and sovereign
for the understanding, as the first is for the affections; for
friendship maketh indeed a fair day in the affections from
storm and tempests, but it maketh daylight in the understanding, out of darkness and confusion of thoughts:
neither is this to be understood only of faithful counsel,
which a man receiveth from his friend; but before you
come to that, certain it is, that whosoever has his mind
fraught with many thoughts, his wits and understanding do
clarify and break up, in the communicating and discoursing
with another; he tosseth his thoughts more easily; he mar-

shalleth them more orderly; he seeth how they look when they are turned into words: finally, he waxeth wiser than himself; and that more by an hour's discourse than by a day's meditation. It was well said by Themistocles to the King of Persia, "That speech was like cloth of arras, opened and put abroad; whereby the imagery doth appear in figure; whereas in thoughts they lie but as in packs." Neither is this second fruit of friendship, in opening the understanding, restrained only to such friends as are able to give a man counsel, (they indeed are best,) but even without that a man learneth of himself, and bringeth his own thoughts to light, and whetteth his wits as against a stone, which itself cuts not. In a word, a man were better relate himself to a statue or picture, than to suffer his thoughts to pass in smother.

Add now, to make this second fruit of friendship complete, that other point which lieth more open, and falleth within vulgar* observation: which is faithful counsel † from a friend. Heraclitus saith well in one of his enigmas, "Dry light is ever the best;" and certain it is, that the light that a man receiveth by counsel from another, is drier and purer than that which cometh from his own understanding and judgment; which is ever infused and drenched in his affections and customs. So as there is as much difference between the counsel that a friend giveth, and that a man

---

* *Vulgar, i. e.* common.

† Offering advice is the most delicate office of friendship. Counsel is not always sincerely sought; and too often, men in the act of asking advice are seeking only approval of, or agreement with, either the conclusions of their own judgments or the wishes of their own hearts. Pope, who took an unfavorable view of human nature, prescribes this rule for the adviser: —

> "'Tis not enough your counsel shall be true, —
> Blunt truths more mischief than nice falsehoods do;
> Men must be taught as tho' you taught them not,
> And things unknown proposed as things forgot."
> —"*Essay on Criticism.*"

giveth himself, as there is between the counsel of a friend
and of a flatterer; for there is no such flatterer as is a man's
self, and there is no such remedy against flattery of a man's
self as the liberty of a friend. Counsel is of two sorts; the
one concerning manners, the other concerning business:
for the first, the best preservative to keep the mind in
health is the faithful admonition of a friend. The calling
of a man's self to a strict account is a medicine sometimes
too piercing and corrosive; reading good books of morality
is a little flat and dead; observing our faults in others is
sometimes improper for our case; but the best receipt (best,
I say, to work and best to take) is the admonition of a friend.
It is a strange thing to behold what gross errors and extreme
absurdities many (especially of the greater sort) do commit
for want of a friend to tell them of them, to the great damage
both of their fame and fortune: for, as St. James saith, they
are as men " that look sometimes into a glass, and presently
forget their own shape and favour: " as for business, a man
may think, if he will, that two eyes see no more than one ;
or, that a gamester seeth always more than a looker-on ; or,
that a man in anger is as wise as he that hath said over the
four-and-twenty letters; or, that a musket may be shot off
as well upon the arm as upon a rest; and such other fond *
and high imaginations, to think himself all in all: but when
all is done, the help of good counsel is that which setteth
business straight; and if any man think that he will take
counsel, but it shall be by pieces; asking counsel in one
business of one man, and in another business of another
man; it is well, (that is to say, better, perhaps, than if he
asked none at all,) but he runneth two dangers; one, that
he shall not be faithfully counselled; for it is a rare thing,
except it be from a perfect and entire friend, to have counsel given, but such as shall be bowed and crooked to some
ends which he hath that giveth it: the other, that he shall
have counsel given, hurtful and unsafe, (though with good

* *Fond, i. e.* foolish.

meaning,) and mixed partly of mischief, and partly of remedy; even as if you would call a physician, that is thought good for the cure of the disease you complain of, but is unacquainted with your body; and, therefore may put you in a way for a present cure, but overthroweth your health in some other kind, and so cure the disease, and kill the patient: but a friend, that is wholly acquainted with a man's estate, will beware, by furthering any present business, how he dasheth upon other inconvenience; and, therefore, rest not upon scattered counsels; they will rather distract and mislead, than settle and direct.

After these two noble fruits of friendship, (peace in the affections, and support of the judgment,) followeth the last fruit, which is, like the pomegranate, full of many kernels; I mean, aid and bearing a part in all actions and occasions. Here the best way to represent to life the manifold use of friendship, is to cast and see how many things there are which a man cannot do himself; and then it will appear that it was a sparing speech of the ancients, to say, "that a friend is another himself; for that a friend is far more than himself." Men have their time, and die many times in desire of some things which they principally take to heart; the bestowing of a child, the finishing of a work, or the like. If a man have a true friend, he may rest almost secure that the care of those things will continue after him; so that a man hath, as it were, two lives in his desires. A man hath a body, and that body is confined to a place; but where friendship is, all offices of life are, as it were, granted to him and his deputy; for he may exercise them by his friend. How many things are there which a man cannot with any face, or comeliness, say or do himself? A man can scarce allege his own merits with modesty, much less extol them:* a man cannot sometimes brook to supplicate, or beg, and a number of the like: but all these things are graceful

---

* "It is an abominable thing for a man to commend himself."— *John Beal, "Divine Art of Meditations." A. D. 1610*

in a friend's mouth, which are blushing in a man's own.
So again, a man's person hath many proper relations which
he cannot put off.   A man cannot speak to his son but as a
father; to his wife but as a husband; to his enemy but
upon terms: whereas a friend may speak as the case
requires, and not as it sorteth with the person: but to
enumerate these things were endless; I have given the
rule, where a man cannot fitly play his own part, if he have
not a friend, he may quit the stage. *

OF EXPENSE.

Riches are for spending, and spending for honour and
good actions; † therefore extraordinary expense must be
limited by the worth of the occasion; for voluntary undoing
may be as well for a man's country as for the kingdom of
Heaven; but ordinary expense ought to be limited by a
man's estate, and governed with such regard, as it be within
his compass; and not subject to deceit and abuse of servants; and ordered to the best show, that the bills may be
less than the estimation abroad.   Certainly, if a man will
keep but of even hand, ‡ his ordinary expenses ought to be

* "It must be confessed that a pretended affection is not easily
discernible from a real one, unless in seasons of distress. *For
adversity is to friendship what fire is to gold, the only infallible test
to discover the genuine from the counterfeit.*" — *Cicero, Epistles.*

† "Money is power, cash is virtue," says Byron, and it would
seem, from the struggle of men for wealth as for the greatest
good, that the sneer has more truth than poetry in it.   Bacon
defines the uses of riches in the hands of a man who has gotten
wealth honestly, — who loves it not for itself, whose heart is not
hardened by success, who recognizes every gift, whether material
or mental, not entirely as his own, but as shared by his God and
his fellow-man, — a talent not to be buried away from the latter,
and to be accounted for to the former.

‡ *Keep of even hand, i. e.* be prudent, not extravagant.

but to the half of his receipts; and if he think to wax rich,
but to the third part. It is no baseness for the greatest to
descend and look into their own estate. Some forbear it,
not upon negligence alone, but doubting * to bring themselves into melancholy, in respect they shall find it broken:
but wounds cannot be cured without searching. He that
cannot look into his own estate at all, had need both choose
well those whom he employeth, and change them often; for
new are more timorous and less subtle. He that can look
into his estate but seldom, it behooveth him to turn all to
certainties. A man had need, if he be plentiful in some
kind of expense, to be as saving again in some other; as †
if he be plentiful in diet, to be saving in apparel: if he be
plentiful in the hall, to be saving in the stable, and the like;
for he that is plentiful in expenses of all kinds will hardly
be preserved from decay. In clearing of a man's estate, he
may as well hurt himself in being too sudden, as in letting
it run on too long; for hasty selling is commonly as dis-
advantageable as interest. Besides, he that clears at once
will relapse; for finding himself out of straits, he will
revert to his customs: but he that cleareth by degrees
induceth a habit of frugality, and gaineth as well upon his
mind as upon his estate. Certainly, who hath a state to
repair, may not despise small things; and, commonly, it is
less dishonourable to abridge petty charges than to stoop to
petty gettings. A man ought warily to begin charges, which
once begun will continue: but in matters that return not, he
may be more magnificent.

* *Doubting*, *i. e.* fearing.
† Thackeray illustrates this rule of prudence in detailing how
Pendennis ruined himself at Oxford by breaking it.

OF SUSPICION.

Suspicions amongst thoughts are like bats amongst birds,
—they ever fly by twilight: certainly they are to be
repressed, or at the least well guarded; for they cloud the
mind, they lose friends, and they check* with business,
whereby business cannot go on currently and constantly:
they dispose kings to tyranny, husbands to jealousy, wise
men to irresolution and melancholy: they are defects, not in
the heart, but in the brain; for they take place in the stoutest
natures, as in the example of Henry the Seventh of England; there was not a more suspicious man nor a more
stout:† and in such a composition they do small hurt; for
commonly they are not admitted, but with examination,
whether they be likely or no? but in fearful natures they
gain ground too fast. There is nothing makes a man suspect much, more than to know little; and, therefore, men
should remedy suspicion by procuring to know more, and
not to keep their suspicions in smother. What would men
have? do they think those they employ and deal with are
saints? do they not think they will have their own ends,
and be truer to themselves than to them? Therefore there
is no better way to moderate suspicions, than to account
upon such suspicions as true, and yet to bridle them as
false: for so far a man ought to make use of suspicions, as
to provide, as if that should be true that he suspects, yet it
may do him no hurt. Suspicions that the mind of itself
gathers are but buzzes; but suspicions that are artificially
nourished, and put into men's heads by the tales and whis-
perings of others, have stings. Certainly, the best mean, to
clear the way in this same wood of suspicions, is frankly to
communicate them with the party that he suspects; for
thereby he shall be sure to know more of the truth of them

* *Check, i. e.* interfere.
† *Stout, i. e.* proud, haughty.

than he did before; and withal shall make that party more circumspect, not to give further cause of suspicion; but this would not be done to men of base natures; for they, if they find themselves once suspected, will never be true. The Italian says, "*Sospetto licentia fede;*" * as if suspicion did give a passport to faith; but it ought rather to kindle it to discharge itself.

OF DISCOURSE.

Some in their discourse desire rather commendation of wit, in being able to hold all arguments, than of judgment, in discerning what is true; as if it were a praise to know what might be said, and not what should be thought. † Some have certain commonplaces and themes, wherein they are good, and want variety; which kind of poverty is for the most part tedious, and, when it is once perceived, ridiculous. The honourablest part of talk is to give the occasion; and again to moderate and pass to somewhat else, for then a man leads the dance. It is good in discourse, and speech of conversation, to vary and intermingle speech of the present occasion with arguments, tales with reasons, asking of questions with telling of opinions, and jest with earnest:

* "Mistrust justifies infidelity, or dissolves the obligation of fidelity."
Italian proverbs are not the place to look for a high code of morality. One wrong cannot justify another; a breach of promise on the part of one cannot excuse a breach of confidence on the part of another; the confidence given by one's friend is none the less sacred, although that friend has become your enemy.

† No society is so tedious as that of professional wits, who, like the metaphysical poets, have but the one wish — of saying "what they hope had never been said before." The talker's mind is on a constant and painful strain after success, and the hearer's is relaxed and wearied by his many failures.

for it is a dull thing to tire, and as we say now, to jade anything too far. As for jest, there be certain things which ought to be privileged from it; namely, religion, matters of State, great persons, any man's present business of importance, and any case that deserveth pity; yet there be some that think their wits have been asleep, except they dart out somewhat that is piquant, and to the quick; that is a vein which would be bridled; " *Parce, puer, stimulis, et fortius utere loris.*" *   And, generally, men ought to find the difference between saltness and bitterness.   Certainly, he that hath a satirical vein, as he maketh others afraid of his wit, so he had need be afraid of others' memory. †   He that questioneth much, shall learn much, and content much ; but especially if he apply his questions to the skill of the persons whom he asketh; for he shall give them occasion to please themselves in speaking, and himself shall continually gather knowledge; but let his questions not be troublesome, for that is fit for a poser; ‡ and let him be sure to leave other men their turns to speak: nay, if there be any that would reign and take up all the time, let him find means to take them off, and to bring others on, as musicians used to do with those that dance too long galliards.   If you dissemble sometimes your knowledge of that you are thought to know, you shall be thought, another time, to know that you know not.   Speech of a man's self ought to be seldom, and well chosen.   I knew one was wont to say in scorn, " He must needs be a wise man, he speaks so much of himself:" and there is but one case wherein a man may commend himself with good grace, and that is in commending

---

* "Boy, spare the spur and hold the reins tighter."

† "The mortgagor and mortgagee differ, the one from the other, not more in length of purse than the jester and jestee in that of memory." — *Sterne.*

"Men are satirical more from vanity than ill nature," says a philosopher.

‡ *Poser, i. e.* an examiner, questioner.

virtue in another, especially if it be such a virtue whereunto himself pretendeth. Speech of touch * towards others should be sparingly used; for discourse ought to be as a field, without coming home to any man. I knew two noblemen, of the west part of England, whereof the one was given to scoff, but kept ever royal cheer in his house; the other would ask of those that had been at the other's table, "Tell truly, was there never a flout or dry blow given?" To which the guest would answer, "Such and such a thing passed." The lord would say, "I thought he would mar a good dinner." Discretion of speech is more than eloquence; and to speak agreeably to him with whom we deal, is more than to speak in good words, or in good order. A good continued speech, without a good speech of interlocution, shows slowness; and a good reply, or second speech, without a good settled speech, showeth shallowness and weakness. As we see in beasts, that those that are weakest in the course, are yet nimblest in the turn; as it is betwixt the greyhound and the hare. To use too many circumstances, ere one comes to the matter, is wearisome; to use none at all, is blunt.

OF RICHES.

I cannot call riches better than the baggage of virtue; the Roman word is better, "*impedimenta;*" for as the baggage is to an army, so is riches to virtue; it cannot be spared or left behind, but it hindereth the march; yea, and the care of it sometimes loseth or disturbeth the victory; † of great

---

* *Speech of touch*, *i. e.* personalities of any kind, although amiable and well-intentioned.

† " But Satan now is wiser than before,
And tempts by making rich, not making poor."
—*Pope's " Epistle to Bathurst."*

The poet refers to Job's temptation.

riches there is no real use, except it be in the distribution;
the rest is but conceit; so saith Solomon, "Where much is,
there are many to consume it, and what hath the owner but
the sight of it with his eyes?" The personal fruition in
any man cannot reach to feel great riches: there is a
custody of them; or a power of dole and donative of them;
or a fame of them; but no solid use to the owner. Do you
not see what feigned prices are set upon little stones and
rarities? and what works of ostentation are undertaken,
because there might seem to be some use of great riches?
But then you will say, they may be of use to buy men out of
dangers or troubles; as Solomon saith, "Riches are as a
stronghold in the imagination of the rich man;" but this is
excellently expressed, that it is in imagination, and not
always in fact: for, certainly, great riches have sold more
men than they have bought out. Seek not proud riches,
but such as thou mayest get justly, use soberly, distribute
cheerfully, and leave contentedly; yet have no abstract nor
friarly contempt of them; but distinguish as Cicero saith
well of Rabirius Posthumus, "*In studio rei amplificandæ
apparebat, non avartiæ prædam, sed instrumentum bonitati
quæri.*"* Hearken also to Solomon, and beware of hasty
gathering of riches; "*Qui festinat ad divitias, non erit
insons.*"† The poets feign, that when Plutus (which is
riches) is sent from Jupiter, he limps and goes slowly; but
when he is sent from Pluto, he runs, and is swift of foot;
meaning, that riches gotten by good means and just labour
pace slowly; but when they come by the death of others (as
by the course of inheritance, testaments, and the like), they
come tumbling upon a man: but it might be applied likewise
to Pluto, taking him for the devil: for when riches come
from the devil (as by fraud and oppression, and unjust

---

* "In his anxiety to increase his fortune it was apparent that he
sought not the mortification of his avarice, but the means of doing
good."

† "He who hastens to riches will not be without guilt."

means), they come upon speed. The ways to enrich are many, and most of them foul:* parsimony is one of the best, and yet is not innocent; for it withholdeth men from works of liberality and charity. The improvement of the ground is the most natural obtaining of riches; for it is our great mother's blessing, the earth; but it is slow; and yet, where men of great wealth do stoop to husbandry, it multi-plieth riches exceedingly. I knew a nobleman in England that had the greatest audits † of any man in my time, a great grazier, a great sheep-master, a great timber-man, a great collier, a great corn-master, a great lead-man, and so of iron, and a number of the like points of husbandry; so as the earth seemed a sea to him in respect of the perpetual importation. It was truly observed by one, "that himself came very hardly to a little riches, and very easily to great riches;" for when a man's stock is come to that, that he can expect the prime of markets, and overcome ‡ those bargains,

---

* It is a weakness of human nature to rail at the subserviency, low-cunning, absence of self-respect, dishonorable means, sacrifice of the religion, poetry and beauty of life, characterizing the aver-age greedy seeker after great riches in the beginning of his career; but in middle or old age of the millionaire, after the wealth is realized, the railers become worshipers at the shrine; they do not seem to care how the money was made, taking the rich man as he is, not inquiring how he came to be; then

> "They hold Vespasian's rule, that no gain is unsavory."

Having the same opinion which he had in the beginning of his money-making, and which is so satirically expressed by Juvenal: —

> "No! tho' compelled beyond the Tiber's flood
> To move your tan-yard, swear the smell is good,
> Myrrh, cassia, frankincense, and wisely think
> That what is lucrative can never stink."
> —*Juvenal. IV. Satire.*

† *Audits, i. e.* accounts.

‡ *Overcome, i. e.* seize upon; literally, have more than enough ready money to meet the offer.

which for their greatness are few men's money, and be part-
ner in the industries of younger men, he cannot but increase
mainly. The gains of ordinary trades and vocations are
honest, and furthered by two things, chiefly, by diligence,
and by a good name for good and fair dealing; but the gains
of bargains are of a more doubtful nature, when men shall
wait upon others' necessity; broke * by servants and instruments to draw them on; put off others cunningly that
would be better chapmen, and the like practices, which are
crafty and naughty; as for the chopping of bargains, when a
man buys not to hold, but to sell over again, that commonly
grindeth double, both upon the seller and upon the buyer.
Sharings do greatly enrich, if the hands be well chosen that
are trusted. Usury is the certainest means of gain, though
one of the worst, as that whereby a man doth eat his bread
"*in sudore vultûs alieni;*" † and besides, doth plough
upon Sundays: but yet certain though it be, it hath flaws;
for that the scriveners and brokers do value unsound men
to serve their own turn. The fortune, in being the first
in an invention, or in a privilege, doth cause sometimes a
wonderful overgrowth in riches, as it was with the first
sugar-man in the Canaries: therefore, if a man can play the
true logician, to have as well judgment as invention, he may
do great matters, especially if the times be fit: he that
resteth upon gains certain, shall hardly grow to great riches;
and he that puts all upon adventures, doth oftentimes break
and come to poverty: it is good, therefore, to guard adventures with certainties that may uphold losses. Monopolies,
and coemption of wares for re-sale, where they are not
restrained, are great means to enrich; especially if the
party have intelligence what things are like to come into
request, and so store himself beforehand. Riches gotten
by service, though it be of the best rise, yet when they are
gotten by flattery, feeding humours, and other servile condi-

---

* *Broke.* To broke is to employ panders.

† "In the sweat of another's brow."

tions, they may be placed amongst the worst. As for fishing for testaments and executorships (as Tacitus saith of Seneca, " *Testamenta et orbos tanquam indagine capi*)," * it is yet worse, by how much men submit themselves to meaner persons than in service.

Believe not much them that seem to despise riches, for they despise them that despair of them; and none worse when they come to them. Be not penny-wise; riches have wings, and sometimes they fly away of themselves, sometimes they must be set flying to bring in more. Men leave their riches either to their kindred, or to the public; and moderate portions prosper best in both. A great state left to an heir, is as a lure to all the birds of prey round about to seize on him, if he be not the better established in years and judgment: likewise, glorious † gifts and foundations are like sacrifices without salt; and but the painted sepulchres of alms, which soon will putrefy and corrupt inwardly: therefore measure not thine advancements by quantity, but frame them by measure: and defer not charities till death; for, certainly, if a man weigh it rightly, he that doth so is rather liberal of another man's than of his own.

OF NATURE IN MEN.

Nature is often hidden, sometimes overcome, seldom extinguished. Force maketh nature more violent in the return; doctrine and discourse maketh nature less importune; but custom, only, doth alter and subdue nature. He that seeketh victory over his nature, let him not set himself too great nor too small tasks; for the first will make him dejected by often failing, and the second will make him a small proceeder, though by often prevailing: and at the

* "Wills and childless parents taken as with a net."
† *Glorious, i. e.* ostentatious, inspired by vanity.

first, let him practice with helps, as swimmers do with blad-
ders, or rushes; but, after a time, let him practice with dis-
advantages, as dancers do with thick shoes; for it breeds
great perfection, if the practice be harder than the use.
Where nature is mighty, and therefore the victory hard, the
degrees had need be, first to stay and arrest nature in time;
like to him that would say over the four-and-twenty letters
when he was angry; then to go less in quantity: as if one
should, in forbearing wine, come from drinking healths to a
draught at a meal; and lastly, to discontinue altogether:
but if a man have the fortitude and resolution to enfranchise
himself at once, that is the best:

> "Optimus ille animi vindex lædentia pectus
> Vincula qui rupit, dedoluitque semel." *

Neither is the ancient rule amiss, to bend nature as a wand
to a contrary extreme, whereby to set it right; understanding it where the contrary extreme is no vice. Let not a man
force a habit upon himself with a perpetual continuance,
but with some intermission: for the pause reinforceth the
new onset; and, if a man that is not perfect be ever in practice, he shall as well practice his errors as his abilities, and
induce one habit of both; and there is no means to help
this but by seasonable intermissions; but let not a man
trust his victory over his nature too far; for nature will lie
buried a great time, and yet revive upon the occasion, or
temptation; † like as it was with Æsop's damsel, turned
from a cat to a woman, who sat very demurely at the

---

* "He is the best asserter of intelligence who bursts the bonds
that gall him, and ends his grief at once." — *Ovid's "Remedy for
Love."*

> † "No mortal footing treads so firm in virtue
> As always to abide the slippery path,
> Nor deviate with the bias. Some have few,
> But each man has his failing — some defect
> Wherein to slide temptation."
> — *Brooke's "Gustavus Vasa," Act II., sc. 1.*

board's end till a mouse ran before her : therefore, let a man either avoid the occasion altogether, or put himself often to it, that he may be little moved with it. A man's nature is best perceived in privateness; for there is no affectation in passion; for that putteth a man out of his precepts, and in a new case or experiment, for there custom leaveth him. They are happy men whose natures sort with their vocations; otherwise they may say, "*Multum incola fuit anima mea*," * when they converse in those things they do not affect. In studies, whatsoever a man commandeth upon himself, let him set hours for it; but whatsoever is agreeable to his nature, let him take no care for any set times; for his thoughts will fly to it of themselves, so as the spaces of other business or studies will suffice. A man's nature runs either to herbs or weeds; therefore let him seasonably water the one, and destroy the other. †

OF YOUTH AND AGE.

A man that is young in years may be old in hours, if he have lost no time; but that happeneth rarely. Generally, youth is like the first cogitations, not so wise as the second : for there is a youth in thoughts, as well as in ages ; ‡ and yet the invention of young men, is more lively than that of old, and imaginations stream into their minds better, and, as it were, more divinely. Natures that have much heat, and

* "My soul has long been a sojourner."

† "The mind that lies fallow for a single day sprouts up in follies that are only to be killed by constant and assiduous culture." — *Addison.*

‡ "In youth, indeed, there is a certain irregularity and agitation by no means unbecoming; but in age, when business is unseasonable and ambition indecent, all should be calm and uniform."— *Pliny's " Epistles."*

great and violent desires and perturbations, are not ripe for
action till they have passed the meridian of their years: as
it was with Julius Cæsar and Septimus Severus; of the latter
of whom it is said, "*Juventutem egit, erroribus, imo furori-
bus plenam;*" * and yet he was the ablest emperor, almost,
of all the list: but reposed natures may do well in youth, as
it is seen in Augustus Cæsar, Cosmos, Duke of Florence,
Gaston de Foix, and others.   On the other side, heat and
vivacity in age is an excellent composition for business.
Young men are fitter to invent, than to judge; fitter for execution than for counsel; and fitter for new projects than for
settled business; for the experience of age, in things that
fall within the compass of it, directeth them: but in new
things abuseth them.   The errors of young men are the ruin
of business; but the errors of aged men amount but to this,
that more might have been done, or sooner.

Young men, in the conduct and manage of actions,
embrace more than they can hold; stir more than they can
quiet; fly to the end, without consideration of the means
and degrees; pursue some few principles which they have
chanced upon absurdly; care not to innovate, † which
draws unknown inconveniences; use extreme remedies at
first; and that, which doubleth all errors, will not acknowledge or retract them, like an unruly horse that will neither
stop nor turn.   Men of age object too much, consult too
long, adventure too little, repent too soon, and seldom drive
business home to the full period, but content themselves
with a mediocrity of success.   Certainly it is good to compound employments of both; for that will be good for the
present, because the virtues of either age may correct the
defects of both; and good for succession, that young men
may be learners, while men in age are actors; and, lastly,
good for external accidents, because authority followeth old
men, and favour and popularity youths: but, for the moral

---

* "His youth was full of errors and even of frantic passions."
† Are not careful in innovating.

part, perhaps, youth will have the preëminence, as age hath
for the politic. A certain rabbin upon the text, "Your
young men shall see visions, and your old men shall dream
dreams," inferreth that young men are admitted nearer to
God than old, because vision is a clearer revelation than a
dream: and, certainly, the more a man drinketh of the
world, the more it intoxicateth: and age doth profit rather
in the powers of understanding, than in the virtues * of the
will and affections. There be some have an over-early ripe-
ness in their years, which fadeth betimes: these are, first,
such as have brittle wits, the edge whereof is soon turned:
such as was Hermogenes † the rhetorician, whose books are
exceeding subtile, who afterwards waxed stupid: a second
sort is of those that have some natural dispositions, which
have better grace in youth than in age; such as is a fluent
and luxuriant speech, which becomes youth well, but not
age: so Tully saith of Hortentius, "*Idem manebat, neque
idem decebat;*" ‡ the third is of such as take too high a strain
at the first, and are magnanimous more than tract of years
can uphold; as was Scipio Africanus, of whom Livy saith
in effect, "*Ultima primis cedebant.*" §

OF BEAUTY.

Virtue is like a rich stone, best plain set; and surely
virtue is best in a body that is comely, though not of delicate features; and that hath rather dignity of presence, than
beauty of aspect; neither is it almost ‖ seen, that very beau-

* "We abandon not vices so much as we change them." —
Montaigne.

† "The vivacity which augments with age is not far from
folly." — *Rochefoucauld.*

‡ "He remained the same; but the same was no longer
becoming to him."

§ "His last deeds fell short of his first."

‖ *Almost, i. e.* generally.

tiful persons are otherwise of great virtue; as if nature were rather busy not to err, than in labour to produce excellency; and therefore they prove accomplished, but not of great spirit; and study rather behaviour, than virtue. But this holds not always: for Augustus Cæsar, Titus Vespasianus, Philip le Bel of France, Edward the Fourth of England, Alcibiades of Athens, Ismael, the Sophy of Persia, were all high and great spirits, and yet the most beautiful men of their times. In beauty, that of favour, is more than that of colour; and that of decent and gracious motion, more than that of favour. That is the best part of beauty, which a picture cannot express;* no, nor the first sight of the life. There is no excellent beauty that hath not some strangeness in the proportion. A man cannot tell whether Apelles or Albert Durer were the more trifler; whereof the one would make a personage by geometrical proportions: the other, by taking the best parts out of divers faces, to make one excellent. Such personages, I think, would please nobody but the painter that made them; not but I think a painter may make a better face than ever was; but he must do it by a kind of felicity, (as a musician that maketh an excellent air in music) and not by rule. A man shall see faces, that, if you examine them part by part, you shall find never a good; and yet altogether do well. If it be true, that the principal part of beauty, is in decent motion, certainly it is no marvel, though persons in years seem many times more amiable; "*Pulchrorum autumnus pulcher;*" † for no youth can be comely but by pardon, and considering the youth as to make up the comeliness. Beauty is as summer-fruits, which are easy to corrupt, and cannot last; and, for the most part, it makes a dissolute youth, and an age a little out of countenance; but yet certainly again, if it light well, it maketh virtues shine, and vices blush.

* "Beauty is the lover's gift." — *Congreve.*
† "The autumn of the beautiful is beautiful."

OF STUDIES.

Studies serve for delight, for ornament, and for ability. Their chief use for delight, is in privateness and retiring; for ornament, is in discourse; and for ability, is in the judgment and disposition of business; for expert men can execute, and perhaps judge of particulars, one by one: but the general counsels, and the plots and marshalling of affairs come best from those that are learned. To spend too much time in studies, is sloth; to use them too much for ornament, is affectation; to make judgment wholly by their rules, is the humour of a scholar: they perfect nature, and are perfected by experience: for natural abilities are like natural plants, that need pruning by study; and studies themselves do give forth directions too much at large, except they be bounded in by experience. Crafty men contemn studies, simple men admire them, and wise men use them; for they teach not their own use; but that is a wisdom without them, and above them, won by observation. Read not to contradict and confute, nor to believe and take for granted, nor to find talk and discourse, but to weigh and consider. Some books are to be tasted, others to be swallowed, and some few to be chewed and digested; that is, some books are to be read only in parts; others to be read, but not curiously;* and some few to be read wholly, and with diligence and attention. Some books also may be read by deputy, and extracts made of them by others; but that would be only in the less important arguments, and the meaner sort of books; else distilled books are, like common distilled waters, flashy things. Reading maketh a full man; conference a ready man; and writing an exact man; and, therefore, if a man write little, he had need have a great memory; if he confer little, he had need have a present wit:

* *Curiously,* i. e. very attentively.

I

and if he read little, he had need have much cunning, * to seem to know that he doth not.   Histories make men wise; poets witty; the mathematics subtile; natural philosophy deep; moral, grave; logic and rhetoric, able to contend; *"Abeunt studia in mores;"* † nay, there is no stond or impediment in the wit, but may be wrought out by fit studies: like as diseases of the body may have appropriate exercises; bowling is good for the stone and reins, shooting for the lungs and breast, gentle walking for the stomach, riding for the head. ?. ͟ the like; so, if a man's wit be wandering, let him study the mathematics; for in demonstrations, if his wit be called away never so little, he must begin again; if his wit be not apt to distinguish or find differences, let him study the schoolmen, for they are *" Cymini sectores;"* ‡ if he be not apt to beat over matters, and to call upon one thing to prove and illustrate another, let him study the lawyers' cases: so every defect of the mind may have a special receipt.

OF PRAISE.

Praise is the reflection of virtue, but it is as the glass, or body, which giveth the reflection; if it be from the common people, it is commonly false and naught, and rather followeth vain persons than virtuous: for the common people understand not many excellent virtues: the lowest virtues draw praise from them, the middle virtues work in them astonishment or admiration; but of the highest virtues they have no sense or perceiving at all; but shows and *"species virtutibus*

---

* "The wit of one man can no more countervail learning than one man's means can hold way with a common purse."— *Ad. of Learning.*

† "Studies grow into habits and manners."

‡ *Splitters of cummin, i. e.* hair-splitters.

similes," * serve best with them. Certainly, fame is like a river, that beareth up things light and swollen, and drowns things weighty and solid; but if persons of quality and judgment concur, then it is (as the Scripture saith) "*Nomen bonum instar unguenti fragrantis;*" † it filleth all round about, and will not easily away; for the odours of ointments are more durable than those of flowers.

There be so many false points of praise, that a man may justly hold it a suspect. Some praises proceed merely of flattery; and if he be an ordinary flatterer, he will have certain common attributes, which may serve every man; if he be a cunning flatterer, he will follow the arch flatterer, which is a man's self, and wherein a man thinketh best of himself, therein the flatterer will uphold him most: but if he be an impudent flatterer, look wherein a man is conscious to himself that he is most defective, and is most out of counte- nance in himself, that will the flatterer entitle him to, per- force, "*spreta conscientia.*" ‡ Some praises come of good wishes and respects, which is a form due in civility to kings and great persons, "*laudando præcipere;*" § when by telling men what they are, they represent to them what they should be: some men are praised maliciously to their hurt, thereby to stir envy and jealousy towards them; "*Pessimum genus inimicorum laudantium;*" ‖ insomuch as it was a pro- verb amongst the Grecians, that, "he that was praised to his hurt, should have a push ¶ rise upon his nose;" as we say, that a blister will rise upon one's tongue that tells a lie; cer- tainly, moderate praise, used with opportunity, and not vul- gar, is that which doth the good. Solomon saith, "He that praiseth his friend aloud, rising early, it shall be to him no

* "Appearances resembling virtues."
† "A good name is like fragrant ointment."
‡ "Conscience being turned out of doors."
§ "To teach by praising."
‖ "Flatterers are the worst enemies."
¶ *Push, i. e.* blister, pimple.

better than a curse." Too much magnifying of man or matter doth irritate contradiction, and procure envy and scorn. To praise a man's self cannot be decent, except it be in rare cases; but to praise a man's office or profession, he may do it with good grace, and with a kind of magnanimity. The Cardinals of Rome, which are theologues, and friars, and schoolmen, have a phrase of notable contempt and scorn towards civil business, for they call all temporal business of wars, embassages, judicature, and other employments, *sirrbirie*, which is under-sheriffries, as if they were but matters for under-sheriffs and catchpoles; though many times those under-sheriffries do more good than their high speculations. St. Paul, when he boasts of himself, he doth oft interlace, " I speak like a fool;" but speaking of his calling, he saith, " *Magnificabo apostolatum meum.*" *

OF JUDICATURE.

Judges ought to remember that their office is "*jus dicere*," and not "*jus dare;*" to interpret law, and not to make law, or give law; else will it be like the authority claimed by the Church of Rome, which under pretext of exposition of Scripture, doth not stick to add and alter, and to pronounce that, which they do not find, and by show of antiquity to introduce

* "I will magnify my apostleship."
Sir Walter Scott says that undeserved or exaggerated praise is the worst kind of satire.

† In this essay, and in the two succeeding extracts from Bacon's works on "The Essentials of a Good Judge," the reader will recognize, if he has seen of what stuff some judges are made, and has had any experience in courts of justice, how keen an observer Bacon was, how well he knew the qualities of a good, and the failings of a bad, judge.

novelty. Judges ought to be more learned than witty, more reverend, than plausible, and more advised, * than confident. Above all things, integrity is their portion and proper virtue. " Cursed," (saith the law,) " is he that removeth the landmark." The mislayer of a mere stone is to blame ; but it is the unjust judge that is the capital remover of landmarks, when he defineth amiss of lands and property. One foul sentence doth more hurt than many foul examples ; for these do but corrupt the stream, the other corrupteth the fountain : so saith Solomon, " *Fons turbatus, et vena corrupta est justus cadens in causa sua coram adversario.*" †

The office of judges may have reference unto the parties that sue, unto the advocates that plead, unto the clerks and ministers of justice underneath them, and to the sovereign or State above them.

First, for the causes or parties that sue. " There be," (saith the Scripture,) " that turn judgment into wormwood ; " and surely there be, also, that turn it into vinegar ; for injustice maketh it bitter, and delays make it sour. The principal duty of a judge is, to suppress force and fraud ; whereof force is the more pernicious when it is open, and fraud when it is close and disguised. Add thereto contentious suits, which ought to be spewed out, as the surfeit of courts. A judge ought to prepare his way to a just sentence, as God useth to prepare His way, by raising valleys and taking down hills : so when there appeareth on either side an high hand, violent prosecution, cunning advantages taken, combination, power, great counsel, then is the virtue of a judge seen to make inequality equal ; that he may plant his judgment as upon an even ground. ‡ " *Qui fortiter emungit, elicit*

* *Advised, i. e.* careful.

† A just man, failing in his cause before his adversary, is as a troubled fountain and corrupt spring.

‡ "English jurisprudence," says the great English lawyer, Dunning, "has the good of the people for its basis, and the accumulated wisdom of ages for its improvement." The people are

sanguinem ; " and where the wine-press is hard wrought, it
yields a harsh wine, that tastes of the grape-stone. Judges
must beware of hard constructions, and strained inferences ;
for there is no worse torture than the torture of laws : especially in case of laws penal, they ought to have care that

made up of individuals as a bucket of water is made up of drops
of water; color one drop and the whole body is affected, although
in an almost imperceptible degree; let injustice be done to one
man by the instruments of justice, and the whole body of the
people, society, is affected, for every private wrong is in some
sense a public injury. The theory is, that our lives, liberty and
property are subject to the administration of justice, and the
agents of justice are the judge on the bench, the lawyer at the
bar, the jury in the box.

The lawyer is in one sense as much an agent of justice as a
judge; he is a sworn officer of the court, and has moral as well
as legal obligations to society. The theory of a lawyer's duty is
to take the straight and honest path to the goal of truth. If
his client and client's cause are not false and fraudulent, they will
not fall by the wayside. In the Harlean MSS. is the following:
"In this peerless Queen's (Elizabeth) reign it is reported that
there was but one sergeant-at-law at the Common Pleas · bar
(Sergeant Benlowes) who was ordered to plead for the plaintiff
and defendant, for which he was to take of each party ten groats,
and no more; and to manifest his impartial dealing to both parties, he was therefore to wear a parti-colored gown, and to have a
black cap on his head of impartial justice, and under it a white
linen coif of innocence."

Things as well as theory have greatly changed since the virgin
queen's virtuous time. Macaulay, speaking of the modern road
to justice, says, in substance, that the English judge goes
straightway to the right of a cause, after it has been most unfairly
and deceitfully argued by the lawyers on both sides.

It is a sad reflection, that "for time whereof the memory of man
runneth not to the contrary," courts of justice have been too frequently regarded as asylums for the unjust; and that although
partisan judges and corrupt juries have often contributed to the
creation of this feeling of mistrust, the bar itself is most to blame

that which was meant for terror be not turned into rigour; and that they bring not upon the people that shower whereof the Scripture speaketh, *"Pluet super eos laqueos;"* * for penal laws pressed, are a shower of snares upon the people: therefore let penal laws, if they have been sleepers of long, or if they be grown unfit for the present time, be by wise judges confined in the execution: *"Judicis officium est, ut res, ita tempora rerum,"* etc. † In causes of life and death, judges ought, (as far as the law permitteth) in justice, to remember mercy, ‡ and to cast a severe eye upon the example, but a merciful eye upon the person.

Secondly, for the advocates and counsel that plead. Patience and gravity of hearing is an essential part of jus-

on account of the lawyer, the officer of the court, the agent of government and society, becoming the mere advocate of a client's cause, right or wrong, true or false. "We who are conversant in the real contentions of the bar," says Pliny, "unadvisedly contract a certain artfulness, however contrary to our natural tempers." If so honorable an ancient writes thus of himself and his profession, we should not be surprised that other fingers should be pointed at its frailties. Martial thus describes a certain class of lawyers, *Iras et verba locant*, as men who hire out their words and anger. Charles James Fox speaks of that glorious uncertainty which always attends the law; and Sir Pertinax Macsycophant says the glorious uncertainty of law is of more use to its professors than the justice of it. Horace Walpole calls it — law — a horrid liar, and adds that he never believes a word it says until the final decision. But Lord Bolingbroke truly describes it as in its nature the noblest and most beneficent to mankind; in its abuse and abasement, the most sordid and the most pernicious.

* He will rain snares upon them.

† It is the duty of a judge to consider not only the facts but the particulars of the case.

‡ "Humanity is the second virtue of courts, but undoubtedly the first is justice." — *Lord Stowell. Evans vs. Evans. T. Haggard.*

tice; and an over-speaking judge is no well-tuned cymbal.
It is no grace to a judge first to find that which he might
have heard in due time from the bar; or to show quickness
of conceit in cutting off evidence or counsel too short, or to
prevent * information by questions, though pertinent. The
parts of a judge in hearing are four: to direct the evidence; to moderate length, repetition, or impertinency of
speech; to recapitulate, select, and collate the material
points of that which hath been said, and to give the rule or
sentence. Whatsoever is above these is too much, and
proceedeth either of glory † and willingness to speak, or of
impatience to hear, or of shortness of memory, or of want
of a staid and equal attention. It is a strange thing to see
that the boldness of advocates should prevail with judges;
whereas they should imitate God, in whose seat they sit,
who represseth the presumptuous, and giveth grace to the
modest: but it is more strange, that judges should have
noted favourites, which cannot but cause multiplication of
fees, and suspicion of by-ways. There is due from the judge
to the advocate some commendation and gracing, where
causes are well handled and fair pleaded, especially towards
the side which obtaineth not; for that upholds in the client
the reputation of his counsel, and beats down in him the
conceit of his cause. There is likewise due to the public a
civil reprehension of advocates, where there appeareth cunning counsel, gross neglect, slight information, indiscreet
pressing, or an over-bold defense; and let not the counsel
at the bar chop with the judge, nor wind himself into the
handling of the cause anew after the judge hath declared his
sentence; ‡ but, on the other side, let not the judge meet

* *Prevent*, *i. e.* forestall, anticipate.

† *Glory*, *i. e.* pride of knowledge, display.

‡ Lord Chancellor Ellesmere ordered Lawyer Mylward's head
to be stuck through a replication, on account of its length.— *Lives
of Lord Chancellors, Vol II., 207.*

Lord Chancellor Maynard said, "Law is *ars bablitiva.*"

the cause half way, nor give occasion to the party to say, his counsel or proofs were not heard.

Thirdly, for that that concerns clerks and ministers. The place of justice is an hallowed place; and therefore not only the bench but the footpace and precincts, and purprise thereof ought to be preserved without scandal and corruption; for, certainly, "Grapes," (as the Scripture saith,) "will not be gathered of thorns or thistles;" neither can Justice yield her fruit with sweetness amongst the briars and brambles of catching and polling clerks and ministers. The attendance of courts is subject to four bad instruments: first, certain persons that are sowers of suits, which make the court swell, and the country pine: the second sort is of those that engage courts in quarrels of jurisdiction, and are not truly "*amici curiæ*," but "*parasiti curiæ*," * in puffing a court up beyond her bounds for their own scraps and advantage: the third sort is of those that may be accounted the left hands of courts: persons that are full of nimble and sinister tricks and shifts, whereby they pervert the plain and direct courses of courts, and bring justice into oblique lines and labyrinths: and the fourth is the poller and exacter of fees: which justifies the common resemblance of the courts of justice to the bush, whereunto, while the sheep flies for defense in weather, he is sure to lose part of his fleece. On the other side, an ancient clerk, skillful in precedents, wary in proceeding, and understanding in the business of the court, is an excellent finger of a court, and doth many times point the way to the judge himself.

Fourthly, for that which may concern the sovereign and estate. Judges ought, above all, to remember the conclusion of the Roman Twelve Tables, "*Salus populi suprema lex;*" † and to know that laws, except they be in order to that end, are but things captious, and oracles not well inspired: therefore it is an happy thing in a State, when

* Not "friends of court," but "parasites of court."
† "The safety of the people is the supreme law."

kings and states do often consult with judges; and again, when judges do often consult with the king and state: the one, when there is matter of law intervenient in business of state; the other, when there is some consideration of state intervenient in matter of law; for many times the things deduced to judgment may be "*meum*" and "*tuum*," when the reason and consequence thereof may trench to point of estate: I call matter of estate, not only the parts of sovereignty, but whatsoever introduceth any great alteration, or dangerous precedent; or concerneth manifestly any great portion of people: and let no man weakly conceive that just laws, and true policy, have any antipathy; for they are like the spirits and sinews, that one moves with the other. Let judges also remember, that Solomon's throne was supported by lions on both sides: let them be lions, but yet lions under the throne: being circumspect, that they do not check or oppose any points of sovereignty. Let not judges also be so ignorant of their own right, as to think there is not left them, as a principal part of their office, a wise use and application of laws; for they may remember what the apostle saith of a greater law than theirs: "*Nos scimus quia lex bona est, modo quis eâ utatur legitime.*" *

* "We know that the law is good if a man use it lawfully."

EXTRACTS.

THE LINES AND PORTRAITURE OF A GOOD JUDGE.

HIS LORDSHIP'S SPEECH IN THE COMMON PLEAS TO JUS-
TICE HUTTON, WHEN HE WAS CALLED TO BE ONE OF
THE JUDGES OF THE COMMON PLEAS.

Mr. Serjeant Hutton, The King's most excellent Majesty, being duly informed of your learning, integrity, discretion, experience, means, and reputation in your country, hath
thought fit not to leave you these talents to be employed
upon yourself only, but to call you to serve himself, and his
people, in the place of one of his justices of the court of
common pleas.

This court where you are to serve, is the local centre and
heart of the laws of this realm : . . . here justice opens not
by a by-gate of privilege, but the great gate of the King's
original writs out of the chancery. And therefore it is
proper for you, by all means, with your wisdom and fortitude,
to maintain the laws of the realm : wherein, nevertheless, I
would not have you head-strong, but heart-strong. . . . To
represent unto you the lines and portraitures of a good
judge :

1. The first is, that you should draw your learning out of
your books, not out of your brain. *

---

* " With discretion to conceal ignorance, a little learning goes
a great way on the bench." — *Lives of Lord Chancellors, II., 14.*

2. That you should mix well the freedom of your own opinion with the reverence of the opinion of your fellows.

3. That you should continue the studying of your books, and not to spend on upon the old stock.

4. That you should fear no man's face, * and yet not turn stoutness into bravery.

5. That you should be truly impartial, † and not so as men may see affection through fine carriage.

6. That you should be a light to jurors to open their eyes, but not a guide to lead them by the noses.

7. That you affect not the opinion of pregnancy and expedition by an impatient and catching hearing of the counsellors at the bar.

8. That your speech be with gravity, as one of the sages of the law; and not talkative, nor with impertinent flying out to shew learning.

9. That your hands, and the hands of your hands, I mean those about you, be clean, and uncorrupt from gifts, from meddling in titles, and from serving of turns, be they of great ones or small ones. ‡

10. That you contain the jurisdiction of the court within the ancient merestones, without removing the mark. §

11. Lastly, that you carry such a hand over your ministers and clerks, as that they may rather be in awe of you, than presume upon you.

* "An ignorant man cannot, a coward dares not, be a good judge." — *Bacon's Advice to Villiers.*

† A judge in the Isle of Man takes an official oath which concludes as follows: "I will execute the laws of this isle betwixt party and party as indifferently as the herring's backbone doth lie in the midst of the fish."

‡ " For gold his sword the hireling ruffian draws,
For gold the hireling judge distorts the laws."
—*Johnson's Vanity of Human Wishes.*

§ "The discretion of a judge is the law of tyrants." — *Lord Camden.*

MATTERS CONCERNING JUSTICE AND THE LAWS, AND THE PROFESSORS THEREOF.

But because the life of the laws lies in the due execution and administration of them, let your eye be, in the first place, upon the choice of good judges: these properties had they need to be furnished with: to be learned in their profession, patient in hearing, prudent in governing, powerful in their elocution to persuade and satisfy both the parties and hearers, just in judgment; and, to sum up all, they must have these three attributes: they must be men of courage, fearing God and hating covetousness; *an ignorant man cannot, a coward dares not, be a good judge*. . . . Judges must be as chaste as Cæsar's wife, neither to be, nor to be suspected to be, unjust.

If any sue to be made a judge, for my own part I should suspect him, but if either directly or indirectly he should bargain for a place of judicature, let him be rejected with shame: vendere jure potest, emerat ille prius.—*Advice to Sir George Villiers.*

ANSWER TO POLITICIANS.

PRAISE OF KNOWLEDGE.

For matter of policy and government, that learning should rather hurt, than enable thereunto, is a thing very improbable: we see it is accounted an error to commit a natural body to empiric physicians, which commonly have a few pleasing receipts, whereupon they are confident and adventurous, but know neither the causes of diseases, nor the complexions of patients, nor peril of accidents, nor the true method of cures: we see it is a like error to rely upon advocates or lawyers, which are only men of practice, and not grounded in their books, who are many times easily surprised, when matter falleth out besides their experience, to the prejudice of the causes they handle: so, by like reason, it cannot be but a matter of doubtful consequence, if states be managed by empiric statesmen, not well mingled with men grounded in learning. But contrariwise, it is almost without instance contradictory, that ever any government was disastrous that was in the hands of learned governors. For howsoever it hath been ordinary with politic men to extenuate and disable learned men by the name of pedants; yet in the records of time it appeareth, in many particulars, that the governments of princes in minority (notwithstanding the infinite disadvantage of that kind of state) have nevertheless excelled the government of princes of mature age, even for that reason which they seek to traduce, which is, by that occasion the state hath been in the hands of pedants: for so was the state of Rome for the first five years, which are so much magnified, during the minority of Nero, in the hands of Seneca, a pedant: so it was again, for ten years' space or more, during the minority of Gordianus the younger, with great applause and contentation in the hands of Misitheus, a pedant: so was it before that, in the minority of Alexander Severus, in like happiness, in hands not much unlike, by reason of the rule of the women, who were aided by the teachers and preceptors. Nay, let a man look into the government of the bishops of Rome, as by name, into the government of Pius Quintus, and Sextus Quintus, in our times, who were both at their entrance esteemed but as pedantical friars, and he shall find that such popes do greater things, and proceed upon truer principles of estate, than those which have ascended to the papacy from an education and breeding in affairs of estate and courts of princes; for although men bred in learning are perhaps to seek in points of convenience, and accommodating for the present, which the Italians call "*ragioni di stato*," whereof the same Pius Quintus could not here spoken with patience, terming them inventions against religion and the moral virtues; yet on the other side, to recompense that, they are perfect in those same plain grounds of religion, justice, honour, and moral virtue, which if they be well and watchfully pursued, there will be seldom use of those other, nor more than of physic in a sound or well-dieted body. Neither can the experience of one man's life furnish examples and precedents for the events of one man's life: for, as it happeneth sometimes that the grandchild, or other descendant, resembleth the ancestor more than the son; so many times occurrences of present times may sort better with ancient examples, than with those of the latter or immediate times: and lastly, the wit of one man can no more countervail learning, than one man's means can hold way with a common purse. And for the conceit, that learning should dispose men to leisure and privateness, and make men slothful; it were a strange thing if that, which accustometh the mind to a perpetual motion and agitation, should induce slothfulness; whereas contrariwise it may be truly affirmed, that no kind of men love business for itself, but those that are learned; for other persons love it for profit, as an hireling, that loves the work for the wages; or for honour, as because it beareth them up in the eyes of men, and refresheth their reputation, which otherwise would wear; or because it putteth them in mind of their fortune, and giveth them occasion to pleasure and displeasure; or because it exerciseth some faculty wherein they take pride, and so entertaineth them in good humour and pleasing conceits toward themselves; or because it advanceth any other their ends. So that, as it is said of untrue valours, that some men's valours are in the eyes of them that look on; so such men's industries are in the eyes of others, or at least in regard of their own designments: only learned men love business, as an action according to nature, as agreeable to health of mind, as exercise is to health of body, taking pleasure in the action itself, and not

in the purchase: so that of all men they are the most inde-
fatigable, if it be towards any business which can hold or
detain their mind.

And if any man be laborious in reading and study, and
yet idle in business and action, it groweth from some weakness of body, or softness of spirit; and not of learning:
well may it be, that such a point of man's nature may make
him give himself to learning, but it is not learning that
breedeth any such point in his nature.

And that learning should take up too much time or leisure:
I answer; the most active or busy man that hath been or
can be, hath, no question, many vacant times of leisure,
while he expecteth the tides and returns of business (except
he be either tedious and of no dispatch, or lightly and unworthily ambitious to meddle in things that may be better
done by others): and then the question is, but how those
spaces and times of leisure shall be filled and spent;
whether in pleasures or in studies ; as was well answered by
Demosthenes to his adversary Æschines, that was a man
given to pleasure, and told him, his orations did smell of the
lamp: "Indeed," said Demosthenes, "there is a great difference between the things that you and I do by lamp-light."
So as no man need doubt that learning will *expulse* business ; but *rather* it will keep and defend the possession of
the mind against idleness and pleasure, which otherwise at
unawares may enter, to the prejudice of both.

Again, for that other conceit, that learning should under-
mine the reverence of laws and government, it is assuredly
a mere *deprivation* and calumny, without all shadow of truth.
For to say, that a blind custom of obedience should be a surer
obligation than duty taught and understood; it is to affirm
that a blind man may tread surer by a guide than a seeing
man can by a light.   And it is without all controversy, that
learning doth make the minds of men gentle, generous, *maniable* and pliant to government; whereas ignorance makes
them churlish, thwarting, and mutinous; and the evidence of

time doth clear this assertion, considering that the most barbarous, rude, and unlearned times have been most subject to
tumults, seditions and changes. . . .

And for meanness of employment, that which is most traduced to contempt is that the government of youth is commonly allotted to them; which age, because it is the age of
least authority, it is transferred to the disesteeming of those
employments wherein youth is conversant, and which are
conversant about youth. But how unjust this traducement
is (if you will reduce things from popularity of opinion to
measure of reason) may appear in that, we see men are more
curious what they put into a new vessel, than into a vessel
seasoned; and what mould they lay about a young plant,
than about a plant corroborate; so as the weakest terms and
times of all things used to have the best applications and
helps. And let it be noted, that howsoever the condition of
the life of pedants hath been scorned upon theatres, as the
ape of tyranny; and that the modern looseness or negligence
hath taken no due regard to the choice of schoolmasters
and tutors; yet the ancient wisdom of the best times did
always make a just complaint, that states were too busy with
their laws, and too negligent in point of education. — *Advancement of Learning.*

CHURCH CONTROVERSIES.

The controversies * themselves I will not enter into, as judg-
ing that the disease requireth rather rest than any other cure.
Thus much we all know and confess, that they be not of the
highest nature, for they are not touching the high mysteries
of faith, such as detained the churches for many years after

* The controversies which inspired this tract were those raging
between high-church and Puritan writers. The freedom of the
press had been abolished; printing was restricted to London and
the two universities. Every publication had to receive the

the first peace, what time the heretics moved curious questions, and made strange anatomies of the natures and person of Christ; and the Catholic fathers were compelled to follow them with all subtilety of decisions and determinations to exclude them from their evasions, and to take them in their labyrinths; so as it is rightly said, "*illes temporibus, ingeniosa res fuit, esse Christianum;*" in those days it was an ingenious and subtile thing to be a Christian.

Neither are they concerning the great parts of the worship of God, of which it is true, that, "*non servatur unitas in credendo, nisi eadem absit in colendo;*" there will be kept no unity in believing, except it be entertained in worshiping; such as were the controversies of the east and west churches touching images, and such as are many of those between the Church of Rome and us: as about the adoration of the Sacrament, and the like; but we contend about ceremonies and things indifferent, about the external policy and government of the church; in which kind, if we would but remember that the ancient and true bonds of unity are "one faith, one baptism," and not one ceremony, one policy; if we would observe the league amongst Christians that is penned by our Saviour, "he that is not against us is with us;" if we could but comprehend that saying, "*differentiæ rituum commendant unitatem doctrinæ;*" the diversities of ceremonies do set forth the unity of doctrines; and "*habit religio quæ sunt æternitatis, habit quæ sunt temporis;*"

approval of the Archbishop of Canterbury or that of the Bishop of London.

A series of pamphlets signed " Martin Marprelate," which were secretly published and aimed at the English Church and its clergy, added fuel to the flame. Penry, a young Welshman, and Udall, a dissenting minister, were arrested as the supposed authors; the former was executed and the latter died in prison. A bitter pamphlet war ensued, and Bacon's object was to pour oil on the troubled waters and teach the lessons of conservatism and charity.

religion hath parts which belong to eternity, and parts which pertain to time: and if we did but know the virtue of silence and slowness to speak, commended by St. James, our controversies of themselves would close up and grow together: * but most especially, if we would leave the over-weaning and turbulent humours of these times, and revive the blessed proceeding of the Apostles and Fathers of the primitive church, which was, in the like and greater cases, not to enter into assertions and positions, but to deliver counsels and advice, we should need no other remedy at all: "*si eadem consulis, frater, quæ affirmas, consulenti debetur reverentia, cum non debeatur fides affirmanti;*" brother, if that which you set down as an assertion, you would deliver by way of advice, there were reverence due to your counsel, whereas faith is not due to your affirmation. St. Paul was content to speak thus, "*Ego non Dominus*," I, and not the Lord: "*Et secundum consilium meum;*" according to my counsel. But now men do too lightly say, "*Non ego, sed Dominus*," not I, but the Lord: yea, and bind it with an heavy denunciation of his judgments, to terrify the simple, which have not sufficiently understood out of Solomon, that "the causeless curse shall not come." . . . It is hard in all causes, but especially in religion, when voices shall be numbered and not weighed.† "*Equidem*," saith a wise father, "*ut vere quod res est scribam, prorsus decrevi fugere omnem conventum*

* "The itch of disputing will prove the scab of the church." — Sir Henry Wotton. He directed in his will that this sentence should be engraven on his tombstone : —

"*Hic jacet hujus sententiæ primus author:*
DISPUTANDI PRURITUS ECCLESIARUM SCABIES
Nomlu alias quære."

† Old John Selden had no faith in the establishment of a creed by the majority in theological councils. He said that it was as if they were to claim that the odd vote was the Holy Ghost.

Sir John Harrington has preserved an interview between Dr. John Still, Bishop of Bath and Wells, and one whom Sydney *episcoporum; nullius enim concillii bonum exitum unquam vidi; concilia enim non minuunt mala, sed augent potius:"* To say the truth, I am utterly determined never to come to any council of bishops : for I never yet saw good end of any council; for councils abate not ill things, but rather increase them. Which is to be understood not so much of general councils, as of synods, gathered for the ordinary government of the church. . . . The fourth point wholly pertaineth to them which impugn the present ecclesiastical government. They have impropriated unto themselves the names of zealous, sincere, and reformed ; as if all others were cold minglers of holy things and profane, and friends of abuses. Yea, be a man endued with great virtues, and fruitful in good works ; yet if he concur not with them, they term him, in derogation, a civil and moral man,* and compare him to Socrates, or some heathen philosopher : whereas the wisdom of the Scriptures teacheth us otherwise ; namely, to judge

Smith would call a consecrated cobbler. The bishop conferred with him, in hope to convert him; and first my lord alleged for the authority of the church, St. Augustin. The shoemaker answered, "Augustin was but a man." He (Still) produced, for antiquitie of bishops, the fathers of the council of Nice. He answered, "They were also but men, and might erre." "Why, then," said the bishop, "thou art but a man and maist and doest erre." "No, sir," saith he, "the spirit beareth witness to my spirit; I am the chyld of God." "Alas," saith the bishop, "thy blynde spirit will lead thee to the gallows." "If I die," saith he, "in the Lord's cause, I shall be a martyr." "This man," saith he, "is not a sheepe strayed from the fold, for such may be brought in againe on the sheapheard's shoulders ; but this is like a wild bucke broken out of a parke, whose pale is thrown down, and flies the farder off, the more he is hunted."— *Nugæ Antiquæ.*

* Butler satirizes this class of bigots who substituted imaginary or hypocritical inward workings of the spirit for the letting one's "light shine before men," — for practical Christianity. They laid so much stress on this "inward grace," that they would not credit with being a religious man the benevolent labourer

and denominate men religious according to their works of
the second table; because they of the first are often counterfeit, and practiced in hypocrisy. . . . St. James saith,
"This is true religion to visit the fatherless and the widows."
God grant that we may contend with other churches, as the
vine with the olive, which of us shall bear the first fruit;
and not as the briar with the thistle, which of us is most
unprofitable. *

in the vineyard, who could not or would not cry aloud, "The
spirit beareth witness to my spirit:" —

> 'Cause grace and virtue are within
> Prohibited degrees of kin,
> And therefore no true saint allows
> They should be suffered to espouse.
> — *Hudibras. Part III., Canto I., l. 1293.*

* The true spirit of religion is exhibited by Dr. Tillotson in his
letter to the Earl of Mulgrave, Oct. 23, 1679: "I am, and always
was, more concerned that your lordship should continue a virtuous and good man, than become a Protestant; being assured that
the ignorance and errors of men's understandings will find a much
easier forgiveness with God than the faults of their wills. . . .
I am sure you cannot more effectually condemn your own act,
than by being a worse man after your profession of having
embraced a better religion."

Electrotyped by JAMES S. ADAMS, 299 Washington St., Boston.

www.ingramcontent.com/pod-product-compliance
Lightning Source LLC
Chambersburg PA
CBHW020848020726
47497CB00005B/1316